D0209733

THE
FALL
OF
BUTTERFLIES

THE FALL OF

ALSO BY ANDREA PORTES

Anatomy of a Misfit

WITHDRAWN

BUTTERFLIES

Andrea Portes

HARPER TEEN
An Imprint of HarperCollinsPublishers

Library of Congress Control Number: 2015951379
ISBN 978-0-06-231367-6 (trade bdg.)
ISBN 978-0-06-249780-2 (int. ed.)

Typography by Ellice M. Lee
16 17 18 19 20   CG/RRDH   10 9 8 7 6 5 4 3 2 1
❖
First Edition

For my son, Wyatt,
who is my sun, my moon,
and my stars.

And for my husband, Sandy,
who is my mountain, my ocean,
and my northern light.

PART I

ONE

Bet you'd never thought you'd be sitting at the freak table. It's okay. You get used to it. Trust me.

But there are some responsibilities here, so let's get things straight.

Let's go around the table, shall we? Clockwise it goes . . . Peanut Allergy Boy, Headgear Girl, OCD, and me. You're probably wondering about the names. Look. I'm not gonna sugarcoat it. There's a reason I'm not telling you. We'll get to that. I mean, geez. Why are you rushing me?

You may have to take care of these people when I'm gone, okay? Like Headgear Girl is pretty low maintenance. And, honestly, Peanut Allergy Boy is, too. Other than the fact you have to make sure there are no nuts anywhere near him, even pine nuts, seriously. If he eats nuts he'll blow up like a puffer fish and you'll have to stab him in the thigh with his EpiPen or he'll die. That's not an exaggeration. He will literally die. Don't worry. No pressure. I'll show you how to do it before I go.

Really, OCD is the one you have to watch out for. It's just that if you don't get the salt and pepper, ketchup, and mustard condiment dispensers all in a row, like exactly in a row, parallel to the table edge and centered in the middle of the table, well, he kind of starts flailing all over the place and then crying and shaking and yelling that we're all gonna die. It's okay, though. He's on medication. Small detail, sometimes he forgets to take said medication and then all of a sudden the condiments' positioning will lead to the end of the world, so it's best just to put them there in the first place. Why risk it?

You can imagine all this freakiness in one place might lead to a certain amount of asses getting kicked. Never have you imagined more correctly. It's okay, though. I usually take the brunt of it. That's sort of what I'm here for. It's also, kind of, why I'm here in the first place. I used to just be a normal high school–hating teenager somewhere in the middle of the public school experiment. In a kind of purgatory. A safe space.

But I sort of lost my mind in tenth grade and decided to

defend Peanut Allergy Boy after the zillionth time he had "Penis Allergy" stuck to his back on a sign. It was really that he tried to defend himself. That was not allowed by the jocks, who clearly took a kind of red-faced glee in throwing him into the nearest trash can and rolling him down the hall between fourth and fifth periods.

Look. I don't know what came over me. But whatever it was, it went like a whirl. The first part of the whirl was me yelling at them and calling them idiot Neanderthals with the IQ of maybe a concrete block. The second part of the whirl was them putting me into a trash can and rolling me down the same said hallway between fourth and fifth periods. And the third part of the whirl was me at the freak table from there to forevermore. It's okay. Wanna know a secret?

I like it here.

This is the place for me.

Yeah. The freak table. Holler.

At least here I don't have to dumb myself down or pretend to care about football or talk about the pros and cons of hairspray. Here, it's perfectly acceptable for me to stare into the abyss for an entire hour, and nobody bothers me. All I have to do is make sure the table is sans peanuts, the condiments are in a row, and there's nothing too stringy that gets stuck in headgear. Easy, right?

I would've stayed here happily. I really would have. For, like, ever.

Right now OCD and Peanut Allergy are waxing poetic about next year. About what's gonna happen when I get back from the East Coast, calling it Le Snooty Coast, and how I'll eat lobster rolls and say "Pahk the cah in the Hah-vahd yahd" and get molested by a Kennedy. Headgear Girl thinks I should invest in a lot of navy blazers and maybe even invent a fake family crest.

And I don't have the heart to tell them the truth. I don't have the heart to tell them I won't be back. I don't have the heart to tell them I have a two-point plan. But I'll tell *you*, okay? As long as you keep it a secret. You ready? It's a simple plan, really.

1) Move to the East Coast.

And . . .

2) Kill myself.

TWO

You want to know what happened?

Fine. I can explain everything.

It's because of "should."

Yep, that one word. That's why it all went down.

Does that sound crazy? It won't for long. Not after I tell you the whole story. And this? This is the story you want to hear.

So, yeah. "Should."

If it has to do with "should" or "supposed to be," you are dealing, without question, with my mom.

If it has to do with "just the way things are," that's my dad.

And "just the way things are" is never, ever, good enough.

Nope. Not for my mom.

Not that she even lives here anymore. She lives in France.

Outside Paris. In Fontainebleau. In *the forest of Fontainebleau.* Yes, she's actually a fairy. Doesn't that sound like a total fable? But hold on, we'll get to that later, 'cause that's a whopper.

If you think my dad and I live in Paris or France or *Fontainebleau,* you've got another think coming. No, we come from a very glamorous place you may have heard of. It's all the rage. Beyond *en vogue.* Can you guess where? Okay, here goes.

What Cheer, Iowa.

Yup, you heard me. What effing Cheer effing Iowa. You may have thought I just got distracted while we were talking and turned to the person next to me and said "What?" and that person answered, "Cheer!" but no. No. That is the name of the town. What Cheer.

There are many theories as to how the town got that name. I'm fairly sure the main reason is to make everybody confused when I tell them where I'm from.

The main story most people like to tell is the one where, back in ancient times, all the townsfolk—and I want you to imagine here a bunch of people in overalls, maybe someone with a corncob pipe, someone with a rope for a belt, and then a kindly old gentleman in a black suit with white hair like George Washington—gathered round in the town hall to think of a name for the town. No one could agree. There were insults made. Accusations hurled. Possibly a chair thrown.

Finally, it descended into so much chaos and rabble-rousing that the only respectable person there, who I imagine to be the guy with the George Washington hair, declared, "All right! The next person to come in that door, the first thing they say, THAT will be the name of the town!"

And then . . . out of the blue, a lonely old drifter came sidling in. I imagine this was the moment the hall fell silent. Possibly some tumbleweed blew across the floor. Maybe even the mice froze in anticipation. A kind towns-man said, "Come in, sir. Take a seat." To which the drifter replied, "What chair?" But nobody back then could hear anything, because they had all left their ear horns back home or something, so they all thought he said, "What cheer!" And, lo and behold, the first and most constant source of my awkward discomfort. What Cheer, Iowa.

People in town love to regale folks with this story. They tell it with real verve. At the punch line, everybody laughs and shakes their heads and pretends not to have heard it a thousand times before.

Oh, yes. I can rattle off that and a million other tales about What Cheer that would make the folks back home proud, but right now let's just stick to the fact that the population is 646 people. Actually, 645, if you're counting me.

Because right now, if you're looking at me, I'm on a train. See me there? I'm the girl with the frizzy red hair and the funny mouth. Don't make fun of my mouth—everybody has to have one, and I just got a weird one. Not weird, exactly, just kind of big. I have a big mouth. In all senses. First, the mouth is literally big, and second, the mouth is open a lot, asking a lot—okay, maybe too much—about all kinds of things. But what I want to know is which came first? The big mouth or the "big mouth"? You can't exactly go through life with a mouth like this and not, by default, end up using it a lot to ask things everybody wonders but no one wants to say. If I had been born with a thin mouth, like Kristen Stewart or something, I bet I would just always be quiet and know my place. I bet I would wear a lot of beige. I bet I would bathe in beige.

But that's not what happened here.

What happened here is I got this funny mouth, which by order of the decree of human existence made me a "big mouth." And also, I got a broke dad, because he and my mom are divorced. So, if you start with a kid with a smart-alecky persona, grow her up in a place called What Cheer, and give her zero money (Thank you, broken family!), then you get me. A girl who has to dress from a thrift shop and never stops asking questions.

They call it "quirky."

I call it "If I weren't wearing these thrift-store clothes, I'd be wearing a pickle barrel."

If I had just been born with a small mouth and a rich family I could've worn beige till the cows came home. Or the pheasants. Whatever rich people wait for to come home.

I could've had stick-straight hair and said clueless things like "For a home pedicure, just slather your feet in one-thousand-dollar gel made of rare dodo eggs!" Just like that celebrity woman with that "lifestyle blog." Have you ever noticed how that blondie pale-face over there is always making a complete fool of herself? You know who I am talking about. Admit it. I have a theory, which is not that she's out of touch or too privileged or *just too transcendent* or something. My theory is that maybe she is just dumb. There I said it.

But this is not her story. God, wouldn't that be a bore.

No, this is a story about a girl from What Cheer, Iowa.

And the train has left the station. Literally. Like, the train just left the station fifteen minutes ago and now I am heading out to conquer the world. And by "conquer the world," I mean "get calmly ensconced in a tomb of my own making and then end it all with a dramatic flair." I am still hammering out the details, by the by. I'd like to see the lay of the land before I make any rash decisions.

I'd say I spent eighty percent of the year sitting there between OCD, Headgear Girl, and Peanut Allergy Boy trying to figure it out. What is the best way? When should I do it? Should it be a quiet one, where nobody knows and somebody just happens upon me, like in the stacks of the library? Or should it be a dramatic jump off the top of the giant clock tower they show all over the place in the brochure?

But listen. OCD, Headgear, and Peanut had no idea, saying good-bye to me, that they'd never see me again. I covered. Look, why make them depressed? I think they have enough problems, don't you?

I'd be lying if I said I wasn't gonna miss them. I'm gonna miss the fuck out of them. This whole plan? To make me go east? To make me sophisticated? To make me a respectable member of society? Honestly? It's diabolical.

So I make a pact with myself. Don't think about them. Just put them far away from me in a box and never think about them. Or, at least, try not to think about them. I don't want to cry every day, now, do I? That is not sophisticated.

I bet you're wondering why I'm not heading west. Isn't that where everybody goes? Doesn't it seem like at the end of every movie, book, whatever, the main honcho always shrugs or has a moment of insight or kills the bad guy before taking a train, plane, bus, or horse, west—to where the sun shines free and the palm trees fan you to sleep?

You've got to wonder what everybody does when they get there.

I bet they just look around and say, "Huh."

And then the whole of California just kind of shrugs and

goes back to its juice diet.

So, in case you're wondering, no. No, I am not heading to California. I mean, this is the *beginning* of the story, right? If I headed there now, it just wouldn't be proper. And I bet I'd end up on the streets with a guy named Spike as my criminal accomplice.

No, no. This story is about the "should." As in, I "should" be more sophisticated by now, according to my mother. And I "should" be less of a total freak if I want to get anywhere at the Ivy League university I will no doubt be attending. Sending somebody to California to get sophisticated is like sending someone to the Krispy Kreme to lose weight.

Nope, to ensure this all-important sophistication I am headed to The Pembroke School back east. Oh, you've never heard of The Pembroke School? That's because it's basically a secret and nobody can get in unless their parents are in the Social Register or their great-great-great-great-great-grandparents came over on the *Mayflower* or their names are Sasha or Malia. Other than that, you're out of luck. Don't even think about it. It will just depress you.

So, how does a giant-mouthed, secondhand oddball from the sticks like yours truly get into a place that should obviously reject and scorn me before I even say its name? Well, here's the good part.

So, have you ever heard of that theory of money called

"The Logic of Collective Action"? You know, the "theory of political science and economics of concentrated benefits versus diffuse costs, its central argument being that concentrated minor interests will be overrepresented and diffuse majority interests trumped, due to a free-rider problem that is stronger when a group becomes larger"?

Of course you haven't.

Nobody has.

Except economists. And bankers. And political scientists. And everybody who cares an awful lot about money and power, mainly because they already have money and power and they need to make sure to keep the money and power while everybody else just sits around wondering where all the jobs went, or why they work for forty hours a week and still can't afford to put food on the table.

Well, that theory, that theory, which is impossible to understand, was the main, superimportant work of . . . drumroll, please . . . my mother. Basically everybody in that little microcosm of the world, the one with the money and power, knows that theory and knows my mom.

Not "knows her," exactly. "Worships her" is more like it.

Yes. She is worshipped.

I know, it's weird.

And because of that, she's written a zillion books and been in a zillion brain trusts and served under not one but two presidents. Like, in their cabinets. You get the picture. She's a mucky-muck. A big whoop.

Don't be jealous, she's not a nice lady.

Like, if you're even thinking of being jealous, you might want to take that thought and throw it out the back window and go downstairs and hug your normal mom, who maybe didn't come up with some famous theory of economics but maybe, also, remembers your birthday, or Christmas, or that you even exist. Trust me. If you have a mom, and she went to maybe, say, ONE activity you ever did in your life, little league or the school recital or the Christmas pageant where you played Mary (MARY, for God's sake!)—well, then, you have me beat. And you are sitting pretty, my friend.

Where this comes in handy, however, is The Pembroke School.

Because in places like this, if your attendance isn't assumed by virtue of your birth, then it comes down to someone making a phone call. And when you get a phone call from an ex-president, you answer the phone. Even if this ex-president is, you know, just a pal, making a phone call for his pal. To get his pal's daughter into your school.

It's like that, see. That's how it goes in these places.

Oh, did you think it was about the best candidate?

Wrongo.

This is the kind of thing you're not supposed to know

about. Like there's this gas station right out of town, right out of What Cheer. And my dad had to stop going there. At least, with me in the car. Why? It's because they live there. The whole family. The gas attendant, his wife, their three little kids. They live right there. Above the gas station. You can see the little kids looking out the front door, squinting there, in just a pair of shorts. And the littlest one, the baby, in just a diaper. And my dad just had to stop taking me. 'Cause every time I would throw a fit and tell him we had to go back and give those kids some clean clothes and maybe some food and "it isn't fair, Dad. It's just not fair, it's just not FAAAAIIIIIRRRR."

And there would be my dad, just trying to reassure me. Just trying to calm me down. "Shh, it's okay. Shh, we'll go back if you want. Okay? Okay, honey?" But I could tell there was a part of him that just wondered, you know? Just wondered if maybe his little girl had a screw loose. If maybe his little girl was one of those girls who will inevitably one day get taken away to the funny farm.

But those kids, those kids who live above the gas station? Who makes their phone call? Who picks up the phone and makes sure they get in the good school? Or even something to eat? Or maybe some shoes?

No one. That's who.

So excuse me while I go kill myself.

Just kidding. I can't kill myself. We're not even out of Iowa yet! God, be patient. What is wrong with you?!

So, right now, see, what we're looking at is a broke sixteen-year-old in a thrift-store dress, heading to a snooty school on the Eastern Seaboard.

This sixteen-year-old is recovering from a tearful, snot-stained good-bye to the motley crew from her lunch table—a crew that, despite their obvious shortcomings, she seriously did NOT want to leave. This sixteen-year-old also may or may not be carrying with her a picture of the boy she had been stalking as a junior prom date, the boy whose name she dares not even speak, ripped surreptitiously out of the copy of the yearbook from the school library.

Okay, Gabriel. His name is Gabriel.

Actually, Gabe, but I call him Gabriel. When I am talking to him in my imagination. 'Cause obviously he's like an angel sent from heaven. And he likes it when I call him Gabriel. In my imagination.

I didn't tell you about the good-bye to my dad. Honestly, I feel like if I tell you I'll just start crying all over again. Like sobbing. My dad was trying not to cry. He was trying to be brave. Like a cowboy, kinda. Like a skinny cowboy who squints into the distance. And I'd like to tell you that it doesn't matter. That none of it matters.

But it does. Because you're not supposed to say good-bye

to your dad just because of "should."

Whoever made up those rules can kinda just suck it.

Did you know my mom even sent me a Princeton sweatshirt? As if the whole thing was a fait accompli. Pembroke, then Princeton.

Right now this sixteen-year-old is most definitely not wearing a Princeton sweatshirt but walking through the café car and thinking "I need a drink." But don't worry. She doesn't drink. Because if a girl like her starts drinking, well, let's face it, she's about two clicks away from skid row to start with.

So it's not out of the realm of possibility that she'll end up in the gutter by September.

And it's already August 31.

THREE

What happens is . . . you go from small town to small town, a few stops, a few thoughts of a stop, and then not a stop. Sometimes you'll get someplace big. Davenport. Rockford. Chicago. And then there's a lot of hustle and bustle and everybody going crazy trying to get their stuff, check the seats, check the overhead, check under the seats, maybe even the aisle. They are checking, checking, checking. But it's just a bunch of garbage, really. There's nothing here you actually need. Maybe your driver's license and a few bucks. But that sweatshirt, and that *Us* magazine, and those Cheetos? You don't need them. You think you do, but really nobody does. Just leave them.

By the time the train pulls into Chicago, the café car

bartender has made his intentions clear. He would like to have lunch. In Chicago. With me. He said something about deep-dish pizza but I'm pretty sure he has something else in mind. Another kind of dish.

I'm *way* too young for him, but that never seems to stop them. When your boobs decide to make their appearance, all of a sudden every Tom, Dick, and Cletus starts giving you the hungry eye, and next thing you know you have to start making up excuses so some deranged licky-mouth doesn't try to shove you into the back and make a dishonest woman of you.

PS: I'm sixteen. Nobody with a full-time job and the beginnings of crow's feet should be asking me out for deep-dish pizza.

Of course, it's never Gabriel, it's never that cute boy Alex from the grocery store checkout who is interested. Maybe they don't like deep-dish pizza. Or maybe they don't like me.

But, the thing is . . . I have a little problem. Call it maybe a personal fault.

Curiosity.

I know, I know, curiosity killed the cat. Everybody says that. I can't believe you and your lack of originality.

But it's the next part of the phrase that's the kicker. Do you know it? It's: "Satisfaction brought him back."

I don't know why this cat is a male. Everybody knows cats

are girls. From now on I am officially changing the way I say this. Here goes:

"Curiosity killed the cat. Satisfaction brought *her* back."

There. Try that on for size.

When I was little my curiosity made the day-care teacher think I had been dropped on my head. I hadn't been dropped on my head, my dad assured her. But she couldn't understand how I could just sit across the playground from the jungle gym, staring out at the street the whole time. But, you see, there was a lot of action. The comings and goings of the big people. One time there was even a mom fight in front of the Piggly Wiggly. Involving an Easter basket. Very heated.

But now, right now, my curiosity problem is leading me through the vast marble splendor of Chicago's Union Station. There's vaulted ceilings and pillars everywhere, eggshell-colored but not dark enough to be beige. This is the kind of place you imagine Al Capone shooting up. Or someone from *The Bourne Identity* running through and someone chasing them and everybody freaking out. Although in real life no one would freak out. They'd probably just keep staring at their phones. Tweeting about "cray-cray chase in st8ion."

Movie writers are gonna have a hard time with this pretty soon.

I mean, what's a chase scene if everybody just keeps updating their status? Or recording it on their phone? Or tweeting it? Honestly, I figure we have about twenty years left as a species. Twenty years until the oceans rise enough to kill everybody and we all just stand there recording it as it washes us away.

You watch. On your iPhone.

So this guy is meeting me at a place called Fat Sal's Deep-Dish. *Très romantique.*

He kind of looks like if you crossed Steve Buscemi with Brad Pitt. I know, weird. But what I'm trying to say is . . . he's got bug eyes and he looks supertired but then has blond hair and bright-blue eyes. So he's kind of like ugly-cute, in a way.

He's trying to pretend to care about my well-being.

"Now, your train leaves in two hours, so be sure to get back to the platform by three fifteen."

And that's true. My train does leave in two hours. But if this guy really cared about my well-being he would not have invited me to Fat Sal's Deep-Dish, that's for sure. He would have invited me to stay on the train and given me a magazine. Maybe even a lollipop.

"You're gonna love this pizza! Ever had Chicago deep-dish?"

He's very enthusiastic.

"No, sorry."

I don't know why I should be sorry I've never had this stuff that everybody brags about. It's like people from Seattle talking about coffee. Like they invented it. Like it's the apex of human evolution. Enough, already, Seattle. It's a beverage. Step off.

I don't know, either, why I'm here other than the aforementioned combination of boredom and curiosity that have previously been my downfall and the intense lack of fucks I have left to give.

Also, it helps that I won't be alive soon.

Might as well live it up! Deep-dish pizza for everyone!

Although now it occurs to me this guy might actually be dangerous. Maybe this wasn't such a good, devil-may-care idea, anyway. Maybe this guy is wanted for murder, serial murder, and this is his shtick. The hook: deep-dish pizza.

Cold feet, commence. "You know, I really should be getting back. I don't wanna miss my train."

"You have two hours—" he argues.

"Yeah, but, I tend to space out sometimes. Trust me. I've bumped into lampposts before."

"Is that right?"

He leans in now, whispers.

"So . . . you smoke pot?"

Oh, here we go. This is what they do on TV, right? Get the drugs involved, or the booze. Try to get a girl a little off-balance so she'll make a bad decision. My dad warned me about this rap. Thank fucking God.

"Yeah, no. I'm Catholic."

Like that has anything to do with anything. Yes sir, I'm the only Catholic to ever even think of sinning because the Pope told us no! We are all clean as the driven snow!

"Oh."

"Also, I'm sixteen."

His eyes widen. Then he gets this sad-puppy look. "Sixteen? Are you sure you're not . . . *eighteen?*"

I mean. Gross.

"Look, I better go."

"Aw, c'mon . . . You haven't even tried it yet!"

"Um, no."

"Okay, fine."

Now he just looks pissed. Guys always turn real fast, I've noticed, once they see they don't have a shot. It's like the curtain flies up and you realize right away what a shit bag you've been talking to the whole time.

"Well, nice meeting you. Sorry you didn't get to strangle me or whatever."

He looks up, annoyed.

"Don't flatter yourself. You're not even that good-looking."

"If you're saying I'm not good-looking enough to strangle, then I will take that as a compliment, thank you very much."

See what I mean? Two minutes ago this guy was national treasure Tom Hanks. Now?

Never trust a man who cares so much about deep-dish pizza.

On my way back to the platform, there's a gift store. There's a mirror on the back shelf I am trying to avoid, now that I know I'm not good-looking. In this tiny establishment you can buy all sorts of things to tell the folks back home you were in Chicago. Shot glasses. Mugs. Fridge magnets. And I'd buy one, too. If I had any folks back home.

I do not have folks.

I have folk.

Singular.

Dad.

And he does not want a fridge magnet to show I went to Chicago.

About now, he's probably wishing Chicago never existed.

And, about now, I am wishing I never existed, too.

FOUR

Do you ever have the feeling that you're supposed to do something? That there's this big, dark thing hanging right above you, dangling like a carrot, but it's invisible and unknowable and you have to kind of figure it out because if you don't figure it out, boy, you blew it?

Or worse, maybe you do figure it out. Maybe you figure out that big, mysterious thing you're supposed to reach for and you just can't do it. You just *don't* do it. Like you stare it right in the face and say, "I can't."

Then for the rest of your life you know what you are.

A do-nothing.

It's like this fear that pecks away at my brain, sometimes, lying in bed at night. What is the thing? What is this thing?

Will I ever figure it out? Is there even a thing? There has to be a thing. Doesn't there? Otherwise, I'm a do-nothing.

My mother, on the other hand, is a do-*something*.

She has made it.

Everybody knows who she is and freaks out about her and freaks out even more once they figure out she's my mom. It's obnoxious.

My dad doesn't get to be a do-something. That happens sometimes. Not everybody gets to be famous. Or a renowned something-or-other. Or even a vaguely known something-or-other.

Somehow my dad just kind of missed the boat. Maybe he didn't have that killer instinct or *whatever it is* you need to elbow everybody out of the way and fly up into the stratosphere.

Or maybe he just wasted too much time being a dad. My dad.

See, while my mother was off chatting with heads of state and captains of industry, my father was teaching me how to ride a bike. And perfecting his slow-cooker recipes. And googling step-by-step instructions on how to sew a hem.

So maybe it's my fault.

And here's the other thing. He's still in love with my mom. My dad. He tries to pretend he's over it, but he mentions my mom about three times a day and what she's doing and what award she just got, and how I should care and call her and congratulate her. It's all under the guise of keeping me posted, but make no mistake: he's obsessed. It really breaks my heart. I just want to shake him and say, "Get over it! She sucks, let's just face it!" But he goes on and on about her latest, greatest achievement and something-doing. You can imagine that the fact he never got to be a do-something isn't exactly lost on him. Like maybe it just makes him a little bit crazy.

It's the kind of crazy that repeats itself. It's a kind of grinding gear that goes around and around in a loop. Like this: "You know, you should call your mother because she just got an award for blah-blah." Then, wait two minutes. Then, "You know, you should call your mother because she just got an award for blah-blah." Like, on a loop. Over and over.

And obsessive thoughts. Like a kind of dread. Over and over. About everything. About her. About dry-cleaning chemicals. About smoke detectors. About stranger danger and seat belts and all the things that can go wrong in a world that fits inside a toolshed.

"Whatever you do, don't forget your jacket, Cakey-pie."

Oh, yeah. My dad calls me Cakey-pie. It's because somewhere along the line I developed a dessert habit. Look, it's not something I'm proud of, okay? I just don't seem to be able to resist cake, *or pie*, the way most people do.

My affliction extends to other baked goods. Cupcakes, cookies. God help me, cronuts. No one can resist a cronut. Not even the Pope.

But in defense of my slightly fixated father, there was something he didn't have to stretch to get obsessed by. There was something my mother gave him to fulfill his feelings of blind, pulsing dread.

She ran off with his best man.

Yup, that guy at the wedding who gives the speech about how great the groom is? She ran off with that guy.

There. I said it. I never really like to say it, 'cause I never really like to think about it. Like, I just like to make it small and put it in a box and put it far, far away. But every once in a while, it unpacks itself and comes slithering back to meet me, through the corners and crevices of my shoulders and earlobes, and there it is. The dumb fact.

Your mom cheated on your dad.

With his best man.

And then ran off with him.

There's a stabbing kind of thing about it. A real "fuck you" in it. You gotta wonder what kind of person would do a thing like that. I'll tell you what kind of person. A broken person. A person who would grab a life vest from a child on the *Titanic*.

So, even though my mother is a do-something and

everybody thinks she's the bee's knees and maybe my dad repeats himself a little bit, like that guy in *Rain Man*, I stayed with my dad after the split. My mom says I broke her heart or something, but she's just being dramatic. She's the kinda person who talks big but then misses the Christmas recital.

My dad is the kinda person who is early to the Christmas recital, brings flowers to the Christmas recital, and would practically get up onstage and perform the whole Christmas recital for you if you let him.

So, yeah, I stuck by my dad. And, yeah, it's a humble life. By which I mean we are broke-ass. He mostly works at the pharmacy, and we won't be moving into the Ritz anytime soon. But, still, I'd rather be broke-ass than be, well, *her.*

I know what you're thinking. You're thinking there's going to be some kind of happy family reconciliation at the end of all this. There's going to be some moment where the music swells and all of a sudden an understanding is reached and my mother comes back from Europe and everybody hugs each other and there's maybe a dog involved who we laugh and scruff on the head.

Welp, I'm sorry to break your heart, but that moment is never going to happen. This story is *not* about that. My mother got me in to Pembroke, and that is the end of that. If I graduate with honors, there is a five percent chance she might possibly come to the graduation. That is all. There are no heartfelt apologies, no slurpy revelations, no classical music swells as we ride off in a one-horse open sleigh.

And that's okay.

But, let's get one thing straight. I still do *not* want to be a do-nothing. No sir. I wanna be that person who grabs great things and wrestles them down.

But I also just want that nagging desire, that compulsion, to stop. Just stop. Just fucking stop. Stop tugging me, telling me I have to do more, I have to be more, I have to do something or I'm worthless, or I'm nothing or I'm nobody.

There was a kid who used to sit in the sandbox. He used to sit there all day and build castles in the sand and smash them to smithereens and build them again. Happy as a clam.

I would do anything to be that kid.

But I can put a smile on my face now. I can put a smile on my face knowing that all that will be over soon. As the train pulls out of the station, *chugga-chugga-chugga*, off over the plains, heading east, I can put a smile on my face knowing once I turn out the lights, that thing—that thing in me that is my mother—can never get me again.

FIVE

Look at this place, will you? It's better than the brochure. I'm not even kidding. It's got *gargoyles*. Look! At the top of the giant cathedral, at the end of the green, there they are. Two of them, staring down. Just like that place in Paris they always show in movies when the world is ending. You know, over here they show the White House getting blown to smithereens, and in London they show that giant clock. And, what's the place in Paris? Notre Dame. That's it. They show Notre Dame. With gargoyles. *Avec* gargoyles. That's French. See, I just got here and I'm already more sophisticated.

But, trust me, looking around, it's obvious. I'm the lowest of the low in these digs.

All the buildings look like they're haunted. Gray stone

castles with spires everywhere. Gray arches. Gray stone pathways leading into the trees. Ghost city.

I'm surprised a ghost doesn't float out of the admissions building to greet me.

But it's not a ghost that comes out. It's more like a vampire. A vampire lady with white skin and black hair who has probably been eating blood pudding for breakfast.

She emerges from a building marked Holyoke Commons.

She talks the way you talk to people you have to help. People slower than you. People beneath you.

"Well, hello, Willa. Willa Parker, yes? So very nice to meet you."

Oh, I forgot. My name's Willa. Yeah, I know. It's 'cause my father loves *My Ántonia* and Willa Cather and we live in the Midwest, etcetera, etcetera. Now, go ahead, say it. Lucky he didn't love Hemingway or Wharton or Shakespeare, or I would be named Ernest or Edith or William. I've only heard it, in infinite iterations, like a hundred times. It's okay, though. I forgive you. I know you're excited to be here, too.

The vampire lady introduces herself.

"My name is Ursula Cantor, and I am the head of admissions. We are so very glad to have you here. Did you know they teach your mother's book in our economics courses?"

Don't roll your eyes. Don't roll your eyes. Don't roll your eyes. It's the first impression, remember? Come on. Be nice, Willa.

"Oh, really? That's . . . great. I'll be sure to tell her."

That's a lie. I won't tell her because I never talk to her and even if I did talk to her and tell her she wouldn't care. Or maybe she would. She is kind of like a blind narcissist. It's never enough. The compliments.

But she'd pretend she didn't care.

Wait! False modesty.

A sophisticated skill I should try to master, perhaps?

"It's so kind of you to come greet me. I'm flattered."

See how well I'm doing? I even said "kind." I like this new character. Me. New and improved. East Coast me.

Vampire Ursula smiles. She has lipstick on her teeth. Deep berry. Or it might be blood. From that pudding.

"You will be staying off Radnor quad. Thiswicke. Third floor down the hall. Room three-oh-nine. You'll be pleased to hear it has a lovely view of Shipley's Promenade."

"Oh. I am pleased to hear that."

I have only understood half of those words, but look at me! I'm *pleased to hear things* now. It used to be I just *liked* things.

"Also, I'd like you to know I am here for you if there's anything you may need to make the transition. Just let me know."

"Oh, how kind of you. Thank you."

No one can stop me. I am perfect now. My manners are impeccable.

Vampire Ursula sees something out of the corner of her

eye, and all the polite is wiped off her face and replaced with *irate*.

"Remy! Put that out this minute!"

Remy? Who the hell is named Remy? I thought that was some kind of booze. I mean, I truly hope this girl's last name is not Martin.

I turn to look and see her.

No, it's more like this. I turn to look and see . . .

REMY.

All caps. Or more like this. I turn to look and see . . .

REMY.

Zapfino font. Remy deserves Zapfino font. *And* all caps. Remy deserves to have a giant statue erected in her honor.

This is what she's wearing:

First, she's got a plaid miniskirt on. No big deal there. It's a uniform. But she's wearing it with leg warmers. Those are not plaid. Those are striped. Striped! Horizontally! In rainbow colors! She's got on a burgundy blazer with the school insignia on it. A coat of arms. (What did you think it was gonna be? A duck in a Chevy pickup?) Again—uniform. But then, when you look closely, you see she's like written all over it. With a Sharpie, maybe? All kinds of words, maybe random, maybe not. She's got on a pair of boots, but they have this like ethnic embellishment up the sides, like Mongolian or something. Then . . . And here is the kicker. She has a tie coming down like she is a boy. And braids. With a ribbon wound through them. A rainbow ribbon.

Jesus Christ.

Who is this person I'm looking at?

Remy is, also, smoking a cigarette. And not even an electronic cigarette. A real cigarette. From the olden times, you know. Like fire you stick in your face. Which she should not be doing. Not only because it's not good for her, but, obviously, also because this school costs an arm and a leg and the soul of every firstborn cousin to get into, and the last thing anyone should be doing at this school is something that could get them kicked out. I mean, what kind of a person just stands there on the green smoking an old-fashioned cigarette like that? A person who deeply and truly doesn't give a fuck. That's who.

"Remy, you and I both know that is not allowed. Please put it out immediately or you know the consequences."

Remy looks at Vampire Ursula, looks at me.

"Who's the new girl?"

Vampire Ursula lifts her chin.

"Remy, I am not going to tell you again."

Remy rolls her eyes and puts the cigarette out.

"Sorry, Miss Cantor. I'm quitting, I promise."

Ursula pretends to be satisfied. Remy looks at me and smirks.

It's weird how she kind of turn-disappears around the corner. It's like a pivot, and, *poof*, she's gone. It's a hot move I decide to master.

Vampire Ursula reads my mind because everybody knows vampires are mind readers.

"I truly hope you will not allow yourself to be influenced by bad behavior while you are with us, Willa."

I nod assuringly.

"Absolutely. Of course not. I would never."

And I'm right. In that moment. I mean it. I mean it in every ion of every cell of my body.

I could laugh now, thinking of it. Thinking back on this moment. I would giggle into my shirtsleeve.

If it were funny.

Which it turns out, it was definitely not.

Because, you know, of what happened.

SIX

Did you know this place is haunted? Well, I mean, of course it is. You can't build a place out of cold gray stone with gargoyles everywhere and dark wood floors and not expect a few ghosts to show up. Especially if you go back in time and build it two hundred years ago. It's like a ghost's natural habitat.

This place is modeled after Oxford. And that's part of what makes it snooty. It's funny how in America every time you model something after something in England, everybody thinks, oh, it's the best thing ever. If it's so great, then why are we all here anyway? Why did the fathers of our country take a look at that old place, say no thanks, and jump on a rickety, rat-filled boat with hardly any food and nary a chance at survival to get out of there in the first place?

Because it sucked over there, that's why.

I know, I know. You're not supposed to say that. Everybody is supposed to think it's oh-so-sophisticated and we should be respectful and care about the queen and the monarchy and those guys in red suits and black furry hats standing still all day. But I'm not buying it. A queen? Seriously? In this day and age? You might as well just throw up your hands and say, "Let them eat cake!" Then you could punch all the poor people in the stomach on your way to your castle with those guys in funny hats standing at attention.

Don't get me wrong. I'm not a communist or whatever. I just don't see why anybody is supposed to care about a bunch of people because of who their parents were. Aren't you supposed to care about what someone does? What they do with what they got? Like Maya Angelou, for instance. She wasn't born in some red-velvet bed. She had a hard, horrible, terrible life, and then she just flew up out of the ashes and became a world-famous literary genius. Now, that's what I call a queen. Not some random zygote who hails from a long line of blue bloods mating with other blue bloods. Seriously. It's like we all bought this swampland long ago and we just keep buying it. Hook, line, and sinker.

And, by the way, this place is not only buying that idea,

this place is *selling* it. That's why they copied the plans. This place is selling that idea from every plaque to every statue to every quad.

There's a green. There's a cloister. There's a bunch of gothic buildings facing off, silent and judgy. There's a Thiswicke dorm. Yup, Thiswicke. Say that with a lisp. It's the haunted one. I googled it.

According to the legend there was some girl at the turn of the century taking a bath in kerosene in the middle of the night. Why was she taking a bath in kerosene? Oh, I'm so glad you asked. It's because she thought she had the plague. Obviously. Everybody knows if you ever think you have the plague you're supposed to take a bath in kerosene and, also, put a bunch of candles around said bath because, of course, you are taking the bath in the middle of the night. Taking a bath during the day is just not done. Especially if you have the plague.

Well, you can see what's coming. Of course, one of the candles accidentally fell in the bath and then the girl accidentally caught on fire and then she accidentally ran the entirety of the fourth-floor hall, all the way to the end, where she accidentally jumped to her death out the window and now accidentally haunts the dorm in the middle of the night.

Nice place. Very comforting.

My room, of course, is *on* the fourth floor. Right next to the bathroom. Yes, the bathroom where the ill-fated kerosene soak took place.

Don't worry. I am completely prepared for a haunting. Here is my plan: If I hear the bath in the middle of the night, the first order of business is to crawl under my sheets. That's number one. Then, the next order of business is to pull the blanket up over my head. That's two. Then, the third order of business is to find God.

Yes, I will pray. I haven't decided yet to whom I will pray, but I figure I'll just pray to them all and hope one of them comes to my aid. Even a broken clock is right twice a day.

But it's not even dark yet, so don't get ahead of yourself. We're fine. All I have to do is just unpack my bags. Bag. I have to unpack my bag. Traveling light over here. Mostly because my arms aren't that strong. Seriously, though. Am I the only one whose arms get tired washing my hair?

Don't answer that. I know I'm lazy. God, what I would do to exercise! Wouldn't it be great?! I really would love to do it sometime. And I will. Someday.

I'll get a supersporty outfit and fancy all-terrain shoes for my twenty-mile runs through the woods, over puddles and creeks, through the forest, over the town, maybe even the track. No one will be able to stop me. It will be four in the morning, but I won't care. It will just be me against the world. And against myself. I will be my fiercest competitor. You will see me in the morning light, see my breath coming out in bursts against the cold. I'll follow the path along the river and my face will be stern, thinking about the crime I am solving, because in this fantasy I am suddenly that lady on *Law & Order: Special Victims Unit*. I am sassy and a fox and no one can mess with me. I have seen it all, but I still have hope for humanity. That's why I do this job, and jog next to the levy at four in the morning. I'm a tough cookie. A cookie who jogs.

I really can't wait.

But for now my arms get tired washing my hair.

So, baby steps.

It appears I have this whole room to myself. Maybe no one else wants to live up here in ghost city. Maybe the riff-raff like me gets the last pick of the real estate around here.

That's okay, maybe when I see the ghost, I can ask a few things about the afterlife. I have some follow-up questions from Bible school.

I wonder if the ghost will be able to sense my diabolical plan to hurl myself into the abyss. I wonder if the ghost will be happy to have the company. Maybe the ghost is lonely.

The wood floors here are dark brown, practically black.

And there is elaborate molding involved. I know. They are not kidding around with this Oxford stuff, are they? It's a corner room, so I have windows on two adjacent sides. That means next to each other. I know you probably know that, but in my school back home I had to explain to this cheerleader what "astute" meant. Astute! I can guarantee if you don't know what "astute" means then you probably are not.

Down out the window, four stories down, I can see the green. And everybody walking back and forth to the campus center. It's actually a pretty superfantastic vantage point. It's like the catbird seat. Down below everybody is rushing around, books in hand, backpacked, plaid uniform miniskirts swishing, a few uniform blazers slung over shoulders. One girl's wearing a carefree scarf. And socks. And glasses. Everyone rushing, rushing. You gotta figure at some point, one day, everyone will look back and wonder what the shnook they were ever rushing around for. Like, enough with the rushing already. We're in high school. I'm pretty sure Vladimir Putin is not waiting on the latest dispatch from The Pembroke School quadrangle.

My dad got me a fitted sheet set with owls on it. They are knowing but also kind of eclectic. Also, he's sending me a comforter, so I won't "get a chill." Word has it there are owls involved there, too. My dad. He thinks of everything. Although I bet he will also send me something really weird.

Like a Tuscan-themed welcome mat with vines and trellises everywhere. Or something vaguely French. Or worse, he will try to be "cool" and send something with pink and black scribbles all over the place.

Something with Justin Bieber on it.

Until then, I will have to do with these knowing, alternative owls protecting me. I don't even have one picture to hang. What would I hang? A poster with a cat balancing off a tree? Hang in there! Or what about a picture of the Eiffel Tower? Isn't that what everybody does? It shows you've got class. Or how about that picture where that sailor guy is kissing that girl in Times Square? You know, the black-and-white one? If you look at that picture real close it kind of looks like she doesn't even really want to be kissed. I dare you. Check it out. That girl is totally not into it.

Wait! There is one thing. I take my picture of Gabriel from the front pocket of my backpack. I place it on my desk and stare at his swirling deep-brown eyes, the ones I imagined myself falling into during some cheesy, slow-song sway in the crepe-paper-festooned gym.

Except now, all of a sudden, I don't really get why I imagined it so much. I'm looking at this same picture I drooled over, and all of a sudden it hits me. Meh. Gabriel is actually kind of . . . average. Maybe he is just a Gabe after all. Maybe now that I am here he is too . . . provincial.

I crumple up the torn bit of paper and sink it into the little wastebasket in the corner.

As if on cue, a text from my dad.

Proud of U. Call if U need me. ♥.

I could call him and start blubbering all over the place, but that would just make him worry.

No. Be strong, Willa!

Class doesn't start for two days so that means I have exactly forty-eight hours to sit here in my catbird seat and try to catch a glimpse of Remy. No, I'm not stalking her. I just want to see if she has any friends. And, if she does, how I could be one. Maybe.

But I'm not stalking her.

Please. Never.

SEVEN

Nobody seems to notice me the first day of class. Not in a bad way, not in a good way. Not in any way. It's just like I'm invisible. That's fine, too. I'd rather be invisible than humiliated. There seems to be no open aggression against me, and that's a relief. Back in Iowa, there were days I would get tripped twice before first period. Twice.

Mostly, I just sit in the front row and look up at the teacher. I put on this listening face that makes it seem like I'm really interested and that she is the most fascinating person saying the most fascinating things. Sometimes that's true, actually. But sometimes, not so much. It doesn't matter. The listening face remains the same. Questioning, quizzical, pondering, a rare nod of "I get it." Trust me, it works. I've been a straight-A student since preschool. Day care, even. If there had been classes in the maternity ward, I would have graduated with honors. None of those other babies would ever have stood a chance.

Thus far, my teachers, with a few rare exceptions, have rewarded my engaged expressions, my onslaught of curious but not authority-defying questions, and my general most-inspiring-teacher-in-the-world classroom affirmations with straight As across the board.

That was always nonnegotiable. Everything else could just fall where it may with my mother except the grades. The grades had to be A-plus-plus. That was the only deal she made with my dad when she left him.

See, it helps if you sit in the front row and make the listening face. A slight tilt of the head but not too much. Just enough to imply contemplation. Stay in the front row so that no one can distract you. That's important, too. Focus.

The classes are as follows: English Literature. Contemporary Lit. Calculus. Bio. American History. Art. And Music Theory. Both the art and music classes are kind of cool in that they combine actual learning with doing. Like you have to learn about pop art and then we make our own pop art. Or you have to learn about the jazz age and then a song or two. It's kind of cool, honestly. Much better than anything we had back home. Back home it was more like, "Do this, don't ask questions. Learn this date, spit it back at me!" But today we learned about Billie Holiday and this song about strange fruit but it doesn't mean fruit at all because it's about how they used to hang people down south just for being black, and that is one of those things that you don't want to hear, or even know about, but you have to hear and have to know about, so you can make sure it never happens again. Or so that you can be ready with a rebuke when some dumb relative says something horrible about that time when "those people used to know their place." Or at the very, very least, you can know better than to say the horrible thing yourself.

I wonder how many girls in this class have racist uncles or grandparents they have to listen to. It's kind of a massive problem, I bet. Old people are supposed to be wise, not jerk-faces. You gotta wonder what happened to sagacity.

Okay, so far, my favorite is the American History teacher. He's got patches on the elbows of his tweed blazer, and his oxford is kind of wrinkled, like maybe he slept in it. He's got light-brown hair and bright-blue eyes and, yeah, he's cute and everything, but I'm not about to ask him on a date. I bet lots of girls get a crush on him, though. You can kind of feel it. Like there's a mesmerized sigh in the room. A collective swoon coming off the desks.

Remy has been AWOL all day, so it's clear she was just a

figment of my imagination. Some kind of hallucination, or a wish I made.

Tonight, I have my first dinner in this place. I'll be honest with you, I'm not looking forward to it. You have to eat in the cafeteria and it's all these long Hogwarts-like tables, and I don't know anyone, so basically I'll just be sitting there alone. Like a jerk.

Then I remember.

There's a vending machine in the campus center. So my evening repast will consist of Doritos and Sprite, *en suite.*

It's getting dark early now, with the lights streaming out of the cafeteria onto the green, but everything else is starting to look spooky. There's a full moon tonight, and it's so big it looks like you could just reach out and pull it down and roll it around the quadrangle.

Something weird about it, though. Something strange. And insistent. It takes my feet step by step, moving me forward toward it, across the green. Past and away from the chatter and *clang, clang* of silver coming out of the cafeteria.

Now, it's just me, beneath the moon, somehow on the other end of the green from my window. There's a bench at the end, under a row of trees. White marble and too big, really. Not even elegant. Just a giant alabaster bench glistening in the moonlight. Waiting.

It's not cold out, but you can tell it's gonna get cold soon.

Something crisp in the air about to smell like burnt leaves. Something dying.

That bench is waiting for me, and before I know it, there I am sitting on it. Looking across the green at the light streaming out the caf, a warm glow and the chatter floating up into the night sky, I feel a world shutting me out. You know what I mean? Like I don't belong here, or there, or back home, or anywhere. I'm just kind of this weird girl with no place to go. There's a part of me that always feels like that, you know? Like a fox in the snow. Somewhere deep in that arctic, my face sticking out of the tundra. (See me.) Surrounded by crisp, white freezing edges curving down to the horizon with nothing in them. (See me.)

But nothing.

No shelter.

Maybe there's a part of me that *wants* to be that fox in the snow that never gets to come inside. Maybe there's even a part of me that's scared to. You always hear about guys trying to be lone wolves and whatever, but what about girls? Maybe there are some weird girls who wanna howl at the moon, too. Some weird girls who are me.

Looking into the little windows, tiny across the green, it's like a picture show. And looking in, I can't help but wonder what all those silhouette moving heads are talking about and how do you even talk about anything? How do you even come off as normal? Some people are so good at it. Have you ever noticed that? Like they can just smile and be happy and talk to anyone and they're just content. Normal.

But I'm not normal.

I'm a malcontent.

Restless. Always looking for a rock to hide under, or a room, or a cave, or a bench at the end of the green at dinnertime, when everybody else just goes inside, lets it ride, makes it look so easy. And I look up at the moon and wonder—why a malcontent? Why a fox in the snow? Why never at home? What's the point in making someone like that? Or maybe there's no point. Maybe it's just a mistake. A malfunction. A flaw in the design.

My dad's face flashes into my head, and before I even know it, it's happening again. The stupid tears, cold in the night air, rolling down my face. I wipe them with my forearms and sigh. You can see all the way down this row of trees to the bell tower.

I ponder it a moment. Now, *that's* a place you could kill yourself.

"Doesn't it look like a play?"

The words come out of nowhere, and I jump out of my skin. Turning from the bench, there she is.

Remy.

"Sorry. Did I scare you? I didn't mean to."

"No, I just—"

I just what? I just was thinking how isolated and lonely I am? Jesus. I never know what to say.

"But don't they? The people in there? With the light behind them? It feels like the curtain went up and there they are. Act one."

She nods toward the cafeteria.

"Yeah, it does kinda."

She's leaning up against an oak and she's wearing another just-as-weird combination of clothes. It's like she threw everything on in the dark, but somehow it looks like Isaac Mizrahi put it together. It makes sense but doesn't make sense. And I don't know what to say about her, except that she is *everything*.

"So, what's the matter? Don't like cafeteria food? Me neither. It used to be worse. Seriously. Now they've gone organic or whatever."

"Oh."

See, I'm a real wordsmith at the moment.

"Let me guess. It's not the food, it's the company."

". . . Sorta."

She takes out another old-timey cigarette. Lights up.

"You wanna try? Menthol. Tastes like a Junior Mint on fire."

I shake my head.

"They actually have better food at the boys' school. So unfair."

Oh, you didn't know there was a boys' school? Yup, it's the "brother school" to Pembroke. One mile on foot or one stop over on the R5 Paoli local train. Founded in 1805. Are you ready for it? Are you ready for the name? Don't laugh. It's called Witherspoon. I know. I mean, it's almost like they want their kids to get beat up. But that's what it's called, and it's our brother school. That means we're supposed to care about them. Like their lacrosse games and cotillions and dumb plays and stuff.

"Ya ever been over there?"

"Where?"

"Witherspoon?"

"No, um. Sounds too . . . withery."

She chuckles. "Trust me, it is."

We stand there a moment. I still don't quite understand why she's talking to me.

"Well, um, I have a test tomorrow, so . . ."

I start off toward Thiswicke. I don't even know why I'm leaving, other than I'm just embarrassed and can't think of anything to say. And that was a lie. I have no tests tomorrow.

"Hey!" she calls after me. "Where you from, anyway?"

God, should I tell her? She's gonna think I'm so lame and never talk to me again.

But then I think, who cares? It's not like I'm long for this world anyway.

Fuck it.

"Iowa."

"What? Are you serious?"

"Yeah." Resigned.

"Where?"

Here we go.

"What Cheer."

"Excuse me?"

"What Cheer. I'm from a place called What Cheer, Iowa."

"Oh my God, that is the greatest name for a place ever!"

What? I wrinkle my forehead at her, confused.

"I've never met anyone from Iowa before. Do they all look like you?"

"Um . . ."

"Because then I'd know where they grow all the cute people."

I'm not sure she actually said that. Did she just say that? Or what if she did? Or why? Or if she was talking about me. Was she talking about me?

All I know is I better leave. Before I say something stupid. And she realizes what a loser I am. I don't know what to say. I have nothing to say. I'm awkward. I'm weird, and I better leave. Like right now.

I enact a completely wooden gesture, something resembling a wave good-bye, mated with a salute and a bow, and turn to walk back to Thiswicke.

"Okay, then. See ya round . . . Iowa."

She smiles and takes a drag.

All the way across the green I get the feeling she's watching me. Parsing me. Sizing me up. But here's the strange thing. I don't get the feeling that it's bad. I get the feeling that somehow, and I don't know why, but somehow this girl, this coolest girl ever invented—

—actually might possibly perhaps like me.

EIGHT

The next day in Con Lit we start reading *The Bluest Eye*, by Toni Morrison. Our teacher is named Ms. Ingall. She's got light-brown hair and fish-white skin. I mean, she's practically green. But there's something about her. Something kind. You get the feeling she's got to be a vegan or something. No one who ever ate meat could be that pale. I bet she has a "Free the Orcas" sticker on her car. Not that I mind that. I'd like to free the orcas, too. If I could, I'd free the dolphins as well. And the sea otters. Honestly, I'd spend the whole night going tank to tank, emancipating all the marine mammals and shouting, "Swim! Swim! Be free!" Why should they have to suffer just so people can ogle them and applaud on cue? If you want to see an orca, go on a boat. Or watch the

Discovery Channel. Why does anyone have to coop up some poor marine mammal just so you can eat a waffle cone and point at it at the same time?

Ms. Ingall has kind eyes. There's still a light in them. She's not married. So maybe that explains the light. She's wearing Mephisto shoes for comfort and a long, flowy skirt. Maybe she'll never be married. Or maybe this is just her teach-wear. Maybe when she goes home she lets her hair down and puts on red lipstick and kills all the boys with her rapier wit and stacked heels. Or maybe she has a cat. Named Mr. Snuffles.

It is not lost on me that I may end up just like her one day. Alone. With a cat herd. If my station in this class is any indication, I'm a shoo-in. You see, I'm at the back of the room. All alone. Yup, that's right. No one sitting next to me. Or even thinking about sitting next to me. All of my usual seats in the front row? Taken.

I might as well start naming the cats now.

Mr. Fritz. Senator Snuggles. Miss Whiskers. Chairman Meow.

There are going to be at least fifty, so feel free to add to the list. I'm sure I will run out of ideas anytime now.

"Excuse me? Is this Con Lit?"

The whole class turns and there in the doorway . . . is Remy.

The girl in front of me elbows the girl next to her and whispers.

"That's the girl I was telling you about . . ."

Ms. Ingall shushes them.

"Yes, this is Contemporary Literature. And who, might I ask, are you?"

"Remy Taft. This is my class, I think. I should be on the roster."

"Yes, you are on the roster. And . . . you were on the roster yesterday, when you weren't here."

"Oh, yeah, we just got in last night. Sorry."

"Well, Miss Taft, I trust you will not *get in* late again. Take a seat."

Remy walks down the row. There's a silence. A trepidation. Even . . . a hope. I get the feeling Remy is a hot ticket. I get the feeling everyone is hoping she will bless them with her presence, her smile, her last name. Taft. Like the president.

And now she sees me. And now she smiles. And now she sits.

Next to me.

"Well, hey! It's you. I can't believe you're in this class. Thank God."

And the two girls in front of me, who were totally ignoring me and acting like maybe I had leprosy before, take a long look at me and decide it's possible they should have tried to be friends with me. They look at each other. Dumbfounded. They are telepathically communicating with each other: *Oh. We messed up.*

I'm sort of having an out-of-body experience right now.

Remy sits down.

One of the girls leans in.

"Hi, Remy."

Remy barely hears them; she looks up and gives a cursory "Oh, hey."

"Do you remember me . . . ? We met last summer? Fourth of July, actually? The Hamptons?"

"Oh. Maybe. I was kinda drunk . . ."

The girl looks vaguely humiliated, a little disappointed. But she tries to cover.

"Oh, yeah . . . me, too."

The girl doesn't really pull it off.

Remy gives her a polite smile and turns back to me. And now I know.

Remy rules the school.

Of course she does. Her last name is Taft. She dresses like she just got out of the dryer. And she is a chronic, illegal, old-fashioned Junior-Mint smoker.

So, now that we've established that, the question is . . . why is she being so nice to me? I mean, seriously. Maybe it's a trick. That could be. Maybe she's playing a trick on me. To humiliate me.

"Hey, can we look off the same book? I sort of lost mine."

It is the second day of school.

"What? Oh, yeah . . . sure . . ."

"Did I miss anything yesterday?"

"Um, no, we just kind of took these weird tests that had nothing to do with anything."

This gets a laugh, although I'm not sure why.

And I wonder if she knows how nervous I am. Or how I feel like an idiot. Or the fact that my hands are practically shaking when I hold up the book to share with her. Ugh, hands! Stop shaking, you nerds!

My hands *continue* to be total nerds. Look at me. I'm a *mess!*

I can feel the eyes of the two girls staring at me. I can feel them trying to figure out who I am. I can feel them boring a hole in my blazer, but I don't have the courage to tell them the truth. To tell them I'm no one.

And that I get the feeling, just at this second, that Remy has made me *someone.*

NINE

What I'm doing now is lying low. Just staying quiet and keeping away from everybody. Here's the thing: All of a sudden I've got this, like, spotlight on me. Because of Remy.

Ever since that day when she sat next to me in Con Lit. Ever since that day, it's like there's this laser on my back. Like everybody looking. And wondering. But not asking. Parsing. Discerning. Analyzing. But not asking.

And me? I'm just keeping quiet.

Look. Remy sits next to me in class. That's it. We talk. We exchange notes. That's it. One time she walked me across the green. That's all.

But whatever she's been up to before must have been a whole lot of nothing, because I never see her with anyone at school and all of a sudden everybody is being a lot nicer to me than before. It's like before I was Walmart and now I am Comme Des Garçons.

And that's not all. Last time I went to lunch, this girl next to me in line at the salad bar named Abigail—because people around here are named things like Abigail. And Martha. And Betsy. And other mothers of the American Revolution—turns to me and asks me *if I want to sit with her and all her friends.* I look over and they are all staring at me. Expectantly. Like they had talked about it. Like they had planned it. Like they were trying to nab me.

Now, I've never been nabbed before.

I've never even been slightly detoured.

It's weird. But what's weirder about it is I don't even know anything about Remy. It's not like I hang out with her. It's not like she's coming over to my room and we're having a pillow fight. It's just . . . nothing. It's a smile and a shared book in Con Lit. Because she always forgets it.

I mean, I don't get it.

And I don't know quite what to do.

My dad always says that if you don't know what to do, do nothing. So, my solution is . . . lie low. I'm just keeping my head down, going to class, asking insightful but not controversial questions, raising my hand with the answers but not too much, studying and handing in my tests but not too much. I'm basically still just a bookworm, but now I'm a bookworm with eyeballs on my backpack.

But even tonight, tonight when I got out of the shower and was brushing my teeth in the mirror . . . You know, in the haunted bathroom? Even tonight, this girl from down the hall starts brushing her teeth next to me. She starts brushing her teeth next to me and looking at me. Awkward. When you're brushing your teeth: not looking time. Then, after she's done she starts talking to me. Out of the blue.

"Hey, aren't you in my Lit class?"

"Um. Yeah. I think so."

"Cool class, right? I like the teacher."

"Ms. Ingall? Yeah, she's nice."

Then she looks at me a little longer, and I can tell she's about to say something else, or she wants to say something else, but she doesn't. She just stands there. And it's getting uncomfortable.

"Well, um, see you in class . . ."

And I turn to walk back into my haunted room from the haunted bathroom.

"Hey! We could study together. You know, since we're hall mates."

I turn around, "Yeah, okay. That would be nice."

"My name's Emma, by the way."

"Oh, okay."

"What's your name?"

"Huh? Oh, um . . . Willa. My name's Willa."

I always do that. When I get put on the spot like that, I always forget my name for, like, three seconds. It's embarrassing.

"Oh, cool. Well, see you in class, Willa."

"Yeah, okay."

I mean, this is a long conversation to be having in your towel, especially when it's cold outside. I mean, not winter cold. But definitely fall-coming-soon-could-catch-a-cold-any-minute cold.

And I know that now that girl is gonna come up to me in class tomorrow. When I'm next to Remy. Watch. I'm telling you. It's like the whole school has been trying to forge this connection to the elusive Remy Taft, and now that she has anointed me with her friendship I am the conduit.

But it's just me.

Lil' ol' me.

And I'm not a conduit to anything . . . am I?

TEN

You're never gonna believe what happened. I swear to God, I'm not making this up. Remember that thing I told you about the legend of the bath? Okay, so here goes.

That same night, the night where that girl Emma accosted me during my dental hygiene routine . . . well, that same night, at about three in the morning . . . I heard the bathtub. Yes, bathwater running. And that's not all. I woke up, with a start, kind of sweaty, honestly. And as I lurched up in bed, I heard it. The bathwater.

No big deal, right? Maybe someone was just taking a bath at three in the morning. Stranger things have happened.

Well, that's what I thought. So, I sat there. And I sat there. And I listened. And I sat there. But then it wasn't stopping. Like for an hour. An hour-long bath.

So now I'm starting to wonder. Is something wrong? Maybe someone fell asleep in the bath. Maybe I'm supposed to help them. Maybe that's why I flew awake in the first place.

So, now that I know I'm supposed to be the hero of this moment, now that there is some poor girl asleep in the bath and I am the only one to save her . . . I jump out of bed and tiptoe across the hall to the bathroom.

And I walk in.

Except . . .

There's nobody there.

There's not even the sound of the bath anymore. That's gone, too.

Okay, so there are two bathtubs in there. Four showers, four sinks, four toilet stalls, and two bathtubs. I guess they figured when they built this place that only two girls on this floor would ever take a bath at the same time or something.

But here's the thing. There's no one in the showers. Check. There's no one in the stalls. Check. There's no one at the sinks. Check. And . . . *there's no one in the bath*. Not the first one. Check. But, now, the second one, there is a curtain drawn around the second one, and the second one obviously is the one hiding the ghost. Or not hiding the ghost. (Schrödinger's ghost?)

I mean, seriously, how am I even supposed to look around this white tall wall when there could possibly be a ghost girl in the bathtub right there? I mean, what if she's soaking wet and purple and she looks at me smiling and then makes a mean face and her fangs come out? These are the questions, these are the questions . . .

I hold my breath.

Inhale.

And pull back the curtain.

Exhale.

Nothing.

But now I'm getting even more freaked out.

Guess why?

There's no water in the bathtub.

Nope, not even a tiny drop. Nothing. Nada. Dry as the Sahara.

One of these baths was running for an entire hour, I swear to God, I heard it. It woke me up, and now nothing. Zip. Zero.

So now I start backing up. Because now I'm getting really freaked out. Like my heart is pumping in my chest and I'm starting to get the feeling that someone, or some*thing*, is watching me. It knows I'm there and is looking at me, but I can't see it. And I can imagine it might be that soaking-wet ghost girl who is gonna smile but then grow fangs and maybe even start laughing demonically as she corners me.

So I'm basically backing my way slowly, slowly away from the bathtubs, past the showers, past the sinks, out of the bathroom, and back to my room.

And then I'm just standing there.

I'm standing there in my room and trying to figure out what just happened and trying to calm myself down. Breathe in. Breathe out. Calm breaths. Soothing breaths. I start talking to myself. I'm not crazy, don't think that, I'm just trying to talk myself off the cliff here. I'm trying to yoga myself out of this situation.

"Okay, okay, Willa . . . that was just, that was just a coincidence. Maybe you didn't hear the bath after all. Obviously, you didn't hear the bath. Because there's no one in there. Maybe you were dreaming. Or maybe it was downstairs or something. Maybe that's the bath you heard."

But I know that's not true, either. Downstairs the bathroom is way on the other side of the hall, all the way down. Like, someone could scream in there and there's no way I could hear it. Let alone the bathwater.

Okay, so then I decide it was just nothing and I'm just being silly and I decide to go back to bed. I get under the covers, and decide to just talk myself down to a nice sleep. And this works. For about five minutes. Until I'm just about to go back to sleep.

And then I hear it again.

The bathwater.

My eyes open and I look up at the ceiling.

This seriously can't be happening.

And it goes on and on. I try to think of all the things it could be, all the different random explanations, but nothing. Nothing. It really just sounds like bathwater.

Well, now I am really getting annoyed. Obviously, there's someone in there playing some sort of trick. There just has to be.

So I get up again and slowly make my way in, superquiet so I can catch whoever is playing this trick on me.

And I go in.

And, again . . .

There's no one there.

ELEVEN

I make an executive decision.

I. Am not staying. In this room. Tonight. In fact, I am not staying in this room ever again.

I swoop over to the closet, pack my bag, my books, my clothes for tomorrow, my toothbrush, and anything else I ever want to see again. I throw everything in my backpack and bound down the stairs to the first-floor study room. It's a nice room, actually. It's got sofas and lamps and cherry-wood tables and desks. There's even a fireplace. And a wall of built-ins filled floor to ceiling with books.

I throw my stuff on the table and plunk down on the sofa. This is my bed for the night—I don't care if it makes me seem crazy. Clearly, there is some kind of purple ghost girl in that bathroom and I have no intention of meeting her in person. Yes, I know that sounds like I may possibly be insane. No, I'm not going up there ever again.

#sorrynotsorry

I've got enough problems. Jesus.

I'm not religious, but I think I've reached the part of the plan in which it's time to find God.

"Dear God, Allah, Vishnu, Yahweh, Buddha, and all the god-type Super Friends in the sky-located Hall of Justice. Please make whatever that thing is go away and leave me alone and please protect me from ghosts in general forever and into eternity. Amen."

I look up to the stars, to make sure my point is made, and that whatever God is on duty knows I really mean it.

"Thanks. I really appreciate this. You're doing a great job. Except in the Middle East. Might want to send some angels down there or something. But other than that, great job. Keep it up. And again, I know I'm repeating myself, but maybe not so much with the ghost visits."

And I know you think this is probably all ridiculous, but I swear this bathtub thing actually happened, and seriously, tomorrow I'm gonna have to think of a way to get out of that room.

But how?

I can't tell them it's haunted.

Are you kidding me? They'd send me straight back to Iowa in a straightjacket. And then no one would hear the end of it.

And I'd be haunted by a far more frightening specter. My mother.

TWELVE

By the time Contemporary Lit comes, I look like I've been up for two days straight. What can I say? I barely slept last night, thanks to the visitation from beyond.

"Whoa. Look at you. Have you turned to a life of crime and prostitution?"

It's Remy. Of course.

"Nope. My room is haunted."

"Really?"

"Well, it's my bathroom, actually."

"Oooo-oooo. The case of the haunted bathroom . . ."

"Basically, the whole area of my floor where they put me is haunted by some sort of bath ghost."

"You are . . . *odd*." Remy stares at me, openmouthed. Brow

raised. But that open mouth . . . is in the shape of a smile.

Ms. Ingall comes in and everybody sits up in their chairs.

"Now, class, I'm assuming we've all read the book in full? Show of hands?"

Everyone raises their hands but Remy. She's too busy writing me a note on the corner of her paper.

It says: "What are you gonna do?"

Ms. Ingall calls on someone in the front row. It annoys me I'm not in the front row, but it's assigned seating. How am I supposed to make my quizzical face from not in the front row?

I write back to Remy, on the corner of my paper: "Move."

Remy writes back: "How?"

I write back: "Ask?"

Remy scribbles back: "They won't let you."

I gulp.

She shakes her head at me.

Ms. Ingall is writing something on the blackboard. Something about "the other" and "living in the margins."

I whisper to Remy. "But . . . they have to. I'm desperate."

Ms. Ingall turns around.

Remy scribbles back: "I know what to do. You have to pretend you're gonna kill yourself if they keep you there. Then they have to move you. Or they'll be *liable*. Like in court. You know, if you actually try to go through with it."

Oh, that's interesting. All this time I had to pretend I *wasn't* gonna kill myself, now I have to pretend I *am* gonna kill myself. Up is down, America!

Also, Ms. Ingall is on to us.

"Willa? Remy? Do you have something you want to share with the rest of us?"

"No, Ms. Ingall." We say it in unison.

"Good. Now, Willa. What do you think it means? Living in the margins?"

"Um . . . I think maybe it means that the whole world, the whole story is focused on something else. Like men. Rich men. Rich white men, actually. And their hero stories. Like, American history. It's not about you. Not if you're a woman. And especially not if you're an African-American woman or a Latino woman. And especially if you're poor. So, you're, like . . . in the margins, living in the margins, making your case in the margins, trying to make a difference maybe, from the margins . . . but nobody really wants to listen to you. To see you. 'Cause you're not the story they want to tell."

Ms. Ingall looks at me. And so does the rest of the class.

"That's right, Willa."

Ms. Ingall turns around. Waits a beat. Turns back to me.

"And Willa . . . why is it not the story they want to tell?"

"I guess because . . . if you tell your story from the

margins . . . it kind of weakens their story, their storyline . . . kind of like their brand. It threatens them. All of their justifications for doing all kinds of horrible things go out the window if anyone listens to you."

"Good, Willa. Very good."

Remy looks at me, whispers, "Totally! Wow, you're smart! Or that ghost took you over and now you are possessed by a nerd. Either way, nice."

I smile. It doesn't make sense, right? Remy Taft. Related to the president Taft. Rich Remy. Born-with-everything-and-then-some Remy. Agrees? What does she know about coming in from the margins? How could she?

She IS the story. Hasn't she always been the story? A rich, pretty, white girl who comes from a rich family who lives in a rich house.

There's no reason *she* should be interesting.

And I'm ashamed to say it, but I don't trust her.

I don't trust her because of where she comes from and how easy it is, how easy it must be. And also because I see her in Con Lit and then she disappears to wherever effortlessly fascinating people go and I don't see her again till the following class. Where. Does. She. Go?

But then she says something hilarious and I like her so much, I can't help myself. It's like she doesn't care about anything. With her thrown-together clothes and her never talking to anyone. She's just kind of doing everything in her own weird way and damn the torpedoes.

And that must be why everyone is so obsessed with her.

'Cause they can't figure her out. They can't put her in a box.

Ms. Ingall is wrapping it up, writing our assignment on the board. "Write a moment of your life when you felt like you were in the margins. Three pages." We are all writing it down, getting nervous, thinking about what we'll do. How to impress Ms. Ingall. How to get an A.

The bell rings and the room turns into nothing but movement and books and pages flying everywhere and backpack buckles buckling.

Ms. Ingall stops me on the way out.

"Willa, do you think you could drop by my office hours sometime when it's convenient for you? I'm there from two to four p.m. Monday and Wednesdays."

"Sure . . . um. Is everything okay? I know my last paper was a bit of a stretch, but I was . . ."

"No, no, it's nothing like that. I'd just like to talk to you about something."

"Oh, okay. Yes, of course."

"Fourth floor, Wharton House. It's the alcove in the back."

"Oh, okay. Thanks."

Remy and I walk off down the hallway.

"What do you think that's about?"

"Maybe she wants to haunt you. In your pants."

"Gross, Remy! Shut up!"

But I laugh. Oh, do I laugh.

We walk past a gaggle of girls near the doorway. They stop talking and stare at Remy like she is the moon landing. One of them waves a meager little wave and the girl next to her bats down her hand, embarrassed. The first girl looks duly humiliated.

I notice this.

Remy doesn't notice this.

She doesn't seem to notice anything.

She leans in to me, devilish, and whispers.

"Come on, let's go commit fake suicide."

THIRTEEN

When I'm next to Remy I feel famous.

I know. I know that sounds stupid. But here's the thing. All my life I've felt like everybody else is at this invisible party. And you get glimpses of this party, fleeting, on TV or online or in movies or magazines. And it's this amazing, thrilling, whirling party where everybody is superfantastic and skinny and glamorous and nobody ever has to worry about money or food or anything quite so gauche. No, this is a party full of starlight people, and there's just this one thing about this party, which is . . . I'm not invited. Because I'm not exceptional or tall or skinny or some rich old Social Register name's daughter. I'm just some girl. And even if I ever got invited to the party it would be a total mistake. Like

I'd be some cousin's uncle's niece and everybody could tell and if they had their way they would kick me right out.

Because I don't belong at that party. That party is for the fabulous people. And I'm not fabulous. I'm from Iowa.

But not with Remy.

When I'm with Remy I'm invited to that party. When I'm with Remy we are that party. And everybody is looking at us and wanting to be with us and smiling and coming over just to be *superfriendly*. And it's not me. I know it's Remy. But still. Still, with Remy, all that feeling, all that doubt and nervousness and shame, shame for just existing, goes far, far away, and it's just me and Remy, just me and Remy in our own private movie where we are famous and everyone around is there just to shine a light on us.

Which is why I have temporarily moved from my room into hers.

But by the looks of it, she hasn't even moved into hers. I mean it; there's nothing in here. There's one bedsheet, a fitted sheet, strewn over the mattress but not even fitted. Clearly, Remy is on the lam.

"Can you drool?"

"What?"

"Do you think you can make yourself drool?"

"Um . . . what are you talking about?"

"Here. Just think of a lemon. Think really hard."

"You're weird."

Remy is leaning over the bed, sideways, with her mouth open, trying to make herself drool. She looks like a spastic flying fish.

"Why would you want to make yourself drool?"

"I don't know. It kind of seems like if you can make yourself drool, or blush, then you can make yourself cry. And you are gonna have to cry to get out of that haunted bathtub."

"It's not a haunted bathtub. It's a haunted area. It's a haunted bathtub area."

She giggles. "Would you say it's a bed, bath, and beyond the grave?"

I have to bite my cheek to keep from smiling. "I would say that you can joke all you want, but I'm never going back there, I swear."

Okay, we are supposed to be studying. It's three p.m. and we're done with class for the day, but all we are doing is leaning over her bed trying to make ourselves drool.

"This is dumb."

"Okay, let's just practice the crying."

"Okay."

I sit up and we start the scene. Remy plays the imaginary dean of student affairs.

"Okay, I'm gonna get in character. Mi-mi-mi-mi-mi . . . okay, I'm ready."

She sits up, purses her lips.

"And why do you wish to switch rooms, young lady?"

"Because I'm thinking of killing myself."

There's something here. Something fast that happens to my face. It's a tell. An accident. But my eyes almost give it away. My plan. About *actually* killing myself.

Remy stops. She looks at me. A different kind of look.

"Wow. That was . . . really good."

"Thanks."

"Like I really believed you."

Her eyes are on me now.

"Oh. That's weird." I shift around in my seat.

And they're still on me. Laser focus.

I shrug. "C'mon, we have to practice."

Remy raises her eyebrows and continues the charade.

"Okay, okay. My, young Willa. That sounds like a bit of hyperbole."

"It's not, Mrs. . . ."

"Mrs. Persnickles."

"It's not, Mrs. Persnickles. I have a great fear of heights, and this room is one of the highest on campus. I mean . . . it's really high. Like I'm on an airplane or something. I get vertigo. I feel like I'm gonna fall off. Like just fall off into the abyss forever."

"Okay, now cry."

"What?"

"Cry. That's our cue. When Mrs. Persnickles looks most doubtful."

"Okay, but I'm not going to do it now. I'm saving it up."

"That's good. Lightning in a bottle. Save that stuff."

"Wait. Do you know how to cry?"

"Sure."

"Where'd you learn?"

"In rehab."

"Wait. What?!"

"I know. Can you believe it? I got busted once, ONCE, for pot at Spence. It was seriously no big deal. Like nothing. Like a dime bag."

"I don't really understand pot lingo, but I'm going to nod and pretend I do."

"Good. Because it's nothing. Seriously. And everybody acted like it was the end of the world and the sky was falling, and next thing you know I was in the most ridiculous depressing place with everybody *sharing* in a circle all the time. Ugh. What a joke."

"Okay, but maybe it was—"

"It was stupid. Totally pointless. Except that I got to take 'drama therapy.' Incredibly useful, calling up your emotions at will and such. I mean, I wouldn't mind making a career of it."

Welp, she shut that one down. I get it. Rehab. Maybe she's embarrassed. I try to change the subject. Make her like me again.

"Is the dean of student affairs really named Mrs. Persnickles?"

"Yes. Her name is Billybottom Persnickles the third."

"Oh, good, I wouldn't deign to meet with Persnickles the first. Or the second."

"Of course not, darling," Remy drawls. "It would be beneath you."

It's starting to get chilly out, and we only have two hours until the office closes, and I am not going to sleep in that haunted room one more drafty night, so this is it.

"Okay, wish me luck."

I grab my blazer and leave Remy back to her pretend drooling.

"You know I'm gonna get this," she says.

"What?"

"The drooling. I'm gonna make myself drool."

"Are all rich people this weird?"

It's an authentic question.

"Yes. Not the nouveau riche, of course. They're too bougie to be weird. Like they are trying to be this idea of rich or something, but they just always come off as ridiculous, and a little pathetic."

"Do I come off as ridiculous and pathetic?"

"No. You come off as maybe a little bit crazy."

I blink. "Really?"

"Well, I'm not the one switching rooms because of a haunted toilet."

"It's a bathtub. A haunted bathtub."

"Exactly."

FOURTEEN

By the time I make it to the office of student affairs, I've pretty much lost all hope. Of course they're not gonna let me move. Ghosts. What difference does it make? I know my days here are numbered and it's only a matter of time until I, too, am lost to the endless stream of souls wading around in purgatory. Or is it waiting? I think they are wading and waiting. But aren't we all doing that, really?

Huh. Maybe this *is* purgatory. And we just don't know it.

Wait a minute.

Maybe this is hell.

No, no, this can't be hell. Too many flowers. And sunsets. And my dad. He would never be in hell.

But maybe hell is nearby.

Like New Jersey.

The door opens and suddenly the dean of student affairs is standing there. Ms. *Smith*. Totally boring. Mrs. Persnickles was much better.

"May I help you, young lady?"

She actually seems kind of nice. Much more crunchy than I had imagined. Like she eats a bowl of granola cereal for breakfast, a granola bar for lunch, and for dinner . . . a granola sandwich. She's wearing Birkenstocks. With socks. Of course. She has a mane of curly, wiry hair that sticks up all around her head.

"Hi, yeah, um . . . well, I'm here to ask for a possible room change, actually."

"Oh. I see."

She gestures for me to sit down. I'm not gonna lie to you. There are a lot of Navajo tapestries in here. There is even a dreamcatcher. I wonder if it will catch my dreams of getting a new room.

"Yeah, um, it's just . . ."

I was really expecting a snootier-looking person in this scene. Not this Incense Lady. My lines are all wrong. I'll have to improv.

"May I ask what's wrong with your current room?"

"Honestly?"

"Yes. Honestly."

"It's haunted."

I hate my mouth I hate my mouth I hate my mouth! Shut up, mouth!

"Really?"

Okay, this is falling apart fast. First of all, I was never, ever supposed to say that, and second, she was not supposed to respond as though I had some kind of point.

"Yeah, I mean. Okay. This is what happened . . ."

She listens to my terrifying tale about the haunted bathroom. The whole thing. In detail. She doesn't quite seem to be calling the men in white coats just yet. But any minute, I suppose she will press a button and there they'll be—or else I will be ejected out the roof.

"And you feel you won't be able to get any of your work done if you stay?"

"I mean, would you?"

She's on the fence. This is gonna take some waterworks.

"I fear that if I stay there I might . . . kill myself. Like the spirits will convince me or something. The ghost-girl spirits."

She raises an eyebrow.

Oh God. This is not working. Okay, think of something sad, think of something sad, think of something sad . . .

I know. Here's what. Think about how unfair it is that your mother is out there gallivanting around the rolling hills of France even though she's a horrible person and your dad, who is the sweetest, best person, is stuck back in What Cheer, Iowa, with not any cheer at all and a whole lot of bills he can't pay. Think about the fact that you are pretending you're gonna kill yourself when you were actually going to kill yourself because all of it, the whole world, is so deeply unjust.

And here's the good part. Here's what makes this work. I try holding back the tears. Yes, that seems to be the trick. Try to hold back the tears. Nobody ever *wants* to cry, right? So, even though my eyes are swelling up with tears just thinking about the injustice of my folks and the weight of the world and the elaborate suicide ruse I am simultaneously faking and hiding . . . I am holding back.

"Willa? I'm sorry . . . Willa?"

Now she is trying to get my attention. To free me of this weight.

"This endless weight of being a human-type person on this spinning orb next to the sun in an infinite universe in a sea of the evermore infinite multiverse!"

That's what comes out. Of my mouth. I say the sentences and I can't control them. Worse. I keep going.

"What does it all mean?! How can there even be a multiverse?!"

"Willa! It's okay. It's . . . it's going to be fine. Here."

She hands me a tissue. I pant, trying to regain control of

my breath, of myself.

I peek out of my left eye. Clearly, I am done. She's going to throw me out of this place and my only refuge will be the Barnum & Bailey circus. I will be a sad clown and life on the road will be hard, but we will get by with booze and cards every night by the lion cage. One day I will let the lion out of his cage and he will maul the greedy circus master before sprinting off into the setting sun.

"There's a very simple solution here," Ms. Smith says.

"Th-there is?" I say it through sniffles, like the last urchin left at the orphanage.

"Yes, of course. Now just take a deep breath and I'll figure out the best course of action."

Now our hippie lady is going through her files, peering into folders, scrolling through pages. She's not quite talking to herself, but she might as well be. If she could solve this problem by squinting it would have been solved an hour ago.

I whisper, "I'm sorry I got upset about the multiverse."

She pretends not to hear me.

"Okay. Here we are. Denbigh Residence Hall. Perfect. It's on the far side of the green, and you're on the fourth floor. It's a beautiful room. There's even a fireplace. That sounds lovely. Don't you think?"

"Yes! Er, I mean . . . oh, that would be so fantastic. I can't thank you so much for your kindness in my time of woe."

Woe? Yes. I just said "time of woe."

"Oh, it's nothing. That's what we're here for. And"—she wiggles her eyebrows—"I am giving you one of the best rooms on campus."

"Really?"

"Absolutely. You know, I probably shouldn't tell you this, but . . . you're not the first one to opt out of that room."

"Are you serious?"

"Well, I mean. Look, I don't believe in ghosts. But it does seem that room ends up empty quite a bit. Who knows why . . ."

"Wow."

She winks at me and hands me the key.

Is she stoned? What's going on? This is all very strange. I thought everyone at this school was supposed to be terrible and stuffy and full of themselves. And like Dean Hardscrabble in *Monsters U*. But this lady. This lady in socks and sandals, she's all right.

And this all worked out—because Remy told me what to do.

"Listen, Willa. I know it's sometimes hard to transition from . . . other places, maybe even other worlds . . . so if there's anything you need, just feel free to knock. I'm always here. Well, I'm not always here, that would be weird, but my office hours are posted, and I'm here during office hours—you get the idea. But I don't want you to feel like you're all alone here. Because you most certainly are not."

Huh.

Do you think this is because of my Golden Globe–worthy dramatic performance in a leading role? Or do you think it's because I'm a freak from What Cheer, Iowa? Is *that* why she's being so nice right now? And why did she wink? That, too, is a mystery. The Mystery of the Dean of Student Affairs's Eyeball.

Welp. Whenever anybody's nice to me, my instinct is to run away as fast as possible. And that's just what I'm about to do.

"Um, well. Thanks."

"You're welcome, Willa. Remember, you are here for a reason."

"What, like here at Pembroke or like here on earth in general . . . ?"

She smiles, amused. "Both. And, Willa, I, too, am baffled by the concept of the multiverse. But maybe it means that the universe is full of infinite possibility."

Ooo-kay.

I could sit around and contemplate this interaction for five days, but I'm too excited to see my new room. I mumble another thank-you to the Dean of Infinite Possibility and scurry off to the new digs. Now I am in Denbigh dorm with an even bigger room, equipped with a fireplace and, of course, a view.

I should make up stories and cry more often. I should ask more about "what would Remy do?"

I resolve to get the rest of my things tomorrow. Not tonight. It's dark out, and the ghosts are probably camped out in my old room, smoking pipes and reading the *New Yorker*.

FIFTEEN

"It worked!"

I am practically flying across the green like some kind of ghost myself. Nothing is getting me there fast enough, because I am dying to tell Remy and I am still not there yet.

Flying into the dorm and up the stairs and into Remy's room, which is open, I am brimming with tales and quips about my magnificent performance and the ensuing room and let's go see it right now. But Remy's not there. Not a signal, not a sign. Nothing doing. Unmade bed. Check. Clothes all over the floor. Check. Remy. No check.

But the door is open, so that's weird.

"Remy?"

Maybe she's in the bathroom. I walk down the hall and

see a serious-looking girl with a furrowed brow furrowing at me.

"Hi. Sorry. Have you seen Remy?"

She shakes her head and retreats back into her lair.

The bathroom smells like chlorine and more chlorine, but there is no Remy here.

Maybe she's in the study room. The study room in this dorm is unusually beat-up compared to my old study room. It's as if they put all the other study rooms together with a calculated, magnificent plan and then realized they forgot one. This one. This one with furniture in it from the sixties. Put it this way, this study room will not be going in the brochure.

There's a redheaded student who is possibly a descendant of Strawberry Shortcake cuddled up in the reading nook. She looks up at me with annoyance. Then something registers, and she changes completely. Now she is a smile. A redheaded strawberry smile.

"Hi, um, have you seen Remy? Remy Taft?"

"Yeah, I know. I mean, I know her. I mean, not like you, but I know her."

This is getting awkward. She's sort of falling all over herself and now she's turning red but her hair is red, too, so everything is red over there in the reading nook.

"Oh, um. Okay, well, if you see her could you tell her Willa is looking for her. That's me. I'm Willa."

"I know."

I don't understand what is happening right now. No one is supposed to know who I am. That's Remy's job. I am just the sidekick. The trusty sidekick who is not the star of the show but can be counted on to laugh at jokes, attend activities, and generally make everyone else feel better about themselves. I am the frozen yogurt, not the sprinkles.

"I'll tell her. No problem."

Strawberry goes back to her book after an assuring smile. I decide I like her. She reads books in the reading nook in the worst study room on campus. That's a girl after my own heart. Maybe she's like me. Lone wolf. Not good enough for the fancy study room.

Sauntering out of the dorm, into the late-afternoon light, I have the feeling that maybe everything is possibly gonna be okay. Not just okay—maybe even better than okay. Maybe perfect. The sun is turning the sky dusty pink and orange and that means there is infinite possibility in a place where you can cry and get dorm rooms with fireplaces and a view. Where you get to be friends with Remy Taft. Where people know your name is Willa.

SIXTEEN

Denbigh dorm is across the green from the library, hidden away amid the spruce and the pines. From my room, on the fourth floor, I can actually see over through the treetops to the comings and goings along the green, but I am high enough to hear only silence and the occasional chirping birds, which are actually flying dinosaurs.

Don't even talk to me about birds. I can't even.

My only sadness, which is a goofy sadness, is that Remy wasn't here when I opened the door. See, what would've happened then is that we would've held our breath, unlocked the door, opened the door, and then squealed with glee and delight and immediately had a pillow fight when we saw how superfantastic my new room was.

That did not happen. Instead, I crept up the stairs to my lonely little room on the far end of the dorm, wiggled the key in the lock without any ado, opened the door, and peered in on *the best room ever*. But there was no squealing. And no pillow fight.

There was only a brief sigh to be noticed by no one. Not even the leaves on the trees seemed to care. And the only room anywhere near mine in this small alcove, at the end of the hall, is this tiny room next door, which appears to be empty. It's open, but, really, this adjacent room barely counts as a room. More of a large closet.

But *my* room! Oh, ladies and gentleman, it is a grand affair! It is an affair with different-colored wood in the floors, like little designs in the wood. What will they think of next? Back home, if you wanted designs on your wood floor you would have to use a marker.

But wait, there's more! The fireplace has tile around it with little designs in the tile. Like little pictures. One is a scene of a girl sitting by a lake. In the tile. That scene is in the tile.

And out of the windows, I kid you not, there is a little squirrel, just sitting in the space between the window and three of the little turrets that seem to have spawned all over this campus. The squirrel is standing still, in a sort of pro-file, holding on to an acorn, pretending not to notice me, or to exist at all. The squirrel is sizing up the situation. The squirrel is attempting to figure out if I'm going to try to eat him.

"Hi, squirrel." I say it in a singsongy voice. To alert the squirrel to my intentions. Happy intentions. Non-squirrel-eating intentions.

"Hi, little squirrely. Hi there."

The squirrel decides I am not his evil nemesis and decides to pay attention to the acorn he is holding and nevermind me anyway.

I mean, you know you got the best room if there is a squirrel there to greet you. That is a sign from the good Lord above that this was meant to be. The only thing not meant to be is that I am alone in this room. I want to share this room. I want to jump up and down in this room and scream and giggle. I want to hold grand affairs in this room and maybe even a tea on Sunday.

But it's a holding pattern.

I'm on standby. In this room.

Alone.

SEVENTEEN

Two days later, she hasn't even made it to class. It's okay, though. I've analyzed my behavior and decided I was maybe being a little obsessive and maybe she didn't like me all that much anyway. I don't blame her. So it's fine. I am acceptance now. Everything is as it should be. I am Yoda. You can't stop me.

Except . . .

When I get back to my brilliant, amazing dorm room, there is Remy. Just sitting there on my bed like the cat that ate the canary.

"Now, do you know how to fake cry or do you know how to fake cry?"

I laugh, a little taken aback. How did she even get in here?

"Well, Iowa, I think we can both agree that this is the best room of all time and I didn't even know it existed. That's how good it is."

"I know. Can you believe this? It's like I won the lottery or something."

"Who's next door?"

"No one. The room's too small. Like it's probably the size of your closet."

"Maid's quarters."

"What?"

"Maid's quarters."

"Um. I don't exactly have a maid."

"I know. But they used to. People used to send their kids here, *avec* maid."

"Really?"

"Oh, yeah. And . . . they used to have a lady who would wash your hair for five dollars. In the basement."

"What, like she lived there?"

"Yes, she was a troll." Remy smiles, stands up. "No, but she was there all week. And they just abolished that as 'classist' in the '90s. The 1990s. It's true."

"Wow. I kind of wish she were still there—I hate washing my hair. It hurts my arms."

But Remy isn't listening to me. She's too busy walking past me, into the tiny room next door, grabbing the bed, and *bringing that bed into my room.*

"Um. What are you doing?"

"Um. Moving this bed in here."

Now she is arranging the bed in the room, neatly under the window.

"That's where that wants to be." She nods, approving her work, before going back into the other room and reemerging with the mattress.

She plops the mattress down on the bed frame and brushes the dust off her hands, surveying her work.

"That's perfect. I'll go get my stuff."

Before I can say anything, or even process what the hell is going on, Remy is out the door and down the stairs. I see her rushing excitedly across the green, presumably to get her stuff, presumably to move in with me, presumably to start sleeping on that bed she just brought in here.

Huh. I guess I was not being obsessive after all. I guess I was being . . . normal?

I guess next to Remy anybody looks normal.

EIGHTEEN

Our first *en suite* study session goes like this: I organize our work space. Remy orders sushi. I put the books down. Remy goes to the other side of the room. I crack my book open. My phone buzzes next to me.

And now I realize Remy is texting me. From the bed. Across the room.

Y U NO CALL ME NO MO?

I text back.

U CRAY CRAY

I continue to study. Or try.

And now Remy.

MY LUV IS TRUE

My turn.

U R A NERDFACE

And now her.

UR 2 QT 2 B 4GOT

And my turn.

I DIE. IT IS SLO DEATH.

And now, back to studying.

Remy stays quiet and I am just about to launch into an amazing chapter about the importance of the railroad and industry to the outcome of civil war. Except.

Darth Vader ringtone.

I glance down at my phone.

And look who it is!

I pick up.

She is on the other side of the room, but we're not looking at each other.

"Hello? Hello?"

I answer.

"Hello, who is this?"

"This is Ryan Gosling. I'm calling to tell you that I've fallen in love with you even though I've never met you."

"That's great, Ryan, but the problem is I'm studying right now, so you will just have to call later and also marry me."

"If I marry you will you gallivant in the rain like in *The Notebook?*"

"Yes, Ryan."

"Okay, good. Bye."

Remy hangs up.

Well, this is all very exciting, but I do have to study. Here I go, back to the genius of Abraham Lincoln.

Darth Vader ringtone.

"Hello?"

"Hi, this is Robert Pattinson. I was just calling to tell you you've won a trip to my penis."

I try not to laugh.

"That is really tempting, Robert, but I have to study."

I hang up.

Nothing.

Nothing. Back to studying . . .

Darth Vader ringtone.

I pick up.

"Trip to my penis!"

That's it. We both start laughing, and no studying is happening. Okay, I know how to do this now.

For to study: get the hell away from Remy.

For to laugh.

For to be happy.

For to not kill myself . . .

Stay next to Remy.

But Remy is over it now. Now she's ducking into the maid's quarters next door, which she seems to be doing a lot of lately. And now I can study. I can.

NINETEEN

There's this thing they're doing at the boys' school, Witherspoon. The more I hear about these boys, the more I feel sorry for them. Like they all listen to Phish. And play Hacky Sack. And inevitably someone has a bongo drum.

Witherspoon Prep.

I mean, seriously.

These guys should really start breeding out of their circle. Half of them look like they couldn't lift a suitcase. Not that they'd ever have to. But that they actually couldn't. It's pathetic. I mean, what is going to become of them? If they don't get their trust funds, they are all goners for sure.

Anyway, I guess they're putting this thing together. A

play. It's an obvious ploy to get girls over there. Theater girls. But still girls.

I saw the flyer on the wall. Auditions. Guess what's the play? Actually, it's a musical. Don't squeal. God. What is wrong with you? You are so embarrassing sometimes.

Okay, here goes:

It's *Grease.*

Yup. These Witherbottoms over there are gonna put on a production of *Grease*, and we're all invited to be a part of the magic. Of course, everyone will want to play Sandy. That's obvious. (Even though everyone knows the coolest part is Marty. Marty's the hot one. She dates college guys. And Marines. And that famous TV guy who emcees the Rydell High dance contest.)

So I'm busy making fun of this in my head, having a blast internally, really, but next thing I know Remy is next to me, looking at the flyer, and now, get this.

"What? *Grease!?*"

"I know. So lame."

"So lame that we are doing it."

"What? No way."

"C'mon. At the very least it will get us out of this godforsaken place. For a few hours at least. Otherwise we are destined to be shriveled-up old maids who play cards all day. Possibly pinochle."

"You must be joking. Are you high?"

"What? No. Why? You wanna get high?"

"No, it's just an expression."

"Oh, c'mon, it'll be fun."

"Wait. You're serious? I mean, I know you were all into your drama therapy or whatever, but this?"

"Yes. This. I definitely think we should go over there for the auditions. What could it hurt?"

"I know what you're counting on. You're counting on the theater bug. You're counting on it biting me and turning me into a theater spaz."

"Maybe. But really I'm really counting on us having an excuse to blow this popsicle stand."

"I think it's more like you want to blow some guy's popsicle."

"Ew."

I shrug. "I'm just saying."

"Look, it'll look good on your transcripts. How 'bout that?"

Ugh. The magic bullet. "I dunno . . ."

But I already know I'm doing it. If Remy wants to do it, I want to do it. Just to be with Remy. Just to have more to laugh about and make fun of. Just to be in her world. To be next to her. To outsnark and outjoke and outgiggle and out-text from the same room and be silly but act as though we are part of our own personal movie.

"Besides. I bet Milo will do it."

"Milo?"

"Oh. Nobody told you about Milo."

"Um, what are you talking about?"

"Wow, you really are from Nebraska."

"Iowa. And no, I was making it up. To impress everyone."

"Milo. Milo Hesse. Aka the guy you're about to be in love with."

"Yeah, right."

"Trust me."

"How do you know?"

"Because everybody is."

"Even you?"

"We're just friends. But trust me. The guy's irresistible. Like french fries."

"I don't like french fries."

"Well, you'll like this french fry."

And now all I can think about is this unknown irresistible fry guy who even Remy cares about. And it's weird because I'm simultaneously scared of this guy and also jealous of him. Like why does Remy like this guy so much? He's just some stupid guy. And she's *Remy. The* Remy Taft. Why should she demean herself by even liking anyone? Isn't she above that? Everybody's supposed to like her, remember?

I resolve to hate this Milo.

TWENTY

If you ever want to see a bunch of people look like idiots, go to an audition. Any alien from Andromeda Galaxy beamed down into this auditorium would assume he had just blasted his way into the funny farm. Trust me.

We were supposed to show up wearing loose-fitting clothing. To dance. To sing. To move around and pretend we're blissful. Or sad. Or waiting for a bus. The whole thing is kind of ridiculous. There are girls here doing vocal exercises. And boys. Teenage boys singing scales.

I mean, it's shameful.

What Remy doesn't know is that I have set myself a clear goal for this audition: to fail.

No sir, I have absolutely zero, nil, nein intentions of

wasting my time pounding the boards or whatever they call it and singing some song about losing my virginity to a hunky greaser in front of a bunch of strangers. I'd rather cover myself in blood and jump in a shark tank. So, whatever it takes, come hell or high water, I am burning this thing to the ground.

Remy, on the other hand, has her heart set on Sandy. She is focused. She is giddy. She is inspired. She is also the only person here who is somehow managing to pull off this look. This loose-fitting, laissez-faire drama look. I would categorize her look as early eighties meets après-ski. There is definitely something about the furry boots that is throwing the whole thing over to Switzerland. Whatever it is, she looks like she just stepped out of *ELLE* and everybody else looks like they just stepped out of Walmart. You gotta hand it to Remy. There is no clothing assignment she cannot ace. I mean, her sartorial flair is something to be admired.

"Okay, thespians! Gather round. Now, I want you to use this space creatively. Think outside the box. And please do not be inhibited. There are no right or wrong answers. For this is a place of . . . magic."

I look at Remy like this is ridic. She gives me a stern look of dramatic seriousness.

"Now, I want you to find a place in the auditorium, it can be anywhere, somewhere that speaks to you, somewhere that is calling you. And I want you to pretend to be an ice-cream cone."

I roll my eyes so far into my head I almost sprain a socket. Remy tries not to crack a smile.

"A cool, refreshing ice-cream cone. Yes, yes, that's it. Very nice."

Everyone is acting very globby and slow. Not me. No sir! I'm an orange sherbet ice-cream cone, and I have style and pizazz. Maybe the other ice-cream cones are slow, but I am choosing to embody the general zinginess of orange sherbet. Vanilla says, "I'm boring." Chocolate says, "eat me now or die." Rocky Road says, "I'm overcompensating for something." But orange sherbet? Orange sherbet says, "I'm weird. I'm zany."

And thusly I am dancing a very strange dance, which is making the rest of the would-be Rydell High Sandys and Rizzos cast a glance sideways, but not too much, lest it make me seem interesting . . . i.e., interesting enough for the role. And it is also making Remy unable to achieve any ice-cream cone personification because she is trying so hard not to laugh she is burying her face in the red velvet theater curtains, which is really just making her look like an ice-cream cone molesting a drape.

My dance is fast. And uncoordinated. And full of joie de vivre!

Remy is on the ground now, in a ball. She is a ball of melted ice cream. She is looking at me, peeking out from under her armpit, and her face is bright red.

Some of the other dancers have stopped.

Mostly they are just looking at me and grimacing.

The drama teacher is named Mrs. Jacobsen. She kind of looks like if Peppermint Patty grew up, gained sixty pounds, and put on a smart teal suit with a pencil skirt and matching jacket. There are glasses involved. They are tortoiseshell. She is also wearing a scarf. There are birds involved. Both on the scarf and I am fairly certain at home.

"Excuse me . . . Willa, is it?"

"Yes." I continue dancing. The show must go on!

"What kind of ice-cream cone are you, exactly?"

"I am orange sherbet."

"Please stop dancing now."

I stop. Remy is still peeking out from under her armpit, in a ball next to the downstage fly system.

"Can you please explain, Willa? I'm not sure I understand your ice-cream cone. It seems very different from the other ice-cream cones."

"Exactly. Exactly, Mrs. Jacobsen. Orange sherbet *is* different. All the other flavors say generally the same thing. But not me. No. Orange sherbet says 'I'm zany. I don't care. I march to the beat of my own drum! Pick me! I'm not really soothing like vanilla or chocolate or even strawberry.'"

There is a silence in the room.

It's clear I will be kicked out of this audition. Mission accomplished.

Mrs. Jacobsen comes closer.

Now she is close enough to me that I can smell she is wearing some kind of rose perfume, and I am here to tell you it smells pretty good.

And since Remy has inspired me to be all that I can be, and in this case, all I can be is someone who definitely does not want to be cast in this play, it's time to end this charade—for good.

"Wow, that's nice."

"Excuse me?"

"Your perfume. Is that roses? Or gardenias? Jesus, that smells really good. Subtle yet bold. Well played, Mrs. Jacobsen."

Remy is sitting up now, leaning against the wall, with amusement.

"Oh. Well, thank you. Now, where are you from again, Willa?"

Ugh. I brace myself for the snickering.

"Iowa."

A nearly imperceptible smattering of scoffs snakes its way around the room.

I prepare myself for the axe.

"Well, Willa. Congratulations. You're Frenchy."

The floor drops out of the room.

"What?"

"You're Frenchy. You're perfect for it."

"Um . . . really?"

"Yes, Willa. You are the first person I have cast in this year's production!"

"Now, okay, not to be contrary or anything, but don't you think I'm more of a Marty? Because . . . I mean, she's pretty cool, you have to admit, what with those Marines and all those pictures in her wallet and stuff—"

"Sorry, Willa, but Marty you are not."

"Seriously?"

"Hate to break it to you."

"Wait. Really? Why am I not Marty?"

"You're just not, dear. No offense."

"Well, who is, then? Just out of curiosity . . ."

"She is."

And Mrs. Jacobsen points around the room and I follow her hand, and there she is . . . of course . . . Remy.

Right. Of course Remy is Marty.

Remy looks up.

"Me?"

"Yes, you. What is your name?"

There is a silence in the auditorium. It's as if no one in the vicinity can actually believe there is someone on earth who has not heard of Remy Taft. It's just short of a gasp.

"Remy."

"Well, Remy, congratulations. You're officially Marty."

"Wait. So I got the part? And she got the part? We haven't even read yet; this is weird."

And Mrs. Jacobsen smiles. "It's all about casting. Some things can't be acted. Trust me."

The entirety of the room slumps and wants to kill us.

Remy looks at me and give me a thumbs-up. She's actually glowing.

"Okay, now, everyone, let's take a break. When we come back we'll do the reading. You girls stay. Obviously."

So that's that. Remy brought me to this dumb spazfest, and I tried with all my heart to fail, and now I've got Frenchy.

I make a note to try to fail more often.

Remy hops over to me in a hoppery of happiness.

"Aren't you excited?! We can be actresses! My mom will be so annoyed!"

"Wait, what? Really?"

"Yeah. 'It's just not done.' That's how they put it. But screw it, I am going to do it!"

I blink. "Uh, wow. I never realized you were that serious about it, honestly."

"Well, I am. Except I can't be."

"Remy, you can be—"

And I am just in the very middle of that thought when my arm is grabbed in a sudden violent death grip. Remy clutches me and drags me back into the red theater curtains.

"There."

"There what?"

"There. You see him?"

"See who?"

"Milo. That's Milo. Right over there. By that naked Greek statue."

And I hadn't noticed there was a naked Greek statue on the other side of the room. It's just a small one, but it sits there, perched next the arched doorway in a kind of dare against leaving.

But that naked Greek statue is causing me to look down and see that person standing next to it in the doorway. That person who just walked in and is framed by the light in a kind of emanating halo of classical proportions.

And that guy, standing in that doorway, surrounded by that glowing halo, is not like anybody I've seen before—

—and now I know why I was supposed to know about Milo.

TWENTY-ONE

I know what it's like to see somebody and be scared of them. To see somebody and think all the zillions of things you're not supposed to think about how you're not cool enough or too small or too big or too something you don't even know what it is. I know what it's like to see someone and practically melt the minute you see them because everybody told you there would be someone like that. It's in every book. It's in every movie. It's in every poem since the beginning of time and maybe even written on walls somewhere in cave drawings. Everyone tells you that person is coming. That person who's gonna knock your socks off. Everyone tells you for so long and in so many ways that finally you don't believe them.

Until you see them. Him.

Milo.

Milo Hesse.

Now I'm gonna tell you what he looks like.

You know that movie? The one with the cowboy who finds out he's got AIDS and then he starts getting medicine and bringing it over the border? Okay, not that guy. The other guy. The one that plays the transvestite.

That guy.

Now imagine that guy, but imagine him when he is not playing a lady. Now make him about six feet tall and put jeans on him and a dark blue T-shirt that says something in Japanese but it's a Wild West movie poster. Yes, a Wild West movie poster, with Japanese writing, on a T-shirt. I'm pretty sure it says, "*The Good, the Bad and the Ugly,*" but I'm not about to keep looking at this guy's chest to figure it out because I'm already cowering in my boots and I'm not even wearing boots.

That's how bad it is.

Also, there are green eyes involved. And either he is wearing false eyelashes or he should pick up the phone right now and call his mama and tell her thank you for the beautiful eyelashes. And for the mouth. Oh, you didn't know he had a sweetheart mouth? Yes. Check. Chestnut-brown hair that is slightly a swoop but not too much of a swoop? Check.

Camouflage Vans? Check.

What is happening now is Remy is looking at me and smiling like the cat that ate the canary. She is reading my thoughts like a scrawl on a news channel going around and around my head, but that doesn't matter because I am slowly dissolving into the ground anyway.

"Told you."

"What?"

"You know what."

"I have no idea what you're talking about."

"Mm-hm."

Milo doesn't see us yet, but he certainly is looking for someone. Either that or he is auditioning for the play, but you and I both know that is not why he's here.

"Remy!"

Oh, I guess Milo is here to see Remy. Maybe Milo is in love with Remy. That would make sense. Although Milo and Remy? Kind of too much, if you ask me. But maybe they are meant for each other. Like Titania and Oberon.

Before I can evaporate, Remy grabs my hand and brings me over to meet this person who is clearly a robot developed in a lab in order to destroy hearts.

"Oh, hi."

Milo looks surprised Remy's not alone. Not a good sign.

"This is Willa. She's from Iowa."

Kill me. Kill me now.

"What? Really? Wow, I've never met anyone from Iowa."

It's okay if this building just falls into the ground now. No problem.

"I know. Isn't that cool?" This is Remy trying to make me feel better. Fat chance.

"What's it like there?"

"Everyone's blond."

"Really?"

"Yeah, Scandinavian or something. Like that's where everyone went. When they fled. The famine or something."

God, what am I talking about? The famine?!

Now Milo is really sizing me up.

"And would you say you're a typical Iowa specimen?"

"Um . . ."

"I just never really pictured people from Iowa looking like you. Can't tell if that's me being closed-minded or if I never really thought about it, honestly."

What?

What just happened?

Remy sees me blush, and now her smile is from ear to ear. Seriously, you could just pull off the rest of her head now from the top.

"Oh, wow. You're blushing." Milo turns to Remy. "People do that?"

I feel like the biggest hillbilly of all time. I feel two feet tall.

Remy leans in to Milo. "Don't get too cocky. She's smarter than you."

Okay, this is just getting weird.

"So, Milo, are you going to the Fall Ball?" She says it like a dare.

"Definitely not."

Silence. Somehow Milo feels maybe that was the wrong answer.

"Why, are you guys going?"

"Yes," Remy proclaims.

"Then definitely yes."

"Willa's never been."

"Ah. Then I envy her."

"Um, what is the Fall Ball?" I could play it cool, but they know I don't know.

Remy waves her hand around. "It's like this ball to celebrate the harvest or whatever."

"The harvest? So is it like . . . hay rides and apple cider . . . ?"

"More like fancy dresses and people puking." Milo smiles.

"Puking?"

"Yes, everybody dresses up, everybody spikes the drinks, some people dance, some people frolic."

"There will be frolicking?" I turn to Remy for confirmation.

"Oh, there will be frolicking."

"Will *we* be frolicking?"

"Oh, we will frolic."

Milo seems charmed by Remy. The way he's looking at her. Wistful, in a way. There's a magic here, between them, shaking electrons that keep bouncing back and forth, back and forth, trying to form something.

"Okay, well, I'll see you guys there, then."

"So you're going, Milo?" She chides him.

"I'm definitely going. Maybe."

And with that, Milo is definitely-slash-maybe out the door, leaving Remy and me to contemplate.

"Told you."

"Told me what?"

"About Milo. And how he's a stone-cold fox."

"Right. I lost track. Is he going to the fall thingy?"

"Sixty percent with a chance of scattered maybes."

"So you're saying that Milo is as unpredictable as the weather."

"I'm saying Milo is *less* predictable than the weather."

We're walking back now, heading through the front gates of Witherspoon and back to Pembroke. All the boys around wear the uniform, navy blazers with a coat of arms on the pocket, tan pants. They look over at us and quickly look away. They whisper to one another and look again.

All of a sudden they seem adorable. Not pale and blue-veined. But shy and sort of embarrassed. If I were queen of the world, I would make all boys wear that uniform. Seriously, there's nothing more sweet on earth or in heaven than a big-eyed boy, carrying books, almost too skinny, in a navy blazer.

Adorkable. That's what they are. And it's possible I may have died in that audition and now this happens to be heaven.

"Is that why you broke up with Milo?"

"Broke up! What are you talking about, crazy? We're just friends."

"So, you never went out or anything? Not even a little?"

"No way. We're too close for that."

"Of course. Why would anyone want to go out with someone they were close to? Gross."

She nudges me playfully with her elbow. "Oh, Iowa, you're so cute. In some ways, you're actually very traditional. I guess they can take the girl out of the farm but they can't take the farm out of the girl."

"Moooooo."

"Is that supposed to be a cow?"

"Yes, Remy."

"It sounds more like a ghost."

"Maybe it's a cow ghost."

Remy and I are through the gray stone gates of Witherspoon, making our way over the cobblestones back to Denbigh. It starts to rain in little droplets, then big droplets, then cats and dogs, then a typhoon.

We are screaming like banshees and running through the rain and getting soaked. Soaked. Drenched. Annihilated.

By the time we get back to Denbigh, we might as well have just jumped in the ocean. We reach the front doors breathless and laughing, and everybody in the lobby is staring at us.

We look at them, they look at us, and that just makes us laugh more.

And, you know, this is the moment. Right here. If I could go back in time and stop everything. It's right here. This feeling of everything hilarious and nothing bad and everything heart-shaped and shimmering.

What I would give to just stop the tape here.

But life isn't like that. Life keeps unspooling. Whether we want it to or not.

TWENTY-TWO

I have resolved *not* to go to the Fall Ball. Let them celebrate their harvest on their own! Besides, celebrating the harvest by dressing in superexpensive dresses and puking booze seems more like celebrating the fall of western civilization.

There is no way I'm going.

"Remy. I have something to tell you. It's about the Fall Ball."

"Ooh, this sounds official. Yes, Willa Parker. I am all ears. Please be very serious."

Remy is lying on her bed with her legs up on the wall, contemplating her brand-new blue toenails. It's a funny way to sit, but I have tried it and I find it very comforting.

"Okay, fine. Here goes. I've decided not to go to the Fall Ball."

"What?"

"I, Willa Parker, being of sound body and mind, have decided not to attend the Fall Ball."

"No. No, no, no. You have to go. I have to take you. It will be fun. There will be frolicking, remember?"

"I do not wish to frolic."

"I do not wish to frolic without you."

Now it's my turn to lie on my bed and contemplate my toenails. Mine are orange. Neon orange. I don't know why I made this choice, but now I'm stuck with it.

"Besides. Milo will be there."

"Nope. Not falling for it. You said sixty percent with a chance of scattered maybes."

"Yeah, okay. I did say that. But you have to go."

"Nope."

"Please. Pretty please with sugar on top."

"Look, Remy, even if I wanted to go, which I don't, I couldn't, because I don't have anything to wear, and so the night will be ruined and I'll just turn into a pumpkin or whatever."

"Okay, that is not how that story goes. Like, at all."

"Look, I just don't have those kinds of things lying around. Like . . . if it were a real harvest ball, with hayrides and candy apples, maybe, but not dressy stuff. Nope. No way. Just don't have it. Cannot get it."

"Oh, well, that's easy."

"Please enlighten me, o wise one."

"You can just borrow something of mine. I have a zillion things. And they're just sitting there. In my closet. Feeling lonely."

"I don't know . . ."

"I'm serious. Some of them even have the tags still on; it's shameful. Come on. You have to come. Please?"

"Are you sure?"

"Yes, of course. I'll just go get them."

"Go get them?"

"Yeah, I'll go now. Be right back."

Remy is up and throwing on a jacket and almost out the door in a whirlwind of dress-scavenging activity.

"Wait, where are you going?"

"It's called New York. Maybe you've heard of it? Crowded place with very tall buildings."

"So . . . you're just going to New York now. Even though we have a test tomorrow?"

"Yes, this is much more important."

And there she goes, Remy Taft, off to forage for a dress for her poor, pathetic, huckleberry friend. I don't know how to take this. On the one hand, I'm grateful. I've never had a friend forage for me before. On the other hand, this is not exactly honor-student behavior. It's not even student behavior. We have a test to study for, and she's . . . gone.

She calls up to me as she barrels down the stairs.

"Leave the door open! I left my key!"

Of course she did.

TWENTY-THREE

I guess Remy is really taking her time looking through her closet, because it's two days later and she's still not back. Maybe her closet actually leads to Narnia and she is busy fighting the White Witch and communing with Aslan the Lion. That, actually, would make more sense than taking two days to find a dress. For her friend. To go to a ball. That she doesn't even want to go to.

When she finally does comes back, she kind of looks like she just stepped out of a laundry basket. It's late and I am studying down in the Denbigh study room, which puts the other study rooms to shame. I guess with this one they decided to go "full nautical." The room is painted a deep shade of navy blue, with white trim, and everywhere there are pictures of ships, or nautical maps, or anchors, and even kicky pillows that have coral on them in embroidery. Maybe what happened is some salty dog sent his seaworthy daughter to Pembroke and dedicated this room in her honor. Either that, or someone in the housing department has a flair for interior design that will never be squashed!

Either way, I seem to be the beneficiary of this aquatic revelry, as no one else is in here and, now that I think about it, no one ever is. Maybe there is some sort of macabre rumor about this place. Maybe when no one is looking that octopus will crawl out of that painting and grab you. Never to return!

Speaking of never returning . . .

"Mission accomplished."

"Um, Remy, is that you? I used to know someone named Remy, but she left on a quest and was swallowed up in some sort of interplanetary alternate universe. I do miss her."

"Well, miss her no more! She is here. I mean, she is me! I mean, I am here! Get your face out of those books and come upstairs. I have something vast and thrilling for you to see, little farm girl."

Look. I'm annoyed at her. I feel jerked around. And lied to. Or deceived. Or something. I mean, something is just not right here. How does a girl just disappear for three days? Where does she go? What is she doing? Did she forget how to use her cell phone's text function? Why doesn't she just tell me? I mean, it's not like she's smuggling weapons in from Mexico. I hope. And if that's not it, I mean, is there something wrong with her? Is she dying of cancer or something and not telling anybody because she's being supernoble and transcendent and then one day I'll just walk into our room and she'll be gone, never to be seen again?

"Remy, I'm gonna be honest with you here. And I know this may not be that cool, but whatever, maybe I'm just not cool. I don't understand why you just keep disappearing. And, honestly, not to sound like your grandma or anything, but I'm worried."

"What do you mean?"

"What do I mean? Okay. You've been gone for three days. With no text or anything. After taking off like a house on fire. Also, sidebar, you disappeared before that for two days. Also no explanation."

"I don't even remember that."

"Okay, well, I do. Look, it's no big deal, just tell me, okay? There's no reason to be weird about it. I just—it's just worrying me, kinda."

"Wait. Is this really bothering you? Seriously?"

"Yes, it actually is. It's like a trust thing or whatever."

She smiles in this gigantic way that is practically blinding, then grabs me in a hug and smooshes her cheek against mine. "Farm girl! It's like you really care."

My entire body floods with warm fuzzies. My scowl loses its hold on my face despite my effort to keep it there. "Yeah, well. I'm waiting. Explain."

"Okay, okay, okay. I was back in New York and my mom asked me to stay a few days, because she said she missed me, so I did."

"Even though you had a test."

"Well, I can make it up. It's not like they're gonna kick me out."

And that's true. Of course they won't kick Remy Taft out. How could they? Her dad's on the board of trustees. Whoever kicked her out would be fired by the weekend. Remy knows it. They know it. And presumably her mom knows it.

"Okay. Okay, fine. Thank you for telling me. I'm sorry I can't be cooler or whatever."

"Oh, but you are cool, Willa. And you are going to be ice-cold when you see what treasures I have pillaged in me travels."

"It's this room, isn't it? It turns you into a pirate."

"Yar, thar is the secret of the pirate's study cove! Now ye landlubber must die before she tells the tale!"

"Something about being called a landlubber makes me feel fat."

She breaks character. "Maybe it sounds too much like

blubber. Like you feel like a landblubber."

"Sometimes I do feel like a landblubber."

That's how easy it is. To get me to like her again. Here we are, back where we were before. And I am happy. Oh, so happy.

And then that happy turns into giddy when Remy shows me her grand reveal. In the old maid's quarters next to our room, there it is. The room has finally achieved its true calling as a closet. There is a full-length mirror and some kind of upholstered bench/sofa and a little desk thing with a chair and another mirror perched above it, designed, I'm guessing, for sitting and admiring yourself in ultimate comfort.

And then, oh, and then, there is a giant rack of clothes in the middle.

You have got to see this rack of clothes. It's absurd. It's absurd and wonderful and frivolous and exquisite. Slippery silks, poofy tulle, rich velvets, and playful chiffon in a sixty-four Crayola box's worth of colors.

Remy smiles, proud, standing back and observing her work.

"You like?"

Drawn like a magnet, I approach the rack of all these intricate, some embroidered, some bohemian, some simple, all elegant, with-the-tags-still-on dresses. These are not just any old dresses. These are the kinds of dresses that take weeks to make, the kind of dresses you have to order, the kind of dresses that trip you on your way up the stage to accept your Oscar.

The kind that cost as much as a car. And they're beautiful.

"Well, Iowa. Take your pick."

What's funny about this moment is I know Remy has no intention of *lending* me any of these dresses. No, she is planning on giving me one. Whichever it is, whichever I choose. And it's not braggy. And it's not conditional. And it's not proud.

It's just Remy.

"Jesus, Remy, look at all of this. I could never . . . this is . . ." I pause. "It's like—you saved my life."

I meant the dresses. I only meant the dresses. But that's not how it came out. It came out like I was planning to throw myself off the bell tower and then somebody came in and erased, just simply erased, the thought or even *the memory of the thought* of that.

It came out before I could take it back. Before I could grab it.

And Remy looks at me, catches it.

"I don't know, Willa," she says, taking my hand. "Maybe it's the other way around."

TWENTY-FOUR

Hotchkiss Hall is something much grander than it would be in a movie. It's this enormous, cavernous space with dark wood molding and giant iron chandeliers hanging down from the rafters. Said rafters are hand-painted in a colorful style somewhere between *Game of Thrones* and *Aladdin*. On each wall are oil paintings of various extremely respectable dead white people. There is an enormous stone fireplace in the middle of the hall. This fireplace looks like it could eat a normal fireplace. Tonight, the fire is lit. So if you wanted to flambé a small football team, that would be the place.

Remy and I are not matching. Never. That would be gauche! But we are complementary, that's for sure. It's like we're in the same photo shoot. For Valentino. Yes, folks. I am wearing a Valentino dress for the first time in my life, and I almost feel like I should cash it in for tuition.

Shall I describe it to you? I know you are dying to see it. It's a gray tulle dress with the most delicate wool flowers hand-sewn in no pattern whatsoever. They start at the bottom and then spread out as you go up the dress, like the dress is emerging from the woods, until there's nothing but gray chiffon and fabulousness. It's a diaphanous thing, and I feel a little bit like a wood sprite swooping around everywhere. And then there's Remy's dress. Which is hilarious. It's a navy blue tulle dress with a giant red heart over Remy's heart and what look to be hearts and rocket ships embroidered on the skirt of the dress. I know. It sounds insane. And it is insane. I don't know who in their right mind designed this dress and who for. Well, actually, I do. They designed it for Remy. Only Remy could get away with this dress. But, boy, does she ever.

To get into this giant gala event, we have to walk up the marble steps, into the grand room. And when we walk up the steps into the grand room, it is like a record scratch. I'm not kidding. You could hear a mouse holding a pin and then dropping that pin.

Frankly, I'm a bit embarrassed by all of this, but Remy just takes it in stride and glides into the room with the greatest of ease. I guess she is used to stopping rooms. Of course she is. But this is my first room-stopping. I have never stopped a room before. I have never even stalled a room.

There are plenty of Witherspoon boys around, in various interpretations of black tie. My favorite one is the guy next to the DJ, who is wearing a skinny black tux, skinny tie, with a mop of blond surfer hair and checkered Chuck Taylor high-tops.

"Who's that?"

"Who?"

"The cool guy with surfer hair?"

"Oh, that's Zeb. He's from LA. Of course."

"People in LA name their kids Zeb?"

"Um, yeah. They also avoid gluten like the plague but drink a drink called Kombucha that looks like someone jizzed in it."

"Gross."

"He's cool, though . . . wanna meet him?"

"Maybe later . . . Do you see Milo?"

Remy is distracted, looking at something on her phone.

"Wait, I'll be right back."

Aaaaaand she's gone again. Great. If she leaves for two days I'm gonna scream.

But the DJ is playing Yeah Yeah Yeahs and I notice Zeb is spiking the punch. And he notices I notice he's spiking the punch.

"Shh." He lifts up his finger to his mouth and smiles.

I smile back. He's kind of a cute guy. There's something light there.

"I'm improving the recipe. It's an ancient one handed down from my ancestors."

"Really? Is your ancestor Jack Daniels?"

"He's my father, actually. No, wait, that's Darth Vader."

We both stare at each other, a bit nervous.

"Okay, that joke didn't really work."

"I sort of liked it."

"I like your dress. You look kind of like a wood fairy."

"I *feel* kind of like a wood fairy."

"I don't really feel like a wood fairy."

"No. You look more like an ad for . . . people who wear tuxes and . . . ride skateboards."

"That's a pretty small Venn diagram overlap."

I like this guy. This Zeb. I like the fact that he seems to hail from different climes. Breezy ones. There's something gentle about him. I bet he's a Buddhist. Isn't everybody from California a Buddhist?

But there is no more time to contemplate this Zeb, because Remy has come up behind me, captured my arm, and whisked me away toward the cloisters. I look back over my shoulder. "Bye, Zeb."

"Wait, how did you know my name?"

"She's stalking you," Remy chimes in.

#facepalm

Thanks, Remy.

But now we are in the cloisters and all is dark. There's a sarcophagus on the other side of the vault, and it's just plain creepy. In the middle is a fountain, coming out of a shallow well. About six feet down. The water burbles over into the fountain and the music can barely be heard from inside the hall, although you can see the light flickering inside through the giant stained-glass windows.

"Remy, I kind of liked that guy."

"Zeb's supercool. You should like him. Just don't fall for him, 'cause he's got this ridiculously beautiful supermodel girlfriend he's totally in love with. His dad is some famous director, so he's kind of been cool all his life. Like he was raised on sets with everybody fawning over him all the time."

"Ah, bummer . . . Well, now this party just got boring again."

"No, no, this party hasn't quite started, my dearest Iowa."

"Come again?"

"So, remember how you were kind of wondering where I went sometimes?"

"Um. Kind of. By which I mean, of course."

"So . . . one thing that I sometimes have been doing is something that you might be interested in, but I'm scared to mention it because I don't want to freak you out."

"Okaaay."

"Can I tell you? Promise not to be mad?"

"Okay."

"Promise?"

"I promise."

"Okay, here."

And she places something in my hand. Something little and pink and round with a heart on it.

"You've been collecting Valentines?"

"No, no. Much better. Although I guess you could say it's a Valentine, because it fills you with love."

"I'm confused."

"So, okay, this is Ecstasy. Also known as MDMA. And it makes you feel like you're in love. With everything."

"*This* is what you've been doing."

"Doing and recovering. There's definitely a recovery period."

It's getting cold out, and I'm beyond uncomfortable in every way. I shudder.

"Look, you don't have to. You don't. I just thought it might be fun. And maybe thrilling."

I'm frowning down at this small pink thing in my hand. "I don't know . . ."

"Well, maybe just try it. Just to say you did it or whatever.

The world's not gonna end. And if it does . . . wouldn't you like to be wearing that dress?"

She smiles and nudges me.

I can't help it. I know I shouldn't, but I can't help it. There it is—curiosity.

"Okay. Ready?"

"Okay. Ready."

"Stick out your tongue. I'll do it at the same time."

We both stick out our tongues, like little kids at the doctor. She places one pink pill precisely on each of our tongues. Gulp. We wash it down with some bottled water I hadn't even noticed before. I guess her diabolical plan was calculated.

"And away we go . . ." She smiles, mischievous.

I don't know where this "away" is.

I don't know if I'm an idiot.

Ask me in twelve hours. I'll know then.

TWENTY-FIVE

Welp, the Fall Ball is dramatically improved by the introduction of drugs. What before was a boring, contrived excuse for playing dress-up is now a mad, thrilling romp where everyone is adorable and the walls are in love with the ceiling. If you're wondering where I am right now, I'm in the middle of the dance floor, and Remy is doing what can only be described as an interpretive dance next to me, around me, a little bit away from me, and then around me again.

I've noticed that Zeb has left the party. No Zeb, no Milo. I could be sad about that if I weren't flying three feet above the ground and jumping everywhere. There's nothing that could happen that would be wrong right now. No wrong song to dance to, no wrong thing to say, no wrong person to be. Everything is as it should be, and everything is the best thing ever.

I've never been in love before. This is the first time I'm in love. I'm in love with this. I'm in love with the chandeliers hanging from the ceiling, the light off the rafters, the hearts and rockets on Remy's dress, myself, Remy, the DJ, everyone in here and everyone who ever lived. This is what it's like.

I have the thought, it's a quick thought, that maybe this is the way it's supposed to be. Like maybe this is the way you're supposed to live your life. In love. In love with the sky and the trees and each day you're given. Maybe that's how you're supposed to do it.

Remy is grabbing me and pulling me outside, and when the brisk air hits us, that, too, is like the breeze has decided to fan us in just the right way, to lift us off the ground and into the night sky.

"Oh my God. Look."

I look to where Remy is pointing and see nothing. There's a cobblestone path, the side of the library, and a golf cart.

"What am I looking at? What's happening right now? What is my name?"

"Your name is Willa and that's a golf cart."

"Okaaaay."

"And we are going to steal it."

"Um."

"Yes. Trust me. It will be fun."

I wonder how many times in the history of mankind the words "trust me" have been used before something terrible happened. I'm guessing you can round it off to about a million.

"I think we could probably get in big trouble for . . ."

But Remy has not waited for my counsel on this matter. That's because Remy is too busy running to the golf cart, cackling like a crazy person, and jumping on the golf cart.

"Oh my God, the keys are still in it."

"Maybe someone just left it for like two seconds and then they're gonna come back and then they're gonna be mad and then they're gonna put us in jail."

Again, Remy has not waited for me to weigh in on the matter. Instead, she has started up the golf cart, laughed diabolically, and driven up next to me.

"Remy, oh my God, you're insane. I think you might have lost your mind."

"Get in."

"Maybe we should contemplate the pros and cons."

"Willa, as your best friend and friend for life, I hereby decree that you must enter this golf cart."

"Okay, okay, I suppose if you decree."

And with that, I become an accessory to the crime.

We fly down the cobblestone path and wind around campus and over the hill until we are racing down the perimeter of the campus, all the way down down down past Denbigh, past Radnor, past the campus center, past the science center, and all the way to the very end, where there is a gymnasium next to the duck pond.

There's an almost-full moon tonight and I could swear to God the man in the moon is laughing at us, or with us, not yet determined.

It's impossible not to love the wind and the stars and the madness of flying through the campus on an illegal golf cart, our dresses billowing behind us.

Except we are going too fast.

"Remy, I think we're going too fast!" I'm yelling over the sound of the motor.

"What?"

She's yelling, too.

"I think we're going too fast!"

"I know!"

"What do you mean you know? You mean you know and it's okay or you know and there's nothing you can do about it?"

"I mean I know and there's nothing I can do about it!"

"What?!"

"It's not braking!"

"What?! Jesus?!"

And now we are going fast fast fast, way too fast, down the path leading to the gymnasium and the duck pond.

"Turn around! If we go uphill it will slow us down!"

"No, we'll fly out!"

But Remy does try to turn it, and it does slow us down, just enough, just enough so the golf cart runs into the embankment of the duck pond and, yes, into the duck pond with a last final splash.

And now we, too, are in that duck pond.

Remy and I, in our absurdly expensive dresses, have just crashed a golf cart into a duck pond.

And now we just start laughing.

I know. I know we should get up and run away and check that we are not dead or that anything is broken. That is what anyone normal would do. But that's not what's happening right now. No, no, instead, Remy and I are sitting waist-deep in the water and laughing uncontrollably.

This goes on for about five minutes.

You have to admit, it's kind of shocking no one has found us. I guess taking the route around the back of the campus was a stroke of brilliance.

"We are in so much trouble. Oh my God."

"No, we're not! Come on!"

And now Remy is dragging me by the arm, out of the

half-sunken golf cart and up the grass.

"Let's stay off the path so no one sees us."

"Remy, we can't just leave that there. We have to tell someone . . ."

"Oh, no, we won't. I'll be fine, but you'll get kicked out."

And that's true. Oh God, I'm an idiot.

"Don't worry. This is the plan. We'll just sneak back to Denbigh. No one will see us. Everyone's at the Fall Ball—look around, it's like deserted."

"Okay, okay . . . but, um . . . what about the cart?"

"What about it?"

"Well, we broke it."

"We didn't break it; it was broken before. The brakes didn't work. It almost killed us."

"Oh my God. It almost killed us because we stole it and we weren't supposed to. I think that was like karma or whatever."

"Maybe. But it doesn't matter. I'll pay for it, okay? I'll make my dad get them, like, two new golf carts. That way it's, like, a win for them."

"Really?"

"Sure. And besides, that was the best thing ever. You have to admit."

"I do have to admit." I pause. "I feel like we're in that movie with Audrey Hepburn. The one in Rome."

"Europe! We should go to Europe! Willa, will you go to Europe with me? Next summer. I was gonna go, but I couldn't think of anyone I wanted to go with. We can fly into Paris. We have a place there. In the sixteenth. It's kind of bougie, but it's nice. I would've preferred Le Marais, but no one ever listens to me."

"Wait. Are you serious?"

"Yes! It would be so fun!"

And now my mind is racing, thinking of all the things we could do and see and all the trouble we could get into in Paris.

"By the way, I'm freezing." Remy gestures to her soaked dress.

"Me, too. Do you think our frocks will survive this debacle?"

"Sure. It's called dry cleaning."

We walk along, the lights of Denbigh gleaming over the hill.

Remy is just shaking her head and smiling. "I can't believe we crashed a golf cart."

"Into a duck pond."

And now Remy quacks. And I quack, too. And now she attacks me in quacking-duck form. And I pretend run away from the duck attack. And we quack and laugh like that all the way back. And even though we're freezing and even though we just committed a small crime and even though I don't do drugs but I just did drugs, this, so far, is the best night of my life.

And now we're going to Paris.

PART II

PART II

TWENTY-SIX

You should never do drugs and go to class. You should never do drugs and go to class the next day. You should never do drugs and go to class the next day after that. Maybe you should just never do drugs. How about that?

It's two days after the Fall Ball, and I am still in a state of wraith-hood, a state of overwhelming angst and depression. Remy calls it "recovery."

There is no happiness here. No happiness allowed. It's like all the happy got sent out in one shot and now it's gone. And now there's just me. Sad me. Unable-to-be-happy me. Annihilated me.

Remy told me it would be like this. She wanted to prepare

me for it. But sitting here, in Ms. Ingall's Lit class, all I can think is, *I'm an idiot.*

It's the overpowering sense of doom that really is freaking me out. That's the kicker. It's truly difficult to get through the everyday comings and goings of life with an overpowering sense of doom. I wouldn't wish it on my worst enemy.

Not that I have any enemies. What am I, some kind of international superspy?

"Remy, I can't take this," I whisper.

"It's just the crash; it's almost over. I promise."

Maybe she's right. Maybe it is just the crash and then everything will be fine again. Just fine enough so that we'll do it again.

See, that's what I know will happen. Of course it will.

But knowing and doing something about it are two different things.

And I know, looking at Remy, who is also in her own particular state of wraith recovery, that I will do nothing about it.

Absolutely nothing.

And maybe it's not so bad after all. Maybe it's just the price of admission for being friends with someone like Remy. Maybe it's just the price for the ride.

Ms. Ingall steals a long glance over at me, then at Remy,

and I find myself convinced she can read my mind. She knows I'm guilty. She knows I'm blowing it. And I'm not proud of it.

Oh God. Maybe I'll get kicked out before midterms.

TWENTY-SEVEN

I heard a rumor that there's a "New" York. The idea is . . . it's this place with all these tall buildings that everybody is supposed to care about and all the banking happens there and tons of theater and you have to be rich even just to look at it. It's a place that used to be dangerous but now everybody says is a shopping mall and it's Disney-ified and everybody wishes it were dangerous again. Oh, and it's an island. Called Manhattan. That is where the rich people grow.

If movies are to be trusted, you don't have much space, either. Even doctors and lawyers live in a space that, back home, would be considered kind of like a trailer. But here, put that trailer in the sky and call it magic.

But Milo Hesse does not live in a trailer in the sky. Milo Hesse lives in the kind of place they don't even show in movies because if they did, you'd never believe it. If they showed this place in movies everybody would stand up in the theater and say, "No way! Un-unh! I don't believe it!" before storming into the streets and throwing cars everywhere to protest the fact that anybody gets to live like this.

This was Remy's idea. She thought we might enjoy a little sojourn to "the city." I guess there must not be any other cities on earth if this one is simply called "the city."

But there is one place, this place belonging to the family of Milo Hesse, that makes it seem like, of course, there can be no other places.

First and foremost, there is art. And not just any art. No, no. Art that you see in museums. Example: You know that guy who does those paintings of just black with a white date written on the front? I know, I know, they seem ridiculous and like something any fourth grader could do, but they're worth a zillion dollars. Because art. Well, there are two of them, hanging up on the first floor of what essentially looks to be the top two floors of the building, gutted into an empty space, with a spiral staircase at the other end leading to what I can only imagine to be the villain's lair upstairs.

Not your taste? Okay, how about this? There's a giant screen print of Jackie Kennedy, staring across the space at a giant screen print of Marilyn Monroe. Both by that guy with the crazy white hair. There's a sculpture in the middle of the room that looks like a balloon animal, but it's as big as an elephant. And the coup de grace, the pièce de résistance, is the entire back wall. It's taken up by a giant black-and-white photograph, with red writing on it, like you see on those T-shirts. It says: "We Don't Need Another Hero" in giant red letters, in front of a little girl and a boy flexing his muscles. But they look like a little boy and a girl from the '50s. And it's cool. All of it is beyond cool. All of it is designed to make itself look cold and daunting.

And then there's Milo. He just walks past it all like he's at the subway station, ignoring entirely the vast trove of contemporary art, and up the staircase.

"I'll be right back."

He bounds up the stairs to the devil's lair, leaving Remy and me to contemplate the giant painting with the kids on it.

"What do you think it means?"

"I don't know. But it's pretty cool, don't you think?"

I nod.

"Barbara Kruger. She's awesome."

We both nod, looking around.

Across from us, there's a black-and-white photograph of a little Latino five-year-old in a Mexican wrestling mask. He's sort of tubby and happy as a clam. He's so happy you can't help but be happy with him.

"That's a Nan Goldin. Milo's favorite."

"Oh."

"Milo's parents have a wing named after them at MoMA." She senses my vague confusion.

"The Museum of Modern Art. His mom is pretty serious about art, as you can see. And orphans. She's always doing charity stuff for orphans."

"Jesus." I continue to stare at Happy Chubby Boy.

"I know. Don't ask him about it, 'cause it'll just embarrass him."

And now I get it. You can come from this. You can have all of this. But you can't care about it. Like, you have to shrug it off like it's no big deal and act like you're just like the rest of everybody and don't live in a museum and don't care that your family's name is plastered on the side of MoMA and don't care that everybody can trace your folks back to the *Mayflower*. That's how you do it. You just gotta shrug it off. You just gotta pretend the whole thing embarrasses you.

"Don't you think maybe we should get back to school or something? I mean, we didn't sign out or anything."

Remy looks at me and smiles. "Well, we could . . . but I already lied and said we were going to my parents' house for the weekend."

"What?! You did?"

"Guilty."

"And they believed you?"

"Yeah. They pretty much do whatever I want. My dad's on the board."

"Huh?"

"The board of trustees, remember?"

"Oh, right. Of course he is."

I walk around, inspecting the giant balloon animal.

"Jeff Koons. So overrated." Remy rolls her eyes.

If you live like this, I bet they teach eye-rolling in pre-K.

Standing in the middle of that cavernous space, looking around with the art swallowing me up, it dawns on me that I am a zillion miles from home and light-years away from any world I have ever known. This is a world I kind of didn't even know existed. I mean, maybe every once in a while I'd catch a glimpse of this world in the past. Like in a Katharine Hepburn movie. But here. And now. In this time. I didn't really realize there were people who lived like this. And it's like a wash of sadness comes over me. I'd like to think it was a wash of empathy, sympathy for the huddled masses, and everyone else out there living in a trailer, or a shack, or a tiny hole in the wall, scraping by. But that's not what it is. If I'm honest with myself.

It's not that noble.

It's that I'm never gonna have this. It's that no matter what I do, or how much I succeed in the world, or how much I struggle and maybe even someday grab the brass ring and somehow end up in a place like this or even bigger than this, I'm never gonna be the one to casually shrug and walk my way past it and act embarrassed and just let it roll off my back like it's nothing. I'll never grow up with Andy Warhols staring at me. I'll never be in the Social Register. I'll never have the same last name as a president. And even though I spend half my life cracking jokes and making fun of it all . . . the fact of the matter is . . . deep down inside . . . as ashamed as I am to admit it . . . I'm jealous.

I'm fucking jealous.

God, my dad would be so disappointed in me right now.

He really would. He'd lecture me about gratitude and being a good person and never making comparisons. And he'd be right. I know he would be. But that doesn't change the fact that in the pit of my stomach there's this sinking feeling that somehow I just lost.

I lost. And nobody even told me we'd started the game.

"Okay, who's first?"

I look over and there is Milo. He's standing between Remy and me. And he's holding out his palm. And on his palm is a pill. Three pills, actually. One for each.

Remy looks at me and smiles.

"I'll go first."

"What is it?"

"Nothing bad. Just X."

And here we go again. It's not like I didn't think it was coming. I guess I just didn't know how I'd feel about it.

But now I know how I'd feel about it. Here, in this place.

There's something in me. Something that has to do with that last thought. That feeling that I already lost. That feeling that—why not?—what's the point anyway?

"Let's do it together. Like, all of us." It comes out before I know I said it.

Remy nods. "Good idea."

Milo grabs some water while Remy and I stare at each other, waiting.

"Don't worry. Milo always has the best stuff. There might not even be a crash. Seriously."

I'd like to think that this makes me feel good. But it doesn't. I don't like what I'm doing, but somehow I'm still doing it. Thinking maybe, just maybe, that little pill will give me the same thing I just lost in this room about five minutes ago. Whatever it is. I want it back.

It's almost like I don't want to see this. Like there's a truth here I don't want to know. In this place. But if I take the pill. If I take the pill, I don't have to see it. Everything will be just *great*! I don't have to even care.

Milo comes back and the three of us each take a pill. I notice Milo decides to take two. Guess he had extra.

Remy smiles at me with a twinkle in her eye. I smile back, but I can't help but wonder, what's the price this time? What's the price for this ride?

TWENTY-EIGHT

So I guess if you live in New York in the most perfect place ever with the coolest stuff ever, the first thing you're supposed to do is leave. I mean, seriously. Why would we want to stick around a giant, empty, superfantastic space in the middle of this whirling dervish of a town? We couldn't be bothered. How gauche! No one actually stays anywhere superamazing. I mean, why would we want to do that when we could get into a cab and go to Brooklyn to a packed, greasy space filled with weirdos and smoke and something that looks like smoke but kind of smells and tastes like cotton candy and projections everywhere and a zillion people dancing to some kind of throbbing, repetitive mating call?

In case you can't guess, I'm not happy to be here.

There are a couple of reasons for that.

Whatever this drug is supposed to do, it's not really doing anything but making me feel like I'm about to throw up, and then I'm okay, then I'm about to throw up, then I'm okay. Remy says it hasn't kicked in yet. Maybe she's right. Not sure. But if I am gonna be feeling like this, the last place I want to be is around a bunch of people who you have to wonder what they are doing with their lives to be here in the first place.

And then there's Milo. Something odd and tantalizing just happened with Milo. On our way into this godforsaken place . . . there was an incident. You see, there was a girl. And not just any girl. Like, a supermodel-looking girl. With long dirty-blond hair and a gap between her teeth. But a foxy gap. Like, she's the kind of girl that makes a gap between your teeth look glamorous.

Now, normally, this is the kind of girl you would see all sorts of guys rushing over to, but that's not what happens. No, no. Remy and I both step back and watch as this girl bum-rushes Milo, plants two palms on his chest, and literally pushes him back with brute strength.

"WTF?!"

Milo looks vaguely amused but a bit nervous.

"WTF?! WTF?! WTF?!" Just those letters over and over. And now she is just pushing him backward and he is getting pushed. And people are starting to look over. Remy and I exchange the international look for OMG.WTF.com

"Hi . . ." Milo trails off, his cheeks flushed.

"Hi? That's all you have to say to me? HI?!"

"Um . . ."

"Yeah, whatever, *HI*. You know what . . . fuck you!"

And gap-toothed-yet-beautiful storms off.

Now there is just a circle of people staring at Milo, who looks around sheepishly.

"Sorry . . . that was my dentist."

A few chuckles, a few eye rolls, and everyone gets back to the party.

So, as you can see, Milo is becoming more and more mysterious by the minute. I mean, I thought it was pretty clear that he was the most excellent swoon-worthy person of all time, but maybe he isn't after all. Maybe he's a jerk? I mean, that dentist comment wasn't the nicest. Also, I thought it was pretty clear that I was supposed to be in love with him and all, but that's not what's happening, either. And he is presently transforming into some kind of weird turtle who is quiet, withdrawn, and only answering questions with one-word sentences.

Guess that dentist really had an effect.

If you don't believe me, even Remy is noticing. It's like he can't even look at us.

Maybe I shouldn't have admitted I'm from Iowa. He probably just thinks I'm some dumb hillbilly. I mean, the art on my dad's walls is not on loan but was straight-up bought from maybe a garage sale or the ROSS Dress for Less, and there's a kitchen witch involved and also something depicting a cat sleeping in a meadow outside a barn at sunset. There are no giant paintings of Campbell's tomato soup, but there actually is Campbell's tomato soup. If you open the top cupboard to the left, you'll find it.

So there's that.

That might explain the fact that my mysterious future imaginary husband Milo might as well be in Timbuktu right now, let alone standing right next to me in the middle of this sweaty party or bacchanalian festivity or whatever this is. I am noticing that some of these people are probably too old to be doing this. I mean, like . . . I'm not sure what the cutoff point is for gyrating in sparkly clothes, but I can tell you some of these people are really pushing it.

If you think this is Remy's cue to look over at me and say, "C'mon, isn't this fun?!" and then start dancing crazily with that spangly stranger over there in short shorts, then guess what? Wrongo.

Remy looks just as annoyed as me. She's yelling into Milo's ear over the music and he's shrinking and looking around a bit, at a girl wearing what can only best be described as a zebra sequin bathing suit minus the stomach part but with a silver circle attaching the top to a skirt. It's very confusing. And the girl herself looks confused by it. Or maybe she's just wondering where the rest of the zebra went.

Milo nods at Remy, and suddenly I am whisked out as if on a kind of people-conveyor belt back into the brisk Brooklyn air.

"God, that was horrible."

I think it's the first time I've ever heard Remy say anything negative.

"I know. So B and T."

"B and T?"

"Bridge and tunnel."

"Like, the people that have to take a bridge and/or tunnel to get here," Milo fills in.

"Wait . . . didn't WE have to take a bridge to get here . . . to Brooklyn?"

"NO!"

But definitely yes.

Still, they both say it. I think this is the most emphatic they've been all night. Possibly ever.

Here's the good news.

Our Ecstasy is kicking in.

Here's the bad news.

Now Milo is puking in the gutter.

TWENTY-NINE

Don't think I don't know what you're thinking. You're thinking that Ecstasy is fun and doesn't make you puke. But trust me. It does. Or trust Milo. He'll tell you.

But that's over now. All of it. The puking. The nausea. The general grodiness. And what seems to have replaced it is the part that everybody goes through that first horrible part for.

Oh, I forgot to tell you what happened. Milo puked, Remy hailed an Uber, and next thing you know we were back in Manhattan, but this time in a place I didn't know existed. Remy's place. Or Remy's family's place. In Manhattan. Where no one is. Because they are all somewhere called Amasandwich or Amahamburger or something. But whatever the place is, it's not here, and that means they are not here, which is a good thing because Milo is still looking a little green around the gills. In a cute way. Like if Jared Leto were a space alien. Which doesn't seem quite outside the realm of possibility.

Basically, what happens is you walk into this French-blue room with white molding everywhere, even up two feet off the ground. So the French blue just kind of looks like these panels, on the top part of the wall. And there're paintings on them. Discreet ones. Nothing like at Milo's place. Nothing gigantic and modern. No, no. This is shy, coquettish. The floor is wood, but an elaborate wood design with little squares and shapes in it. And there's a cherrywood table in the middle with flowers on it. Also, sconces are involved.

That's just the first room.

The second room, the room with the fireplace that Milo is tinkering with in an effort to either make a fire or burn down the building, has a lot of Chinese-looking panels all around it, but there is also molding and there's a warm glow coming from somewhere and a grand piano in the corner in case you decided to take up the piano. Really, what's odd about this room is that you could actually have a ball in it. Not that you could have fun in it. No, no. You could actually have an actual ball in this space. Like with waltzing and swirling poofy skirts and everything. There are seriously three different seating areas, and that's not even counting the sort of off-to-the-side seating areas, which seem to consist of two chairs and a little table obviously meant to be used whilst conspiring against the queen.

What I love about Remy is that if you saw her on the street you would never, ever know this. She would never tell you. She might look like she grew up in a laundry machine on tumble dry, but you'd never guess she came from this place. It's not this place that makes Remy who she is. It's the fact that she doesn't seem to notice.

The main event seating area is in front of the fireplace, where Milo is busy at attempted arson and can be seen in the giant mirror behind, which was probably taken from Napoleon some time ago. If you're wondering where Remy is, she's rolling on the floor. That's not an expression. Well, it is, actually. But that's not what I mean here. Remy is literally rolling around on the floor, not too far away from the fireplace in question.

If you're wondering where I am, I am on the floor beside Remy and I, too, seem to be rolling around.

What am I doing here? I don't know, but it appears to be all we can muster at the moment.

So, this really turns out to be a very gendered evening. The two girls are rolling around in front of the fireplace whilst the boy is busy building the fire to provide warmth and, also, an activity for himself. Boys are weird. I never would in a million years be trying to build a fire right now. Or tinkering with flammables in any manner.

But there he is. And I must say, for someone who was just puking his face off an hour ago, he's doing swimmingly.

I'm doing swimmingly, too, for that matter, in that I feel like I'm swimming. In this room. In this warmly lit, vaguely playful yet delicate Chinese-paneled room.

I just want you to know. There's marzipan in little shapes of fruit in all of the different little ethnic bowls hanging around. Like a strawberry, a minibanana, a minipear, and even a minipumpkin. The minipumpkin is not an actual fruit. That would be ridiculous. They are all pretending to be fruit but inside they are delicious marzipan. I make a mental note to eat them when I am hungry again. Which should be in about two days. Maybe I should take them with me, if we leave earlier than that, but hopefully we won't leave—earlier or ever.

I would like you to know that my plan has worked. Everything feels great. And I'm in love. With everything. I'm in love with the floors and the marzipan and the fireplace and the Chinese wallpaper and Milo striking matches and Remy rolling around next to me like a demented potato.

Also, Local Natives is playing. So that, too, is making love out of nothing at all.

Remy is looking at me. Now she smiles. She whispers into my ear, "Do you wanna know something funny?"

Local Natives is whispering into my other ear, all about airplanes. They are repeating "I want you back back back."

Remy whispers again, "You're the only person from that dumb school I ever brought here."

I look at her like she's lost her marbles.

She nods. "Yup."

"I don't believe you."

"Milo! Milo . . . answer this question. Seriously. Have I ever once brought anyone back here from school, from Pembroke?"

Milo looks down at me from next to the mantel, through the mirror.

"Nope."

And this is just getting weird. I don't say the thing I want to say, which is, "Why me?" Like, seriously, why on earth, considering that everyone at that school, *everyone* is falling all over themselves to hang out with the one person who is considered the mostest of the most, the allest of the all . . . why does that worshipped person simply decide to reach over and choose me, ME? The biggest hick in the entire school and probably on the entire Eastern Seaboard?

I don't ask that question, but she doesn't seem to mind.

And Milo doesn't seem to mind.

Nobody seems to mind anything.

Everyone is just acting like this is what is meant to be and there's nothing weird about it at all. No sir.

Everyone is just acting like I'm supposed to be here. And I am acting that way, too. Now. Of course I am. I'm not an idiot. I'm not gonna go around this ridiculously beautiful and elaborate but somehow ethereal place with my jaw dropped down, slurping all over the Persian rugs and the parquet floors.

But I can't help wondering what my dad would say. If he saw me. I guess he'd probably tell me to lay off the drugs. Actually, what am I talking about? He'd ground me. Definitely. He'd definitely ground me for life.

But my dad is not here right now, my pretty.

And I'm not in Iowa anymore.

And wasn't that the point of sending me here in the first place? To be with the right kind of people? To do the things they do?

"I have an idea."

It's not Remy, it's Milo. Milo is sitting next to me, and I'm trying not to notice that you could cast him as the cutest person on earth right now.

"Why don't you stay there. Stay as still as you can . . . and tell me if you like this."

I look for Remy. No sign. Guess she's in the enormous

powder room with fancy soaps in the shape of seashells.

But there I am, lying on the floor next to the fireplace, and there is Milo. And what he's doing is, he's touching my skin. Just on my arm. Nothing pervy. He's just touching my skin. Trailing his fingers up my arm, and down my arm. And now my ankles. On the sides of my knees. On the sides of my thighs. And up again. To my arms.

All very PG.

Right?

Except that's not what it feels like.

It doesn't feel PG.

It feels like someone is setting my skin on fire. And that someone is Milo.

And this feels like a secret.

THIRTY

We don't even look at each other on the train ride back to Pembroke. Remy and I. There's nothing wrong, technically. Nothing you could point your finger at and say, "There! That's it. That's why I'm so depressed!" In fact, we were happy as can be, flying high, not twelve hours ago. We were on top of the world. And now? It's like all that just turned inside out on itself and now our heads are killing us, our stomachs are turning, and we both look like we have two black eyes from lack of sleep. Poisoned. We are poisoned.

And it was fun.

Look, it was. I'm not gonna lie to you.

But now, looking out the window of the train with my head pounding and this desperate feeling of certain catastrophe . . . ugh. Again. Here we are again. Not worth it. Seriously not worth it.

"I think I'm fucking up."

"What?" Remy turns to look at me.

"I just don't think I should do this. I think I'm gonna regret it. I already do regret it in a way."

"What? You mean, like, ever? You're never, ever gonna do it again?"

"I don't know. I mean, look at us."

"Yeah."

"It's like we're a couple of scarecrows."

"Yeah."

It's not exactly an agreement. Remy is not committing either way.

"Anyway, it doesn't matter. We have that midterm in two days. We gotta get it together."

"Oh, I forgot about that."

"I'm serious, Remy. We shouldn't mess that up."

I don't say the real thing I'm thinking. Which is that I'm on academic scholarship and if I get kicked out, that's it for me. The whole life is gone . . . never to return again.

Just straight to the trailer park.

Back to What Cheer.

No more Remy.

Do not pass go.

That's the difference. Remy can fuck around all she wants, but that glowy fireplace will always be waiting for her. Not me. I gotta fight for it.

It is strange, wanting to fight for something. When was the last time I wanted to fight for anything?

The last time I can remember actually fighting was at the roller-skating rink when I was ten. It's a long story, okay? But let's just say fighting on roller skates is no small feat. I would like to say I retained my dignity, but that would be a stretch.

"What did you think of that crazy girl, anyway?"

This is Remy changing the subject.

"Which one?"

"Um, the one at the club. With the gap tooth and the stiletto boots, who kept pushing Milo and saying, 'WTF, WTF'?"

I shrug.

But maybe he tried touching *her* in the dark, too.

And maybe she let him.

And maybe she never heard from him again.

I haven't told Remy about the Milo incident. I don't know why. I have this feeling that somehow he belongs to her. Even though over and over she says they're just friends. Somehow he belongs to her. But if I'm honest, I don't want him to.

I want him to belong to me.

"Oh, yeah. I dunno. Do you think he, like, dumped her or something?"

"Mm. I don't think so. Milo is kind of a bunny rabbit. Doesn't sound like something he'd do . . ."

She trails off, staring out the window. Then, she smiles at me, sneaky.

"By the way . . . what did *you* think of Milo?"

I'm not gonna tell her.

"Well, he seems pretty cool. When he's not puking in the gutter. And getting yelled at by supermodels."

And I don't know why I said that. I'm just trying to keep him to me. To keep the possibility of him to me. Safe. Untainted.

"Plus, I don't think he likes me very much."

"Why not?"

"I dunno. He's kind of . . . quiet."

"Well, Milo is not the kind of guy to just jump on top of you after some cheesy line."

She's got that right. He's more the kind of guy to sidle up to you while you're on Ecstasy and gently touch your arm for ten seconds.

"Yeah, I guess."

"Well, he did imply that you were pretty."

"Imply?"

"Yeah, like when we met. He implied that you were

attractive—that Iowa comment? I'm too drained to remember it exactly."

"Well, you both kind of said the same thing. Do they teach you that line in day care or something?"

"What line?"

"That Iowa must be where all the attractive people are. If I'm from there or something."

She shrugs.

"Well, maybe we both actually thought it, ever think of that?"

I shrug. It's like a shrugging contest over here.

"Honestly, I don't know what you're used to back on the farm, but all the guys I know are totally weird and shy and incapable of trying any lines or making any hot moves or whatever."

"Really?" I give an involuntary shiver, thinking of Milo's hand going slowly over my skin in the dark.

"Um. Yeah. Totally hopeless. If they like you then usually they just ignore you. Or say mean things. I think that's called flirting."

Okay, this is the last time I'm gonna ask this question. But I have to know.

"Are you sure you guys aren't in love or something? Like some unrequited thing? Because it sure seems that way. I mean—"

"*Tsh.* No. No way. Milo's not my type."

If that's true, then why do I feel like I'm stealing her boy-friend?

We smile weakly, spent and sick, heads pounding.

"Next time we should drink more water, I think."

The train pulls into Pembroke station. Now everyone's getting up, gathering their things, collecting, looking around.

"Next time?" I ask.

Remy looks at me. Caught.

"I mean, next time *if we decide to do it.* That's all."

We sidle out beside a lady with an orange-and-black umbrella. "Princeton Tigers" on the handle. I look at the lady. She's about my mom's age. Skinny with wispy auburn hair. She smiles politely at Remy and me.

"Pembroke, I assume?"

She talks in that way you only talk if you're from here. It's not snooty or anything like that. It's just a tiny bit nasal, vaguely amused, and the mouth doesn't move that much. Like everybody's a ventriloquist.

"Yes, guilty," Remy replies, in kind.

This is a language they all speak. A language that's always clever, always in on it, and never trying too hard. A language of the unimpressed.

But that's not what I'm thinking about right now. What I'm thinking about, as we get off the train, into the overcast late-afternoon sky, is Remy and Milo and *next time*.

And as we walk through the crowd and off the platform, I swear, that *next time* is following us down the stairs, down the sidewalk, and all the way back to Pembroke.

THIRTY-ONE

Halfway across the green to the library there's an art class set up, painting. All boys. A field trip from Witherspoon. All facing the same direction. The clock tower and the tree-lined path, the sunset in the distance. A serene but majestic vista. Walking past them, you can't help but notice their work. That guy's good. Um, that's average. That's pretty dark. Twenty different interpretations of the same omniscient clock tower.

But then there's this guy.

This joker.

Facing the complete opposite way.

And that is Zeb.

There he sits, easel set facing 180 degrees in the other

direction. Toward the cafe. There's a loading dock there and two guys, smoking. Working-class guys in white aprons, wrapped around sage-green pants. One white, ruddy-faced. The other black, taller. They're laughing about something. A quick laugh. Maybe at the boss. Maybe at us. Maybe they spat in someone's food. Some jerk.

Zeb is painting them.

I can't help it. Curious.

"What do you think they're laughing at?"

"Maybe they're laughing at my painting."

He continues, looking over, dabbling the brush, looking over.

"I like your painting. It's bold."

"Thanks, Iowa."

"You remembered. Great."

"What, you think I could forget?"

He looks up and raises an eyebrow. Such mischief.

"Has anybody ever told you that you have an impish flair?"

"Has anybody ever told you that you should take this class with me?"

"Are you crazy? Painting is not allowed on my transcript."

"Good Lord! Heavens, no! What a terrible idea! Where are you applying that painting would be so frowned upon?"

"If you ask my mother, it's Princeton or death."

"Ugh. Princeton *is* death. You don't wanna go there."

"Really? Why not?"

"Total squaresville. Seriously, I think they hand out, like, light-blue oxfords and gray pants right when you get there. Blech. You'd hate it there."

"How do you know?"

"Because that's a school for, like, future bankers. And I don't want to presume, but that doesn't strike me as you."

"Well, where do you wanna go? Or are you just gonna surf off somewhere into the night with yacht rock playing in the background?"

"I know exactly where I wanna go. USC, documentary filmmaking. I want to change the world! Like *Blackfish*."

The teacher takes note of me and starts to come over, protective.

"You better go. You don't wanna get busted. It won't look good on your *transcript*."

I look back at the two workers, heading in. One of them flicks his cigarette while the other gets the door. Break's over.

I turn to go.

"Hey, Willa," Zeb calls. "If you get into Princeton, I'll come and make a documentary about how boring Princeton is."

He smiles.

I can't help but smile back.

"Funny, Zeb. Very amusing."

And there's something in my step here. A kind of free-dom. There's something to the way Zeb approaches the grass and the minutes of the day. Something playful and never scared.

And I wonder what you have to do to get like that.

THIRTY-TWO

Something totally weird happened with the play, and now it's not *Grease* anymore.

I guess Teal Pantsuit had a nervous breakdown because somebody ate the rest of her Southwestern-Style Enchilada Lean Cuisine in the faculty fridge and she just kind of went ballistic and is taking time off to "refocus," which I think means they almost shit-canned her but felt sorry for her. That's the rumor, anyway. Whatever the case, now she's gone for an undetermined amount of time, so they are bringing in an entirely new director with an entirely new vision. A vision involving Shakespeare. I, personally, would quit the whole thing right now, but somehow the fact that we're already cast means we are by default involved.

Ugh. *Shakespeare.*

This is gonna be a real snore.

And if I have to wear tights, I'm totally quitting.

The play they have chosen is a rather obscure thing called *Hamlet.*

If you like to watch reruns from the '70s, you may remember it from the episode of *Gilligan's Island* where they decide to make *Hamlet* into a musical.

But this is not that version. And there's something else, too. The drama instructor, Mrs. Jacobsen, has been replaced with . . . the Witherspoon English teacher.

Who is—there is no way to sugarcoat this—hot.

Yup. No Frenchy and singing by the bleachers. Now we are straight into medieval tragedy *avec* hot English teacher.

There are a few problems, and the main one is we can't all play Ophelia. There are only so many enviable roles for a young lass. The crazy girl who kills herself over the prince being the tippy top.

So, basically, it's obvious we will all be spear carriers.

Said English teacher is basically a little paler than white bread, with hair the color of ink. Jet-black ink. Set on bold. His hair is set on bold. And underlined.

He's sophisticated. He's elegant. He's unexpected. He

is not blowing his own horn, but there's something to be blown. Ahem.

If you think Remy is not noticing, that is because it's hard to tell what she's doing because she's hiding behind me, using me as a human shield, if you will. Why, you ask? Why on earth would Remy need to use me as a human shield? Well, quite simply, what is happening is that her tongue is basically exiting her mouth and slurping its way to the ground with love for this here English teacher before us.

That's right. She is hiding from her tongue.

"What the fuck is that?"

She whispers it into my ear, somehow able to speak.

"That . . . is the director for our new production of our Shakespeare play."

"Is he a gift from God?"

"I think he might be a gift from the devil, actually. Considering that he's our teacher."

"I think he is my husband."

I laugh. "What're you talking about? It rhymes with something. And that something is grape. Matchutory grape."

Remy is holding me by the shoulders and giggling into my ear like a schoolgirl.

"What should we call him?"

"Um. I think . . . Humbert Humbert."

"Humbert Whatbert?"

"Humbert Humbert. The guy from *Lolita*."

"And that makes me Lolita?"

"Bingo."

"Perfect. I love a starring role."

THIRTY-THREE

I am left to ponder the incredible force of nature that is Remy Taft.

She was cast as Marty in *Grease* by, basically, breathing.

Now she's been *encouraged* by our new director, the one and only Mr. Humbert, to audition for the starring (female) role in Hamlet. Old Bert referred to her *natural presence* when he made the suggestion.

I nearly gagged. "How does he know they're natural?" I joked. But Remy wasn't laughing. She seemed to soak up Humbert's particular brand of attention like a sponge. I could see it actually puffing her up, making her . . . more.

I, on the other hand, am feeling considerably *less* as I make my way to Wharton House.

It's a stoic white colonial across a gravel road, just north of the green. It sits hidden from everything by a grove of trees, and if you didn't know it was there, you'd assume someone just lived there making pies all day.

But no! This place is silverfish heaven. Books, papers, files everywhere, and up a tiny, curving staircase on the fourth floor is the alcove. And in the middle of the alcove is my Contemporary Lit professor, Ms. Ingall.

I received a reminder note from her in my school mailbox. There it was, right alongside the care package from my dad. (For the record, said package included a Tupperware full of snickerdoodles and a novelty pencil. You know, the kind with the crazy felt hair and the googly eyes? I like it. I've decided to name it Fuzzy McGillicutty.)

Ms. Ingall has summoned me to her lair. I am fearful that I am about to receive a come-to-Jesus kind of lecture, here. I have not, *certainly* not, been the kind of laser-focused teach-me-o-wise-one student I have modeled for my instructors historically. And so, it seems, we're having a little heart-to-heart. Who knows? Maybe I can turn this all around. Maybe I can get some sort of extra credit out of it, graduate with honors and some Latin next to my name.

There she is. Peering through her reading glasses over a pile of papers the height of a vacuum cleaner when my head pops up above the staircase.

"Um, hello?"

She looks up, over her reading glasses.

"Oh, Willa! I'm so glad you came. Thank you for taking the time."

"Sure. Um . . ."

Um. What am I doing here? Um, why so mysterious, Ms. Ingall?

"Willa, you're probably wondering why I've asked you here to my rather claustrophobic and extremely chaotic office."

"Yeah, sort of."

"Well, to be honest, I've taken an interest in you."

Wait, what? Interest? Teachers have blessed me with their tacit approval before, but expressed interest? "Um."

"Do you, by any chance, remember those tests we took perhaps? You know. The first day of class?"

"Sort of . . ."

"I know they were very unusual. Probably seemed pointless."

She's got that right.

"Well, the thing is . . . students come in from all sorts of circumstances. Some, well, quite privileged, and others . . ."

"Like me?"

"Well, let's just say, from varied backgrounds."

I mean, she's practically tiptoeing around the silverfish here.

"The point is I like to know a bit more about my students . . . beyond what they might have learned, quite often by rote, at their previous place of education."

"Oh."

"Certain tests can be weighted to favor those who, say, have been exposed to certain kinds of education since . . . well, since preschool."

"Okay."

"And I don't quite think that's fair. So I have researched extensively and found a more analytical test. A sort of way of really seeing who my students are right there on the first day, before any impressions are made."

I nod assuringly.

"Do you mind? I'd like to show you something, if it's not too much bother."

And now she is rooting around in her desk.

"Oh God, I can never find anything . . . oh, here it is."

And now she takes out a blue folder. And now she takes out a piece of paper with a graph from that blue folder.

"You see this, Willa? You see where all these marks are here? These dots?"

"Yes . . ."

"Okay. Okay, good. Now, what these dots represent are just simply analytical skills. Nothing to do with certain books or even certain formulas. Just simple . . . analytical ability."

She looks at me a second, hesitates.

"Do you see this dot here?"

"Um . . . yeah."

"Willa, this dot here is you."

"This dot is me?"

"Yes. And do you see how it's separate?"

And this is true. All the other dots are huddled together having a little dot party, and there is one dot out to the side, left out.

"I get it. So I'm behind. That makes sense."

"No. No, Willa. Oh God. You're not behind. It's the opposite. You are quite literally . . . off the chart. You're . . . an outlier."

"An outlier?"

"Yes. You have a score that is highly unusual and, well, given your classwork so far, and your participation and your papers, I have no reason to believe this is some sort of fluke."

I'm having a hard time not staring at that dot all by itself in the middle of the chart.

"I've looked at your transcripts and your . . . background. And I feel I must tell you . . . I believe it would be possible for you to apply to a number of esteemed colleges, early decision. And, well, Willa, I think you have a good chance—in fact, I think you have a *great* chance of being accepted. Additionally, I want you to know I would be happy to write a letter of recommendation for you. If you wish."

"Doesn't it seem a little early for—"

"Well, yes. That's why it's called early decision. But it does have its advantages. I have a few brochures here, just a few choices, for you to peruse. You can take them. They send out throngs every year. Frankly, it's a waste of paper. Let's see, there's, um . . . Oberlin. Brown. Berkeley. Cornell. Of course, any of the seven sisters . . . Vassar, Radcliffe, Bryn Mawr . . ."

"Huh. Ms. Ingall. I don't really know what to . . ."

"It occurred to me that, with your grades, and your test scores, and your papers, and quite frankly, your unique perspective . . . there might also be some wonderful options for you that perhaps you might not be aware of. Or perhaps no one had told you about. I don't mean to interfere, but, well . . . I know your mother . . . I mean, Princeton . . ."

She hands me the pamphlets gently.

"Some of these places give full scholarships. To those . . . in need."

She's trying to be polite about it. She's trying to not come off like a jerk.

"Willa, you have . . . an interesting brain. I think there are possibilities for you, beyond what I think you may see for yourself, honestly."

Walking down the steps with the stacks of brochures, I can't seem to get out of there fast enough. I'm not sure if I should be swelling with pride or humiliated.

Hurtling down the stairs, my mind is a kaleidoscope. I can't put it together somehow. What all this means.

At least it confirms something I have always suspected. I am what they refer to as "special." They say this word, "special," when what they really mean is "different" or "strange."

Maybe that's why when I was little my dad could never take me to the zoo because I would cry and scream to see all the animals in cages while everybody else just ate kettle corn and pointed and giggled. Maybe that's why half the time I don't understand what's going on around me or who set the rules and why this world outside my head exists the way it exists or even exists at all.

I am, statistically, a square peg. My brain hums a long-forgotten tune. *One of these things is not like the others, one of these things just doesn't belong.*

I'm halfway down the driveway and around the bushes when I realize those things on my face are tears and there are thousands of them and they won't stop.

I'm not feeling sorry for myself. I'm not. That's not what's happening. It's just . . . I understand all those puzzled looks from my dad now. All those times he was trying, trying so hard to figure out his daughter, with the totally bizarre reactions to everything nice and normal like the zoo or the sandbox or the gas station. It's just, he didn't know what to do. It's just, I didn't know what to do.

It's just . . . I never asked for this. I never asked to be a fox in the snow.

THIRTY-FOUR

Remy is running lines now. From *Hamlet*. She told me she's making it her mission to become the English teacher's Lolita. Which makes no sense because she's trying out for Ophelia. Also, I'm not used to Remy getting spastic about anything. Especially some off-limits creep. But that seems to be what's happening, and, honestly, it's having an effect.

She's carrying a worn copy of *Hamlet* around like she's some kind of character in a Salinger novel. And not only does she swoon at him all the time, which is embarrassing, but when he's not there, she talks about him. Incessantly. Like, we'll be having a conversation about pickles and the next thing you know it's on and on about Humbert Humbert.

Sort of like this:

Me: "I like pickles."

Remy: "I like Humbert Humbert."

Or, the other day:

Me: "I think it's gonna rain. I'm gonna wear my rain boots."

Remy: "I think you're right. I wonder if Humbert will drive me home in the rain."

And on and on and on. Name one thing. Anything. And Remy can bring it back to Humbert. It's absurd.

There's another thing, too. She stole all these pill bottles from her aunt. Without telling me.

Yup. Last week she skipped out again for a few days. I didn't worry. I'm kind of getting used to it. She came back with the same "I decided to stick around at home for a while" excuse and then she disappeared into the closet, aka maid's quarters. Where she disappears a lot.

What happens in the maid's quarters stays in the maid's quarters, right?

But it's getting kind of out of hand.

And the fact that she's keeping it secret? Or trying to?

That's not a good sign.

Am I supposed to say something? Is that the idea? Or am I supposed to ignore it, just shrug and say "whatever" and keep a smile on my face?

And it's all happening so fast I kind of can't keep track of it. Like on Monday.

Get this.

Monday after class, I get back to our room. I hear Remy's voice from behind the door. She's talking on the phone, and from what I can gather, it's to her mother. The one side of the conversation I can hear goes something like this—

"So there's this new drama teacher, and—yes, Mom, drama . . . What? No, I'm not *going on about that whole thing again*. It's just a school play . . . fine. So, I'm trying to tell you that I got a part . . . Yes, I auditioned. Aren't you proud of—so what if I *did* let myself get carried away with it? Oh, yes. The family name. You know the Kennedy son did theater, right? Well, maybe he wouldn't have been flying that airplane if he'd been starring in a play that weekend. Mom. I'm just telling you that—"

I feel guilty listening to even that much, so I turn around and make myself scarce, reading in the study room while Remy deals with whatever *that* is.

When it feels like enough time has passed, I head upstairs. No more dialogue. Nope. Just a few slams and crashes. I open the door and WTF. OMG. Gasp. Everything Remy owns or has ever owned is all over the place, like the place was ransacked by a burglar on a cop show, and she's rifling through it all like it's the end of the world. And talking to herself.

Like a crazy person. Or some kind of stressed-out rat, rummaging through her cage.

So I ask her what she's looking for and she totally ignores me. She's actually, honestly, kind of a bitch about it. Sort of like flippant. Then, she finds whatever the thing is, goes back into the ol' telltale maid's quarters, then comes right back in like nothing happened.

She breathes a sigh of relief and apologizes.

I just stare at her.

"Sorry. I was just kind of freaking out."

"Yeah, um, okay."

"It's just . . . my parents. They're being so fucking mean to me. About this play. They're like—they called it embarrassing. They want me to quit."

I feign ignorance. "Really?"

"Yup. They think it's, like, *beneath* me. Or them. Or whatever."

Then she goes to the bathroom and I watch her down the hall. And now, in the maid's quarters, I start rummaging around. Here. No. Maybe here. No. Okay, how about over here.

And then I find it.

Something I have never seen before.

Okay, I've heard of this drug. I have. Everyone basically says it's the greatest thing ever. Like, it makes you feel like you're the greatest thing on earth and everything is just peachy. Better than peachy. Perfect. And it makes you feel like the world is perfect. Like everything is as it should be. Which is kind of like a Buddhist thing. Except in a pill. A Buddhist pill.

But this is also a drug they give pregnant ladies to recover. From giving birth.

So, yeah, not exactly no big deal.

And this is the drug she's hiding in the maid's quarters.

I guess this is a new level of pill-popping. One that makes Remy bitchy and spastic and rummaging and kind of mean. And isn't that kind of the opposite of Buddhism?

I hear Remy down the hall and go back to a completely abnormal "normal" position.

We're supposed to walk over to this stupid *Hamlet* rehearsal, but to be honest, I really don't want to go anymore. At least *Grease* would have been fun. And there would have been singing involved. And now it's all about talking to skulls and jumping into graves and freaking out on your mom.

Remy will, of course, end up as Ophelia. If I'm lucky I'll get to be Gertrude. You know, the mom who marries her brother's killer and then pretends everything's okay, no, really, don't worry about it. I think in modern times Gertrude would wake up, put on her Juicy jogging suit, blend herself a nice vodka milk shake, and move to the OC. But not Ophelia. Ophelia would never move to the OC. Ophelia is the one who gets to be beautiful and crazy and jilted by Hamlet until she crawls up a willow tree, falls into the river, and drowns, and then Hamlet loves her again.

Sidebar: Why do guys always fall in love with girls *after* they kill themselves? Wouldn't it work a lot better to fall in love with a girl *before* she kills herself? And then maybe she wouldn't even have to kill herself? It always seems like guys fall in love with girls who a) don't notice them or b) are dead.

It honestly seems like a guy would never like a girl just standing in front of him, being in love with him, no matter who she was. Even Angelina Jolie.

But Remy is not behaving like Angelina Jolie. No, no slightly aloof, regal glances here. She is, instead, falling all over herself for Humbert.

So far he's kept things professional. Oh, sure, he'll give her acting direction and talk about iambic pentameter. But he's not whispering sweet nothings into her ear or anything slurpy. I just hope he can keep his weiner on straight in the face of whatever Remy has planned.

Exhibit A: Remy comes back in the room and now it's all rainbows and buttercups. Now she's happy as a clam and getting dressed for rehearsal like it's her own personal date with Humbert Humbert.

"You know he can't like you, right?"

"Who?"

"Humbert Humbert. He's not allowed to like you. Even if he does. Or did. He can't act on it or anything. He'd lose his job."

Remy looks at me through the mirror, she's holding up a cool Bohemian-print dress that might as well be a shirt. It's the kind of thing that looks like you forgot your pants. It makes me involuntarily gulp.

"I know. I just want him to notice me, kinda."

"Um, if you wear that pants-optional outfit, I'm sure he'll notice you. As will everyone else."

"C'mon, don't you think he's cute? A little?"

"I think he's old a little."

I could ask her right now. I could ask her about the pills and the maid's quarters and the whole elaborate charade.

But somehow I don't.

Somehow I'm afraid that if I do, I'll break this thing we have. This thing I don't totally understand the existence of in the first place.

"Can I ask you something, Willa?"

"Maybe."

"How come you never talk about your mom?"

"My mom? Why are you asking?"

"Because she's famous. Famous for being logical. Which sometimes you are."

"I'm not anything like her, actually. And besides, economists aren't famous."

"Okay, *world-renowned*."

"Better."

"So . . . ?"

"Honestly, I haven't seen her in, like, ten years. I haven't talked to her on the phone for about two years, and I kind of like it better that way. I used to really care about what she thought, like it bothered me, like I had to be perfect. Then my dad brought me to a headshrinker, and the shrink said I didn't have to care anymore. He said I could just write her off. Even though she's my mom."

"Really?"

"Yup, really. I couldn't believe it. It was like, 'I can do that? I don't have to care what she thinks? Wow!' And then I felt better. A lot better, actually. That headshrinker kind of saved my life. I really liked him. He kind of looked like John Denver. Like he had blond hair and this sweet smile and a big pie face. You sort of expected him to start singing any minute."

"I wish I'd had that."

"What?"

"A shrink that looked like John Denver."

She puts on the non-leg-covering vestige.

"See? It's not so bad."

"People are starving for pants in India. And you, you throw away your pants like garbage."

"Would you say they're pants-starving?" Remy smirks.

"I would say *you're* pants-starving. As in . . . you are dying for Humbert Humbert to get in your pants."

She turns, assuring me.

"Don't worry, *mon amie*. I won't bring him to Paris with us."

"Very funny. Wait. Were you thinking of bringing him to Paris?"

"Not really."

She grabs her bag as if this is all so blissful and there is absolutely nothing that could possibly be wrong. We head out across the green. But don't think I don't notice that Remy ducks into the maid's quarters again on the way out. And grabs that bottle . . . pretending not to grab that bottle.

I guess she thinks she needs sustenance for her pants-free date with Mr. Old.

THIRTY-FIVE

Watching Remy make a fool of herself over Humbert Humbert is a little cringe-inducing. She is focused. She is swooning. She pays attention. She bats her fucking eyelashes, for God's sake.

And I would definitely think this was a total waste of time, breath, energy, and pants-optional outfits, but I do declare, by rehearsal week four . . . I think she is making progress.

Here is the evidence:

Remy is Ophelia. (She got the part, naturally.) She is practicing this speech where she realizes that Hamlet has lost his marbles and she is bummed out to see such a great guy gone ape shit. "Oh, what a noble mind is here o'erthrown."

(That's "overthrown," bdubs.)

("Bdubs" means "BTW," bdubs.)

So, Remy is over there in another all-legs getup, getting all teary-eyed about bat-shit Hamlet, and I happen to take a glance at Humbert Humbert.

Well, let me tell you. The guy is in a state.

Depending on how you look at it, it's either a state of forlorn longing or a look like a toddler just got his cookie taken away or the way a puppy looks at a "No Dogs Allowed" sign in an old-fashioned cartoon. Whatever it is, there is want there. Not even want. Need.

Humbert Humbert is starting to lose it. Just the sight of him induces a kind of half gag I try to conceal.

Remy finishes her (actually kind of great) monologue and everyone sits there, spellbound. Transfixed. Befuddled. Forlorn.

It is as if, in this one moment, all of us plebeians just lose all the studying, and midterms, and papers, and failed diet plans, and we just sit there, for one moment, together in Ophelia's lost love, taking in the madness of her secret boyfriend prince.

I can't help but wonder if Remy's parents would think it was *beneath* her now. If they saw this. What she can do. If they saw what she just did to this room.

And Remy looks at me. And I nod toward Humbert Humbert.

There he is. In all his sage, skinny glory. Riveted.

Oh, Remy!

You did it! You really, truly did it. You hooked the bait. Your reeled him in. You got him.

Truly remarkable.

I really never thought it would happen.

Never ever.

And this is where I wonder, why am I worried about her? I mean, for Christ's sake, she clearly has the world on a string. She's getting the ungettable teacher, and she's moving this entire auditorium to tears!

I should be worried about *me*.

Well, obviously, nothing bad can come of this. Right? I mean . . . it's just an underage girl in love with an English teacher at a school where her dad is on the board.

Please check if you will have chicken or fish at the wedding.

THIRTY-SIX

As you well know, I don't care about Milo at all. There are some people, not me of course, who would obviously be in love with him, but I would never be such a stupidface because I am truly above that sort of thing.

Even if he were the last guy on earth, I would tell him that we are just supposed to be friends, and that is that.

So, don't even think that just because he showed up at my dorm I even care.

Here's how it goes with Milo. Everyone on earth grunts and sweats under a weary life, and he just kind of sails through, not caring, not really trying, and knowing that it will all work out in the end. And why wouldn't it? He will someday, after he's been out and about in the world, be placed lovingly and gently into a position of some repute, nothing too crazy, as there will be enough of a symbolic upward movement for all those involved to feel satisfied. He will be a junior junior something. And then a junior something. And then a something.

From what I can tell, he doesn't even really have to show up at Witherspoon Prep. I mean, he does. He shows up as much as he has to. Which is as little as possible. But just enough. Just like Remy. That's all he will ever have to do. Just enough.

I heard a rumor he went to Bio class once. *Once*. And he passed.

And that's all very well and good. I actually like Milo. Platonically, of course. But it does seem a bit unfair to all those other poor schmucks out there who kind of just toil and toil away, trying to get ahead. I mean, it does kinda seem unfair that all the moves are made before you are born. And then it's just settled.

I know what you're thinking. You're thinking, "No, no, no, you're wrong, what about the Great American Dream?" And I've heard of it. But here's the thing. I keep hearing about it. I hear about it all the time. But I ain't seeing it. Back in Iowa it'd be like a guy would lose his job, and that was that. It's like all the farms and all the factories and all the fisheries and all the widgets and all the gears in this great engine got shipped out to China or Bangladesh or Timbuktu and now the American Dream is more of an export.

I'd love to be proven wrong, though. Maybe you can prove it to me.

But, honestly, Milo isn't a mean guy, or a greedy one, or a jerk. He's humble and shrugging and sort of doesn't say anything. Half the time his shoulders are curved in on themselves. Apologizing. What is he apologizing for? Maybe for having it so easy, I guess.

The fact that he's standing outside my dorm room is shocking, but I am not about to fall all over myself for him. No sir.

And I am definitely not thinking about that part where he touched me in the dark, no talking. Nope. Not doing that at all.

"Um . . . hi?"

"Hi." He looks embarrassed. Caught.

"Um . . . Are you looking for Remy?"

Of course that's why he's here. He's probably extremely disappointed.

PS: If he's looking for Remy, good luck with that. I haven't seen her for three days and I'm a little annoyed—again. No texts. No notes. No messages. Nothing on the interbot. No phone calls. Nothing. Zero. Zip. I'd say I was worried, but there's really no need to ever worry about Remy, is there? It's like if the world were turned upside down and we all ended up living in the postapocalyptic future-scape, Remy would show up on the back of some bad boy's motorcycle and wink, before riding off into the blazing horizon. The ragamuffin bands of dirt-faced children in makeshift postworld leather outfits would run out behind them, cheering them off into their next death race for gasoline. And then they'd win.

"Willa?"

"Oh, sorry, I was just thinking about the gas economy in the postapocalyptic future-scape."

He looks at me, stone-faced. Crap. Big mouth strikes again. What is wrong with me?

"Well, how could you *not* think about it?" he asks. "Clearly, there's going to be trouble."

Wait. Is he . . . playing along?

"Yes, I feel my future will be in fashioning deconstructed leather clothing. Very patchy."

"Uh-huh. And where do you think you will find this leather?"

"I will make it. Out of roadkill. Skinned roadkill. Squirrels, mostly."

"Did they teach you how to skin squirrels in Iowa?"

"No, just outsiders. City slickers. Anyone who hasn't taken *the oath*."

Milo smiles. This is like a moment where there should be

sparkles everywhere around us. And little butterflies.

Singing, glittering butterflies.

"So, I guess I could tell Remy you came by or something. I haven't seen her for three days, actually. She's probably in Bali or somewhere superspectacular. On a whim."

"Yes, Remy is prone to whimsy."

"Would you say she's whimsical?"

"Yes, I would say so. But only off the record. Are you recording this?" His eyes twinkle—actually twinkle—with mischief. My knees nearly buckle. God, I'm a nerd.

Am I recording this, Milo Hesse? Oh, how I wish I were! I would record this and play it over and over again when I'm 103 years old sitting on my levitating easy chair eating Jell-O, staring at the projected wall of memories of the good old days, before the robot takeover.

"So, I'll tell her you dropped by . . . ?"

"Um, actually . . ."

This is awkward. We are both just standing there. Each of us with our own personal ellipsis.

"Um, Willa . . . ?"

The way he says my name. It's purposeful, yes. But there's something else to it. It's kind, like he's stroking my name on the cheek.

"I guess, um . . . well, I'm here to see you, actually."

"Wait? What? Why?"

Okay, that came out wrong.

"Um . . . because I thought it might be sorta fun or cool or something, but if it's not a good time, I totally get it, and I will go away swiftly. With ease. And pizazz."

"How will the pizazz be involved?"

"Perhaps a little soft shoe."

"Is a soft-shoe tap, or is it a different thing?"

"I don't know. I only took one kind of dance."

"What kind?"

"African."

"Really?"

"Of course. I can do a helluva jumping dance. It's the coming-of-age for warriors. I basically jump the warrior spirit into them."

"I'm gonna have to see that."

"You're gonna have to ply me with a lot of alcohol before you see that."

"I'm gonna have to ply you with alcohol to see that and then record it and put in on YouTube and blackmail you under threat of your family disowning you."

"My family would be proud. Especially my mom. She would think it was very PC."

"Oh?"

"Yeah. The only thing she would like more than that is if, at the end of the dance, I came out of the closet."

"Do you think there's any possibility of that occurring?"

Milo has an answer to that. He has an answer that involves him leaning in, before I know it, and kissing me until my feet are one foot off the ground, except they're not off the ground, I'm not exactly floating technically. It's more like I'm levitating. In my mind. With Milo's mouth on mine and his hands, both hands, on the sides of my ears, like he's clutching me to him, like he's been waiting to do this all along, dying to.

And then he stops and we just look at each other.

And he's flushed.

And I'm flushed.

This is the moment I should say something clever, but my mind seems to be wandering up, up, up, into Milo's deep-green eyes somewhere, spinning instead of brilliantly constructing witticisms.

"And now you are coming out of your room with me."

"And now I am studying."

"Nope. Me."

"Studying."

We are both trying to act like what just happened was normal.

"Okay, I'll make you a deal. I will allow you to study now, as you are sure to be a genius lady scientist one day who will solve global warming . . . if, and only if, you promise to frolic with me on Saturday."

"Possible."

"A certainty?"

"Potentially."

"Inevitable."

But I know I am going with him. How could I not? Not after that kiss. Not after that magical conversation with butterflies singing everywhere. I'm not even sure if my feet are touching the ground yet. I think I might have just turned into a hummingbird and flown into a rainbow possibly. And then that rainbow turns into a unicorn.

THIRTY-SEVEN

Ms. Ingall wanted me to meet her here. At the faculty lounge. There's a restaurant for afternoon tea, whatever that is, with white chairs and white wainscoting and the sun coming in from three sides. Everywhere there are vines, clinging to white trellises through the window, trying to get in. Before the cold. Before the winter.

Ms. Ingall is squinting in the bright, sunny room. I don't get the feeling she's used to this much sunlight.

"Thanks for inviting me here, Ms. Ingall."

"Well, you're very welcome. Do you like tea, Willa?"

"Um . . . sure."

"You don't drink tea, do you?"

"Not really."

"They actually do make a respectable iced latte here, if that's more to your liking."

The waiter comes, and before I know it there are cucumber sandwiches all over the place. Who would have ever thought to put a cucumber in a sandwich? It's a revelation.

"Tell me, Willa. Do you have friends back home? Back in Iowa?"

"Yeah. I mean, I did."

"And do you miss them?"

"I try not to think about it, honestly. It'll just make me sad."

"I see."

The waiter brushes past.

"Did you think about what we spoke about, Willa?"

"Um. Sort of."

"Any thoughts . . . ?"

"Well, my mom sort of . . . she sort of has, like, this plan for me. She kind of just wants to just take the reins, you know? Leave it to her kind of thing."

"Your mother. The economist."

I nod. "Well, you know, as you can imagine, she's kinda got it all figured out."

Ms. Ingall looks at me. The waiter pours her tea into a little teacup with pink roses on the handle.

"And you, Willa?"

"Yes?"

"Do you have it all figured out?"

The teacups are so dainty here, you almost feel like you could break them just by looking at them. And Ms. Ingall. She's dainty, too. But I don't get the feeling you could ever break her.

"I don't really have anything figured out, Ms. Ingall, to be honest with you."

"That's okay, Willa. That's part of the adventure."

"Really?"

"Yes, you have to find your way. But . . . it's for you to find, Willa. No one else can find it for you."

The waiter comes by with a three-tiered platter; each tier has minicakes, some pink, some cream, some yellow. There are even some chocolate cream puffs, which I will rendezvous with soon.

"But why does anyone have to find anything? I mean, why can't you just . . . give up?"

I say it before I know I'm saying it.

Ms. Ingall stops for a minute. Puts her tea down.

"Is that what you feel like, Willa? Do you feel like giving up?"

And I don't know what's happening to my face. Suddenly it's lit up, behind my skin, blazing.

"Sometimes."

Saying this. Somehow, saying this makes it all come barreling down the track. And my eyes are trying to cry. Trying so hard to give in. But I'm not letting them. I am not going to cry over cucumber sandwiches.

Ms. Ingall weighs the situation. The waiter comes over, but she waves him off. Not now. Not now, when my student is having a meltdown.

"Is there a lot of pressure on you, Willa? To be . . . perfect?"

It sounds like such a dumb thing. It sounds like such a dumb, easy thing.

"Kind of."

I'm starting to put the tears back now.

"Willa, you don't have to be perfect. Do you believe me? You don't. You just have to be Willa."

And I could gobble up this whole tearoom right now, the pink minicakes and the yellow minicakes and the chocolate cream puffs. I could gobble up this room and these trellises and Ms. Ingall, too. Just for having given me, once, just once . . . a reprieve. A relief from myself. A vacation. A respite from "should."

THIRTY-EIGHT

I bet you thought that Remy was up to no good. Well, you're right. She is so up to no good. She's, basically, in the final last possible seconds before a car crash that seems at this point inevitable. But somehow, even as she's careening wildly forward into the abyss, there still seems to be hope, some hope, that maybe, just maybe, she can still steer clear of the explosion.

As far as I can tell, this is a two-pronged problem.

I will give you the first prong:

Humbert.

"Willa, you'll never guess! I mean, it's crazy."

"What's crazy?"

"Humbert Humbert and me."

It's been five days since I've seen her and there she is, practically leaping out of the bushes onto the green. Everything around us has turned yellow and orange and red now, the very last of the leaves almost gone, only those last few bleached-brown beech and oak hanging on, nervous. Now we are getting cold. But not Iowa cold. Pembroke cold. Wet and damp. The kind of cold that gets under your skin. The kind of cold that keeps you shivering till spring.

There are circles under Remy's eyes and her jaw looks angled, her cheekbones higher.

Gaunt, I realize.

"Um, okay, Remy. You do know this is a bad idea, right?— Humbert Humbert and you."

"Maybe. Or maybe it's the *best idea ever*."

"Oh my God."

I turn to Remy. She really looks out of sorts. I mean, there's something about her that isn't fitting into her own skin. Something shaking and unsure.

"Remy. What do you know about this guy? I mean, he's *old*. He could be *married*."

"No. No way. I asked. No wife. No girlfriend. I would never do something like that and—"

"Okay, let's step back for a second. All of this? Is bad. Don't you think that this little obsession and, say, disappearing for the past three days possibly might have some effect on your grades and, therefore, your future?"

"Not really."

I can feel myself deflate in that moment. The truth is, she's right. It probably doesn't matter what kind of grades Remy gets. I mean, she's already where she needs to be. It's all laid out for her.

"Remy, you just . . . you can't do this."

"Why not?"

"It's just . . . trouble. I mean . . . you could die."

"Oh my God. Hello? Exaggerate much?"

"Okay, well what about when it ends? With Humbert. Have you thought of that?"

"Ends?"

"Yes, Remy. Ends."

"Why are you being so negative?"

She's getting annoyed now. And she has never been annoyed with me before.

Thing is, she's not the only one.

We reach the library. It's a grand old thing with tapestries hanging everywhere inside and huge vaulted ceilings. Iron chandeliers dangling from a million miles above the rafters. There are little patches of furniture, little seating areas lit by porcelain lamps, cozy and just so, wooden coffee tables, and girl after girl curled up, studying, buried deep in their books.

"I'm not trying to be negative. I'm just worried about you, okay?"

"Don't be bougie."

We're whispering, trying not to disrupt this Norman Rockwell scene of study.

"I'm not bougie. And if I am, who cares? I mean, you look like you've lost ten pounds in three days."

Remy doesn't listen, she just goes into her bag, searching. I put down my backpack next to a giant arched window, and when I look back up again she's popping something into her mouth, quick.

"What was that?"

"What?"

"Remy, what was that?"

"What? I seriously have no idea what you are talking about."

We look at each other. It's obvious she's lying. She knows it and I know it. And we both know the other one knows.

Never mind. She doesn't have to tell me. I know what it is. It's the second prong in the two-pronged problem.

The pills. The many, *so many* pills.

That's why she's losing weight. That's why she looks like a lady skeleton. A very big part of me knows—just knows—she hasn't eaten anything but half bites off those little white pills. Breakfast, lunch, and dinner.

"Remy. Listen to me. All of this . . . I know it feels fun and thrilling and like a big fuck-you to everyone, but I'm telling you, it's not pretty."

"Not. Pretty." She glares at me. "You know, Willa, I thought you'd be happy for me. I thought you'd want to hear all about—"

"About how you're losing your mind over some loser teacher who could end up in jail because of you?"

"He's not a loser. And we're in love."

"Are you kidding me right now?"

"Nope. Not at all. This is it."

"Well, does he know you're in love?"

"I think so."

People are starting to look over but Remy stays looking at me, needing something from me.

And the absurdity, the sheer absurdity of all of this is making me want to honestly, literally, scream. So I just say whatever I have to to get out of there. "Okay, well, good luck and amen and *whatever.*"

And I walk away now. I don't know why she needs me to say this is okay. I don't know why she needs me to say anything.

This is so not okay. And the worst part is that I feel

somehow responsible. Like I'm the only person between her and her careening desire to crash and burn everything around her.

But maybe it's always like this. With rich kids. Maybe there's always a drama or something to break and something to put back together. Maybe there has to be something. Otherwise, what would there be to do?

THIRTY-NINE

It's laughable now, to me, what I thought this date was gonna be. I thought this date was gonna be like, you know, a simple kind of Saturday social. Maybe a museum and a stroll through the park. Maybe an ice-cream soda we shared with a straw. At a soda fountain. In the 1950s.

Wrongo.

This misinterpretation might have something to do with the fact that I've never really been on a date. Officially. I mean, that guy on the Amtrak who was trying to get lucky was sort of the closest thing. Also, I went on a few playdates with a kid named Wyatt, when I was three. Apparently, he had a tree house and a pirate hut. That is all.

But there are no tree houses, pirate huts, or Amtrak

creeps here. No, no. This is the kind of thing you don't know is happening until it happens, and then you think . . . um, what the fuck is happening right now?

Here's how it starts.

Milo shows up at my door dressed in what can best be described as a cool turn-of-the-century bartender outfit, minus the bar. There is a vest involved. I mean, he looks cool. But he definitely looks *dressed*. Like, really dressed.

I, on the other hand, was going for a much more casual thing. Like, I am not dressed for an afternoon of timeless romance. More like a picnic of delicious sandwiches, which can sometimes be the same thing. Don't judge me.

Seeing him at my front door, I immediately feel like an idiot and want to cancel the date entirely.

"Um. I'm not wearing the right thing for whatever it is we are doing, am I?"

"No, it's totally fine. Really."

"Okay . . . well, what if you give me like five minutes to come up with something, a little less like I'm going to a football game and you're going to the opera."

"If you want to. You don't have to—"

"I think I have to. Just. Hold on a second."

And with that I slam the door in his face, which I really didn't mean to do but kind of happened anyway. I then swoop into my closet and try to find something, anything, please, lord, to look cool.

Somehow I manage to put together something sort of vintage. It's not that easy to dress when you have only one bag of clothes and two uniforms, and you have no idea where you're going. But I give it the old college try, and I think I get a B for effort. Possibly a gold star.

When I come back to the door, Milo is on the phone, whispering. Clearly he is up to no good. He waves at me, a mischievous smile, and I realize he is really putting an effort into this outing.

He tries to reassure me when we get into the Uber.

"Don't worry. The drive to the coast will only take about a half hour. I know the secret route."

Coast? Route? Secret? What is going on? I thought we were supposed to be, I don't know, five minutes into previews by now. Or maybe catching an open mike at the coffee bar in town.

What. Is. Going. On?

Milo gives me a wink and looks out the window. He's smiling to himself.

"Do you plan on selling me into slavery by dusk? Or sacrificing me to our lizard overlords? I need to know."

"It's our first date, right? I wanted to impress you. I'm kind of nervous, honestly."

What? *He's* nervous? If he's nervous, then I am certifiable.

"Oh, here. I stole this champagne from my stepdad. He's kind of a dick, so hopefully it costs a million dollars and he's going to be superannoyed."

Milo serves up the champagne in two crystal champagne flutes. It's obvious these are stolen from said stepdad's collection, too.

PS: This is illegal.

PPS: Milo doesn't seem to care.

"I didn't know you had a stepdad. Or even that your parents were divorced. Or that your life wasn't completely perfect in every way."

There's a pause here.

"Yeah. Um. My mom's pretty cool, actually. She does all sorts of art stuff, always caring about making art 'available to the disenfranchised.' And she's always raising money for, like, street kids and orphans or whatever."

"That's cool."

"Yeah, she's a real bleeding heart. But she's great. She kind of dotes. Or tends to dote. She calls me her little prince. Still. Like, even now."

"But your stepdad . . . ?"

"Ugh. He's such a fuckwad. He's, like, one of these money guys. Like, you know, the guys who tanked everything. He probably fucks his secretary."

"What about your dad? What's he like?"

"He's like . . . dead."

"Oh my God, I'm so sorry."

"It's okay. It's been, like, a couple of years or whatever."

"I'm really sorry."

"I'm surprised Remy didn't tell you. It was kind of a thing."

"Really?"

"Yeah. I mean, he kind of killed himself."

Jesus.

My plan—the one involving the clock tower—flashes through my brain. And now I feel stupid and melodramatic and incredibly, overwhelmingly, like a total and complete jerk.

Seeing this. What it's like to be left behind.

To be the one left behind.

"Oh, Milo. I had no idea. I'm so sorry . . ."

"It's okay. Maybe that's why I like you. Because you didn't know."

Or maybe he is just attracted to people who have fantasies about killing themselves. I don't say it. Thank God.

The sun is blazing down now, and we're going up and above all the row houses upon row houses. Some brick with old-timey ads painted on it. Old businesses, gone for decades, the hope gone with them, too. You can't help but wonder, looking at the zillion little lives, flying past, some with laundry hanging, some with broken toys on the balconies, faded out by the sun, you can't help but wonder, *Why them?* Why do they get this shitty never-go-anywhere life? Who makes up these rules? You go there. And you, you go there. Oh, you . . . you're down there, sorry. It makes no sense if you think about it. And then there are people like Milo. People with everything. Little princes without a worry in the world.

Except a dad who killed himself.

He downs the rest of his champagne.

"You have no idea how lucky you are to be from Iowa."

FORTY

There are certain things you think you will never experience, or never see, or don't exist. This place where Milo takes me is one those things.

It's an island.

A private island.

Oh, you don't have a private island you can just randomly take your friends to on a Saturday date? Yup. Me neither.

It's funny what's going on here. For a second I thought this was going to get extremely rugged. You know, boats, a dock, craggy rocks, an endless swell of freezing black water. Going down to the dock, I couldn't help but think maybe we were wearing the impossibly wrong attire of madmen destined to fall to their death in a watery grave.

But no.

The rugged part of the trip really just consisted of jump-ing in the boat, where "the boatman" took us across a not-so-placid stretch of ocean, up the coast, just a bit, turn-ing at some cliffs, to reveal, through the perilous whitecaps, in the distance . . . an island, unto itself, no attachments. The sun is getting low in the sky, and it's as if a spotlight is coming off the water onto the island, lighting up the pines and the craggy rocks on the shore. It doesn't look real. An island, just sitting there, being beautiful and mysterious and probably just a ghost figure in the distance.

When the island appears, I look at Milo.

He smiles and gives a cute little shrug. It's not a jerk shrug. It's a shrug that says, "I know, I know, but I couldn't help myself."

I'm just trying to keep my jaw off the floor as we approach, closer and closer. Now there's a clapboard house perched on the island, looking down at us: all white, with turrets, a wraparound porch, and even a crow's nest. When I say "clapboard," don't think there's anything rickety going on over here. This house is huge, and grand, and was probably built by Thomas Jefferson or something.

We reach the tip of the dock, ending the rugged part of the adventure, and the boatman helps us up and out.

"Easy does it."

The boatman smiles. Milo smiles back at him, and I get the feeling these guys have known each other since Milo was a baby. There's a warmth there, a comfort.

"Thanks, Freddy," Milo says.

Making our way up the long dock, up the sloping hill to the house, I see a lone figure coming down from the house. The setting sun flares up through this diaphanous thing of light-blue chiffon, and above it are two hands outstretched, with something sparkling, a glass clinking ice, and lime—a cocktail.

Above the chiffon is an alabaster neck and black bob with bangs, short like a silent film star. A ghost face with light-blue eyes, smiling at Milo like he is the most precious cargo on earth.

"MyMy." She says it like petting a cat, handing him a drink.

Milo turns to me. "This is Willa. Willa . . . this is my sister. Kitty. Her real name is Katherine, but that sounds like someone's grandma."

"Oh! Hi, Kitty. Nice to meet you."

She hands me the see-through drink like it's a done deal.

"Uh, thanks."

"Come in, come in. We almost started without you . . ."

"Oh, sorry, Kit."

"Seriously, Brit is, like, furious because he thinks the

oysters are going to jump off the plate or something totally paranoid. I wish he'd get a girlfriend."

And just like that we are whisked out of the rugged sea and up to the white looming house and Kitty opens the door to reveal . . . what looks like a painting, some kind of oil tableau of a parlor scene. In it, eight figures and a fireplace.

They all turn at once. All dressed. All dressed just so. Like Milo.

"Brit's in the kitchen, but he'll be out soon."

There are four girls and four guys. Or rather, four ladies and four gents. I mean, we are deeply in the "mannered" zone here. I can't figure the ages, but they're definitely older than us. Maybe just out of college? Definitely not working. I'm pretty sure not one of these people will ever have to work a day in their life. And judging by the names, I'm pretty sure they couldn't.

"Igby, Tad, Basil, Win (Winston, but nobody calls him that), Tisley, Paige, Binky, and Cricket. (Her real name is Camilla, but if you call her that she'll get annoyed.)"

Sidebar: Don't worry, you don't have to remember all these names. I'm mostly just telling you because it's an absurd collection in one room. Admit it.

I stand there, next to Milo, feeling like the smallest, dumbest, weirdest person on earth.

"MyMy!"

Okay, so I guess MyMy is his nickname. Short for Milo-Milo.

The one who approaches is the one called Igby. He's skinnier than the other three and somehow more intellectual-looking, but maybe it's just the glasses. He looks like you could open the dictionary, point to a word, and he'd give you five definitions off the top of his head.

Paige and Tisley are up next. They sort of look like a matched set. Both with long brown hair, straight, both with skin that saw the sun last century.

"Milo, you're so *fancy*." They coo.

Yes, this is definitely flirty. A little too flirty for my taste. One of them grabbing his skinny tie.

"Well, you know, I try . . ."

Now come Tad and Win. These guys look like they could probably not die in a bar fight, unlike Igby and Basil. Tad has blond hair and bright-blue eyes. Win has chestnut hair and an adorable bow tie.

"And who, may we inquire, is your young guest?"

They are both smiling at me in a flirty way, and I am smiling back in an awkward, extremely uncomfortable way.

"This is Willa."

Please don't say it. Please don't say it. Please don't say it.

"She's from Iowa."

Ugh. There it is.

And there is the judgment, a wave across the room. Oh, she's no one.

I wish I could bury my head in the sand. Milo didn't mean it. He doesn't know he's the only one who thinks it's cool to be from hicksville.

"Well, well. A farm girl."

Tisley says it. It's not nice. Or even trying to be nice.

Cricket gives her a look. I can't tell if Cricket is colluding or scolding. Either way, I feel like an idiot.

Kitty looks at me. I can tell she gets it. "Don't mind Tisley; she's extremely jealous because all her boyfriends cheat on her."

"Very nice, Kitty."

Tisley walks out of the room, and Cricket turns to us.

"What Kitty is not telling you is that they cheat on Tisley . . . with Kitty."

"That is so not true." Kitty smiles.

Obviously, it is true.

Ladies and gentlemen, welcome to freakyland. Population: this.

Cricket continues. "The good news for you, Willa, is that your boyfriend is not gonna cheat on you with Kitty because your boyfriend is her brother."

Milo and I look at each other. He's not my boyfriend.

Or is he? Is he officially my boyfriend now? Is that what it means to be brought to this weird island of misfit toys? Milo doesn't say anything. Well, at least he doesn't deny it. And I notice that the tips of his ears are turning a kind of alarming shade of red.

"Where's Remy?" Igby leans in.

Okay, what? Time-out.

"I have no idea. She's obsessed with some secret dude, and she is being very bizarre lately."

Aha! So Milo knows Remy is obsessed with someone, he just doesn't know it's Humbert Humbert.

But let's go back. Why, oh, why would Remy be here?

"Do you know Remy?" Win asks me.

"Uh, yeah. She's kind of like my best friend at Pembroke. She convinced me to be in this dumb play I hate."

"Ah! That sounds like Remy."

"Um . . . How do you know her?"

There's a little laugh here, inaudible. But palpable.

"Well, I met her once because she's . . . my cousin."

A titter across the crowd.

"Oh. Okay, I'm an idiot."

"No, you're not. You're adorable."

"What everyone is trying to tell you, Willa, is that we're happy you're here," Kitty adds. "And we should eat."

And with that said, the entire entourage exits to the

dining room, leaving Milo and me to stand there and catch our breath.

"I'm sorry she assumed you were my girlfriend. I hope you're not insulted."

My heart is thudding. Not in a good way. In a what-the-hell-am-I-doing-here way.

I can't help but wonder how I would possibly get off this island all by myself. Like, what if there was a nuclear war, or an undead apocalypse, or maybe everything just got too uncomfortable with all these weird people? Could I do it?

If I make the calculation, between the current, the tides, and my arm strength, my estimation is I could get about nine feet.

That is not involving sharks.

So—

It seems I am stuck here.

It seems I am somewhat of a mascot for the night.

Please, mouth, stay shut—do not say or do anything that will reveal me to be a commoner from the sticks. Just stay shut. Seriously.

Button it.

FORTY-ONE

This dinner is kind of surreal. I think I need to talk about it. I mean, yes, it's dinner, so who cares? But, also, it's, like, a seven-course dinner and every course is tiny but delicious and set up like you are supposed to take a picture of it or something. Now, I'm not one of those people who takes pictures of my food and posts it everywhere, because, let's just face it, that's loserville. But, if I were one of those people, it would be photo session every round. Or course.

Not that I know what any of this is. It seems there are a lot of things that come out of the sea. Also, goose liver. There is a lot of wine, too. And the wine keeps changing, so drink up.

I'm not sure who is preparing the food—in my imagination

there is a very testy French chef involved, but it seems like the guests are taking turns bringing it out from the kitchen.

How normal of them. How down to earth!

Democracy is alive and well on this private island!

Right now, one of these guys, Basil or Cecil or Salad, is going on and on about adorable Cricket and her make-out antics.

"So, there he is, standing in front of her, totally smitten, and Cricket has *no idea* who he is." Basil is holding court.

"That's not true. He looked vaguely familiar."

"Yes, the ridiculous English rock star. He looked vaguely familiar. He had two eyes, one nose, and two ears."

Everyone laughs. The general idea here seems to be: Oh, you, crazy Cricket. What *won't* you do?!

"So, what did you do?" Tisley leans in, curious.

"Well, I made out with him, of course."

Baha! Hearty guffaws all around. Lifted glasses. *Clink, clink.*

"I mean, I kind of felt sorry for him."

More laughter.

Tad chimes in. "I love it. Cricket's reason for making out with someone: I felt sorry for him."

"Or he exists."

"And he's in front of me."

Waves of laughter. I think those last two were Basil and

Win. One of the guys. It's clear that the guys are here to make the jokes. The guys make the jokes and the girls laugh. The girls coo and say clever things, yes. But the guys are the ones in charge of making everyone laugh, of outdoing each other. The guy with the most clever quips wins. It's a different kind of guy contest than back in Iowa.

Back in Iowa I think it had more to do with how big your tires were.

Or your truck flaps.

Suffice it to say, in Iowa, if you had a monster truck with eight-foot tires and truck flaps with naked ladies on them . . . you were the social equivalent of Tad.

But here, on this private island that nobody knows about because it probably doesn't exist, the wittiest man wins. And there are no trucks involved.

Every once in a while, Milo looks over at me, checking in. It's a sweet thing to do, considering this group has obviously known one another since they were in the womb.

There's no one here being necessarily overt or snooty or condescending. I think that initial farm-girl comment was the last of it. I get the feeling everyone here is a bit protective of Milo. He's the kid brother to the group, after all.

There's a moment when I catch Kitty smiling at him, raising her eyebrows. I can tell, now, why Milo is so damn charming. He has Kitty as an older sister. She would never lead him astray. She's probably been dressing him since he was two.

And you can tell she adores him.

It would be easy to hate these people. To think, Jesus Christ, what is wrong with you? Don't you see the world is crumbling to pieces and all you can do is sit around and out-jostle each other and sip wine and eat weird, unrecognizable food in the tiniest portions known to mankind?!

But it's impossible.

Because they're charming. They're charismatic and kind of glowing and adoring—yes, even adoring to each other. It's a strange sort of family. A family of blue bloods, probably all related if you go back far enough.

Fun fact: Paige is an African-American Lit major.

Yeah, bet you didn't see that coming.

She is also an expert in African dance. What is it with these people and African dance?

Meanwhile, I can only assume Paige was named Paige because when she came out into this world she was the color of paper. PS: She is just as thin.

And I am going to have to ask her to show me her hot African dance moves after dinner because I am a horrible person.

Come on. You don't get to be that lily white and be an African-American Lit major with a minor in African Dance if you don't want someone, sometime, to call you on it. I can't tell if this possible cultural appropriation is ludicrous, endearing, or absurd. I guess I will be able to tell by her dance moves.

But we are not going to get to that quite yet. Oh, no.

Because there is something else going on.

We are adjourning from the dining room and leaving behind all the plates and glasses because presumably they will magically vanish into thin air when we exit the room.

Remember how I told you about Milo and Remy and me and how we all did Ecstasy over at her place in Manhattan by the fire and how it was superfantastic except that the next day on the train we felt horrible and promised we would never do it again?

Well, the good news is we are not doing Ecstasy.

However, I feel I would not be being fully honest with you if I didn't tell you that what everyone is doing is a form of Ecstasy, which is the superpure Ecstasy, which is called Molly.

Sorry.

I know.

Don't be mad at me.

I honestly did put up somewhat of a fight.

FORTY-TWO

Okay, we need to talk about Milo. I do not think it's an exaggeration to say that he is kind of slowly but surely killing me and killing my heart.

He is not trying to.

No, Milo does not seem like the kind of guy who would try to hurt anyone, ever, for any reason. In fact, before dinner I noticed he saw a spider in the entryway and he made everyone move out of the way so he could catch the spider, put a piece of paper under it and a shot glass above it, and deliver said spider kindly, gently, into the great outdoors. So, yeah, Milo is not a harm doer, spider killer, or feelings hurter.

Nevertheless! Nevertheless, Milo is turning my head into

jelly and goop because all I can do is think that I shouldn't get a crush on him but I'm getting a crush on him but I shouldn't get a crush on him but maybe he's getting a crush on me but maybe he isn't but maybe he is, otherwise, why would I even be here amid this menagerie of ridiculous names?

By the way, I'm not even going to tell you about the last names. You know what they are, right? What they've got to be? I can only imagine it goes something like: DuPont, Peabody, Carnegie, Picklebottom, Tiffany. Lobstertails. I am not going to ask. Because you and I both know when they say them it's going to be real hard to keep a straight face.

There is a lot of talk about the next round in these here festivities. A lot of shuffling around, trying to attain the right lighting and music. I'd always heard that people who take drugs are unmotivated. Lazy. Layabouts. But if you take into consideration the time and effort Tad and Muffy and, yes, even Milo, are putting into curating and achieving their drug-related experiences, I believe you'd have to beg to differ.

And while this is going on? I'm tiptoeing around, taking it all in.

You know how, back in the day, if you went over to Saddam Hussein's house he had gold chairs, gold faucets, gold toilets? And everything had that same tapestry fabric and then gold on the side of it? Like the whole place was designed to scare you with money. Well, this place is the opposite of that.

This is the kind of place where everything is just so. Small, delicate, intricate, never pointing at itself.

That nautical ship. That mother-of-pearl snuffbox. That Wedgwood ashtray. That Willow Ware vase. That silver engraved pocket watch. That scrimshaw whale tooth. That ivory-handled envelope opener from Nepal.

It's a good thing the drug we are doing is not LSD. If the drug we are doing were LSD, then I'd really be getting lost in this exquisite exhibition of curiosities. As it is, the curiosities are appreciated but not a source of a trip-the-light-fantastic romp I go into in my imagination for the next twelve hours.

And now Milo has come to fetch me.

"Ready?"

"I guess." My frown disagrees.

He takes my hand gently. "Hey. What is it?"

"I just—um, why are we doing this?"

He looks at me like, *Doing what?*

I stare, pointedly, at the pills in his other hand.

"Wait, really?" he asks.

And I know I'm supposed to be enigmatic and inscrutable and mysterious and asking this question is none of those things. I know that. But there is that mouth problem I have.

There it is. I feel my Willa brain revving up, readying all the words, all the thoughts I have to muster. And here it comes, attack of the big mouth—

"I just . . . I feel like this place, and that food, and these things and *that boat* and all of it . . . It's just so incredible, and nobody gets to see these things, or *I* never got to, not before this. And you—this is like *your life*, you know? And, I mean, isn't it all amazing enough? Isn't it all just the dream everyone has? And you are living it! And now I'm here living this little piece of it. So isn't that enough? I mean. I'm asking. I'm just . . . asking."

He stares at me. Blinks once, twice.

Oh God. My cheeks blaze hot and red. I have totally, completely blown it.

"I'll just go now," I say, "before the tide turns. You think I can borrow a bathing suit?" I move for the hallway.

"Willa, wait." Milo squeezes my hand tighter and pulls me deeper into the house. We sit next to each other in the stairwell, on the dark, Persian runner-covered steps. The moonlight is filtering its first rays through the leaded windows in the front of the house.

Milo takes a deep breath.

"Listen. I don't know what you see when you look at all of this. I guess I never thought about it. I didn't mean to freak you out. I just . . . hoped you'd like it. But I grew up here, you know? Every summer, me and my mother and Kitty and my dad. We'd come here. And yeah, I guess I know it's special. But it's also just all I know. And the thing is, Willa, all of this"—he holds his arms out wide—"doesn't make anything better. Or more okay. I mean, don't be insulted. But believe me when I say none of *this* keeps out the horrible things. You know what I mean?"

I open my mouth to argue, but close it again when I see the faraway look in Milo's eyes.

"My father was a good guy, you know? But he was working for some really bad guys. And when he found out how bad they were, how many people they'd stolen from, how many lives they'd ruined, it was like he couldn't take it."

And now it feels like even the moon is listening.

"I found him."

"What?"

"I was the one who found my dad."

My heart feels like it's squeezing in on itself. My stomach becomes a black hole. "Oh, Milo. That is so terrible."

"I know. I just thought you should know because . . . well, everybody knows. And since then it's like I've kind of got this scarlet letter."

"No. Milo, no. Everybody thinks you're sort of God's gift to the world. Honestly! I mean, you should hear Remy talking about you."

"Really?"

"Yeah."

"Hm."

"Does that surprise you? I thought you guys were friends."

"Yeah, um . . . Remy can be hard to read sometimes."

"You're telling me."

He kind of nods. There's a smile here, but a sad little smile. Something pondering.

"Look, I'm sorry to have brought it up. But I guess what I'm trying to say is, people think having all this is the key, right? To happiness? But there is no key. I think . . . maybe there's just whatever gets handed to you. So if you want to know *why*"—he looks down at the fist holding the pills—"I don't know. My feeling is, why not, you know? Why. The hell. Not?"

And I am left wondering the exact same thing.

Did you know when you do Molly you automatically fall in love with the person next to you? True story.

Yes, I said I was never gonna do anything like that again but, right now, I'm just falling in love with Milo. Because he happens to be next to me. And I know it's not real, I know it's just the chemicals, but it seems like, right now, at this instant, Milo is in love with me, too. Like this thing is reciprocal. And I'm not crazy.

"Do you know why I showed up that day?"

"What day?"

"That audition day?"

We're not exactly on the sofa, we're more on the floor, leaning against the sofa and looking into each other's eyes swimming all over the place.

"No. Wait, yes! Because you love *the theater*."

"Wrongo."

He smiles. "Wrongo" is what I say. And now he says it. We're speaking the same language! We're making up a new language—that's how in love we are!

"Okay, why?"

"Because Remy said she'd met the coolest girl from Iowa who she wished she could go out with, but she couldn't 'cause she's not a lesbo, so I had to so she could live vicariously through me."

We look at each other, still smiling, eyes swimming.

"Wait . . . okay, this is a dumb question, but . . . um, forget it. I don't want *to ruin the moment* or whatever." I can't help myself.

"What is it? You won't. Seriously."

Milo looks at me, and I am about to jump into his eyes any second.

"We're not *going out*, are we? I mean, we're just doing

whatever this is. On a private island. Somewhere on the Eastern Seaboard."

Milo smiles. Across from us, in front of the fireplace, Paige, Igby, and Cricket are doing what could only be described as a kind of modern primitive dance. At this moment it seems that Paige is some sort of goddess figure who Igby and Cricket seem to be paying tribute to.

"Why, does that offend you?" Milo says, teasing.

"What? The goddess dance over there?"

"No. The going out . . . with me . . . thing?"

Honestly, I don't know what to say to this. Part of me wants to say no and throw myself around him and tell him he's the most superamazing being on the planet, but part of me wants to say nothing and cry and crawl into a hole because I have no self-esteem. Of course, the Molly is helping with that.

Milo is waiting for an answer, but I'm too busy not knowing what to say.

"To be honest with you, Willa, I don't care what you say."

"Oh?"

"Because I'm gonna make you my girlfriend, no matter what."

"Um."

"I don't care if it takes a year and I have to jump through a zillion hoops and call the president. You are gonna be my girlfriend, Willa. You have no choice."

"Um."

And now his eyes light up, and it's a spooky voice. "Surrender, Suuuureeendeeer, Willa . . ."

He's making Svengali hand gestures at me, trying to reel me into his magical whirling eyes.

"Beeeeee miiiiiiiine . . ."

"Okay can I ask you a question?"

"Yeeeeeessss."

"Do you say that stuff to, like, all the girls?"

"Yeeeeeessss. I have a harem baaaaack hooome in my ciiiiircussss tent."

Oh my God, I don't know what to do with Milo. I want to attack him. I want to attack him with kisses.

Even though, basically, I don't even know how to kiss.

Oh God, please don't tell anybody I told you that.

It's so embarrassing. But, for realz, what am I even supposed to do here? I mean, if Milo tries to full-on make out with me, I'd bet I'd be, like, the worst kisser, like a dragon kisser, and then next thing you know he'd tell everybody and I'd be laughed off the island and they'd probably just force me to swim to the mainland. The mainland.

I'm at a place where you say "the mainland."

"Willa?"

"Milo?"

"You don't have to answer me. You don't have to think. Or worry. Or do anything you don't want to. You just have to be here now. With me."

And I'm looking up at Milo and in the background the weird dance is transforming and I'm thinking to myself, *no one has ever said that to me*. No one has ever let me off the hook.

What if that was all it meant to be in love? That you just let the other person off the hook. That it's okay and nothing has to be like it's *supposed to be*, like everybody says it's supposed to be? And everything can just be what it is. And that's okay.

"Milo?"

"Yes?"

"How many girlfriends have you had?"

"One. In the future. Her name is Willa."

FORTY-THREE

There's something I have to tell you. Can you keep a secret? I kind of did something weird last week that nobody knows about but I kind of did it on a whim. A suggested whim. I don't know. I think my body got taken over by demons or something and the next thing I know I was downloading forms and filling out paperwork and getting letters of recommendation and visiting Wharton House and checking in with Ms. Ingall and writing essays and all sorts of boring stuff that is really annoying and takes forever, but something just made me do it. Maybe it was a ghost. An academic ghost.

Or maybe it was just Ms. Ingall.

Maybe she spiked my tea.

Don't tell anyone, okay? Don't tell Remy. Don't tell Milo. Especially not my mother. Definitely not. Not anyone. Not even my dad. I don't know why I have to keep it a secret, but I do. I guess I don't want to be a laughingstock or something. When I fail. If I fail. Which . . . I probably will.

Okay, here it is.

I applied to Berkeley.

On my own.

Shh.

I said don't tell!

Really, I just don't want to feel like an idiot, okay? I just don't want to feel like I tried for this big, totally unlikely thing and didn't get it and then everybody will make fun of me and laugh at me or, worse, feel sorry for me. So, just don't tell anyone. I'm not getting in, okay? It's just a Hail Mary. Just a *what the heck*.

Just a shot in the dark.

FORTY-FOUR

I really didn't think I'd see Remy before class today. Monday morning is always this bumbling rush of people, half-asleep, trying to make it to Con Lit or Calculus or Chemistry. But, as I was coming out of the campus center, scrambling to get it together, between my iced latte, my backpack, and my books, Remy appeared.

"Willa. I have to talk to you."

She's next to me now, as we rush across the green.

"Um, do you think we could talk after class 'cause I feel like I really need to talk to you, too, but I can't right now 'cause I'm superlate."

There are a zillion things to tell her. Mainly about Milo and the private island and my heart and what to do with it.

"Yeah, of course. No problem. By the way, I slept with Humbert Humbert."

Okay, this stops me.

"You what?!"

"Humbert Humbert. He's mine!"

"Remy, that is so . . . fucked!"

She smirks. "Don't you mean *I* am so fucked?"

"No, I mean *he* is so fucked. Like, he's fucked in the head, and he's fucked in his career."

"Career?"

"Yes, Remy. He's an English teacher. Don't be a snob."

"Well, he could be so much more."

"Like what, like Mr. Remy Taft?"

She doesn't answer.

"Okay, that's it. I am officially quitting the play. You tell Humbert."

"What? Why?"

"Because he's a perv, and I can't risk him molesting me."

"Come on. Besides, what am I even supposed to say?"

"I don't know. Tell him I died."

"Seriously?"

"Tell him . . . I'm allergic . . . to theater. And rapists."

"C'mon, be nice. I need you. I'm feeling kind of vulnerable."

And now I see it. Remy is standing there, in her full

adorable weird mismatched outfit, looking at me, and there it is. She's scared.

"What do you mean?"

"I mean, like . . . I'm feeling kind of . . . I dunno, weird."

"Remy, okay. I want to talk to you about this and I don't want you to feel weird, but I also can't miss class. So, let me just, I guess I'll just drop by later. Okay . . . ?"

"Okay." But she is . . . Is she shaking?

"Um, you're okay, right?"

"Yeah. Yeah, I'm fine."

"Okay, I'll see you after class."

Walking off, I turn around. Remy is just standing there. "Wait, why aren't you going to class?"

"Oh, I kinda just don't have, like, anything to hand in, so . . ."

"So you're just not going to class?"

"Well, I don't really feel very well."

"Remy, just go to class."

"I'm sick."

And this is such a ludicrous self-diagnosis. Obviously, she's not sick. Obviously, she just doesn't want to go. Obviously, she just wants to sit there and pine over Humbert Humbert.

"Remy. If you go to class, it might take your mind off things. Like, it will distract you and you'll feel better."

"Mmm . . . I don't think so."

"Fine. I'll see you later."

There's the clock tower at the end of the cloisters, and I have about thirty seconds to make it across the green into Royce Hall. I can do it. I can do it because I think I can do it and I must do it.

Persevere, Willa!

I could think about Remy standing there behind me fucking everything up or I could think about the fact that I seem to be becoming obsessed with Milo or I could think about the fact that the world is a horrible, unjust place, but none of that is gonna help me make it into the classroom before that bell.

FORTY-FIVE

Milo has sent me a frog.

Literally.

When I get back to my room there is a little frog there, left on my doorstep, in a terrarium with a deeply landscaped natural habitat that either he or a very enthusiastic pet store employee has designed.

It is a red-eyed tree frog, to be exact.

I'm not keeping it. Yes, I understand it's an unexpected gesture that signifies all sorts of effort and thoughtfulness and possibly even love. But the instructions clearly state that tree frogs eat worms and crickets, and that seems awfully slimy to me.

And now there is a text:

if u kiss it, it turns into a prince.

There is also an invite attached. To a New York thing. A charity thing. And, attached to that, a note: "This will be boring, but you have to go with me. It's my mom's thing. I can't face it alone!"

"My mom's thing"? "My mom's thing"?! You know what this means, don't you? This means he wants me to *meet his mother*! Oh my God. Is this even happening right now? Wait. Am I really his girlfriend? I can't be his girlfriend, can I? We haven't even barely done anything. We've just sort of, like, groped. We've drug groped. That's about it. Pretty PG-rated. Except the drugs. And the groping.

But no bodily fluids have been exchanged.

So this maybe is it. Maybe after the charity gala he will ask me officially to be his girlfriend. After I meet his mom. And get her approval. Wait, what if I don't get her approval? I need Remy. I need Remy right now. Only she will be able to guide me through this socialite labyrinth.

Remy!

Before I can put a sentence together, I am down the stairs and out toward the campus center to find her. I seem to recall some vague memory of her random obscure philosophy class letting out near here. Whatever the case, this seems to be the main thoroughfare for all those who trample through the hallowed grounds of Pembroke.

Hallowed grounds? Hollowed grounds?

This is the last thing I think before I see it. Before I see the thing I can't unsee. The thing I wish I could unsee.

Because I see Remy. Yes, that's true. But that's not all I see. I see Milo, too. But that's not all I see. No, no.

This is what I get to see:

Milo's hands all over Remy and his tongue down Remy's throat and Remy holding on to him for dear life. Yep. That's my Remy. And that's my Milo.

Well, apparently he's not mine, after all.

I am frozen there.

And I know what you're thinking. I should say something. I know I should. I should scream out or throw tomatoes or do whatever people do when they see a grand betrayal such as this.

But nope. No way. No sir. This is all about me shrinking down. This is all about me not being seen and not being heard. This is all about me wanting not to exist and wanting to pretend this didn't happen. This is me, see me there, walking backward into the trees and back up the steps and back into my bed in Denbigh dorm. This is all about me not wanting to be me.

And there is that dumb frog in a terrarium. Not a prince, after all. Just a frog.

FORTY-SIX

This gala charity benefit at the Knickerbocker is gonna be great. Oh, you didn't think I was going? Oh, I'm going.

No, I'm not gonna start a scene in front of everyone and ruin the whole night to remember or anything. I mean, this is a benefit for orphans, after all. I know I may be ridiculously preoccupied and obsessed with the dastardly betrayal of my BFF and not-boyfriend . . . but I'm not so self-obsessed as to destroy a night meant to give aid, medical supplies, food, books, and shelter to the orphan children of the Middle East. I am not the Dark Lord Asthmatic or Darth Maul or whatever his name is.

Milo looks great. How do I know? Because he's standing right next to me. Yup, he's standing right next to me, and he has no idea I saw his and Remy's slobbery hookup and/or long-term relationship.

You see, that's why I'm here.

I need to get this figured out.

I don't know how long this has all been going on. I have to know how heartbroken I am supposed to be.

There are a few flyers on the table about this charity and the kinds of things they do to help orphans of all these terrible wars that seem to go on and on. I can't help but pick one up, and next thing I know it stops my heart. I'm not kidding.

I'm not even gonna tell you what's in these pictures, but I wish I could unsee them immediately. And this one. And that one. And another one.

It's the kind of stuff you just don't believe could ever happen. The kind of stuff worse than any nightmare, and, at a certain point, you gotta wonder: How could anyone let this happen? How could this even be happening?

Maybe this is what happens when every country on earth, with the exception of a handful, is run by dudes.

Lookit, you'd never see a lady Hitler. I'm serious. No way. She'd be too busy trying to figure out how to run Germany, how to make sure she doesn't get ousted for having lady parts, who to invite to her kids' birthday party, what to buy everyone for Christmas, what to do about dinner that night, and if she did have a husband, how to keep him from not feeling depressed for being second banana to his wife, the supreme dictator . . . so she would simply not have the time to conceive of, plot, and execute the extermination of millions of people. I know what you're thinking. What if she doesn't have a husband or even a boyfriend? Well, my friends, then lady Hitler would either be single with another huge laundry list of single-lady problems to worry about, or she would be a lesbian. And I think we can all agree that lesbian Hitler would not exterminate nine million people.

Maybe the problem is guys just have too much time on their hands. It's like they just sit around making themselves crazier and crazier, getting themselves more and more riled up in a paranoid frenzy, whether they're screaming about "The Jews! The Jews!" or "The Arabs! The Arabs!" or even "The women! The women!"

It almost seems like the most dangerous thing you could do is put a man in a room with nothing to do. They need to get more involved in, like, building parks, or PTA.

Dudes. It's like they don't know that life blows and they are just looking for something or someone to blame for life's general suckiness. You never have to explain that to a girl. A girl knows. A girl gets to know that the first day she gets her period. It might as well come with a card: "Congratulations! Life sucks! Now you know."

That's why you never see a girl stewing in her room

building an imaginary militia. What are you gonna do? Send a militia out to beat up the sky?

And all that might be well and good, but it doesn't help these kids in these pictures.

Milo is standing next to me sneaking a cocktail. Kind of ridiculous. I'm sure he's not fooling anyone.

"Where's your sister?"

"Oh, she never comes to these things. She finds them depressing."

I nod.

"Oh, shit, there's my mom."

He hides the so-not-secret cocktail behind his back on the table. And there is his mother.

Well, she's blond. With her hair up in a bun at the top of her head, with a little braid around the bun. *Très* regal. She's wearing a strapless black cocktail dress, and she looks like she might as well be Milo's older sister. But she doesn't look weird or plastic surgeried. She doesn't have a duck mouth and giant boobies or anything. And even her blond hair is a pretty shade, pale but natural. Like wheat.

And there's something about her. Her spirit, I guess. She's got, like, a glow. Not like a bottle-orange glow that you always see on those TV housewives. But like a glow radiating around her. Like she's got a lightbulb on inside, emanating.

"Mom, this is Willa. Remember, the one I was telling you about?"

"Willa. Yes, I do remember. Milo's new girlfriend he's crazy about."

"Mo-om." He rolls his eyes. I'm sure this is the millionth time he's rolled his eyes at his mother.

"I know, I know. I'm embarrassing, and everything I say is embarrassing."

She smiles, chiding.

"This is amazing, what you're doing, Mrs. Hesse. Just really incredible."

"Oh, thank you. Thank you so much, Willa. Well, we try. Honestly, you get started and you just realize how much more you wish you could do."

"Well, I'm really impressed. Truly."

"Thanks, Willa."

She gives Milo a little smile. A nod from a mother to her son. I think it might even be a nod of approval.

And did you hear that? *Milo's girlfriend he's crazy about?* I mean, this is really getting confusing. I sort of wish we could have name tags. Girlfriend or Not Girlfriend. Somebody hand me the right one.

One of the donors comes and whisks her away, and Milo gets back to his cocktail.

"Your mom is so sophisticated and kind and international and—"

"And desperately trying to make up for the fact that my family embezzled everyone's money and my dad hung himself."

Welp, that stops everything.

"I didn't mean to—"

"No, I know you didn't."

Someone is about to make a speech, and everyone seems to be wrangling around to the other side of the room. A hush falls over the crowd as one of the donors takes the floor.

Milo and I are facing that side, with our backs to the wall. Everyone is listening, a few hushed whispers here and there. And now I whisper, too.

"Milo?"

"Yes?"

"I know about you and Remy."

FORTY-SEVEN

Milo decided that the only place we could talk about something so personal and convoluted was by the catering station. So, while these guys in white hats and chef jackets are preening over the hors d'oeuvres, Milo and I are having a heated discussion about romance, making out, and the appalling nature of humanity. As if they're not even there.

"I don't know what you think you saw, but—"

"Milo. I think you should stop lying right now. Just get it all out on the table."

"No, but I'm—"

"Milo, I saw you, okay? With my very own eyes in my very own face. I saw you with your tongue down her throat and all the groping and all the slobbering. By the campus center.

Slobbering by the campus center."

A waiter comes and take a grand platter of bacon-wrapped figs with some sort of cream involved. I wish I had an appetite, because normally I would eat the daylights out of that platter.

Milo sighs. Looks at me.

I look longingly at the bacon-wrapped figs before turning back to him. He's calculating, figuring out if he should just spill the beans.

"Okay, okay. You're right."

"Thank you."

"I'm sorry, Willa. I'm really sorry if I bummed you out."

"If you bummed me out? Are you serious right now?"

"Well, what's the big deal? Seriously. We're just friends."

"Just friends?"

"Yes."

"I don't do *that* with my friends." *Or anyone*, I add silently.

"Okay, fine, we're friends with benefits. It's really no big deal, okay? You're the one I'm crazy about. Didn't you hear my mom? Totally embarrassing me?"

"Well, it is a big deal to me. Where I come from that kind of . . . groping is strictly for not-friends or more-than-friends or whatever."

"Okay, okay." He holds up his hands. "Honestly, I think

what we have here is a cultural difference. This is like . . . when people go to Japan and don't understand the high-tech toilets."

"Toilets?"

"The toilets in Tokyo are very confusing. They kind of look like spaceships."

"Really?"

"Yes. It's like a bidet and a toilet and a washer and a dryer all in a toilet. There's even a noise to make it sound like running water for privacy. It's actually kind of brilliant, but *that's not the point right now*. The point is . . . this is a cultural difference between us. Where I come from . . . this is nothing. Because it is. Where you come from . . . this is something. So we just need to create some kind of understanding here, okay? A cultural bridge, if you will."

"Milo, I'm sorry, but I—"

"No, listen. I'm serious. Willa. I really like you. Like, I really, really, really think about you all the time and even told my mom about you, which I never do, and even brought you to the island, which I also never do. Please don't be mad at me. Remy was going on and on crying about some guy, and I just wanted to make her feel better."

"So you groped her?"

"Look, she was crying and acting crazy. I didn't know what else to do!"

"Well, are you just always gonna grope her when she's crying?"

"No. I'm not. Listen. Now that I know it bothers you, definitely not. I will never grope Remy again. Or kiss her or anything. Consider this like an Iowa friendship. Totally G-rated."

From across the room, Milo's mother gives a quick little wave to Milo and me. It's a sweet thing.

"Look, my mom already anointed you my girlfriend, and that's just fine with me, because I want you to be. I want to bring you home for Thanksgiving and somewhere snowy for Christmas and we'll sip hot chocolate, like on a mountain-top, and maybe even take you somewhere superglamorous and kind of hilarious for New Year's. If you'll let me. I want to show you all sorts of cool things and see the look on your face when you see them."

"Like the toilets in Tokyo?"

"Yes, Willa. Even the toilets in Tokyo."

And my head is spinning now. I thought we were break-ing up tonight. I really did. I thought we were breaking up and that was it. But now we are doing the opposite of break-ing up, which is sipping hot chocolate in Christmas chalets and observing the cultural difference in bathroom fixtures.

And I know I shouldn't believe him. And I know his story is thin. But I want it to be true. I want all of this to be true. I want to be Milo Hesse's girlfriend. I want everyone to know it and to shout it from the mountaintops from here to Zermatt to Nepal. It's the opposite of being from Iowa.

And now, total honesty: it's all I want to be.

FORTY-EIGHT

I want you to know, I've thought about this. How to deal with Remy. This is what I've come up with.

She didn't know. She really didn't know about Milo and me. As far as she knew, I barely even liked him. She didn't know I went to the island. She didn't even know I was getting a crush on him. She didn't know he touched me on the arm in a sexy but sort of innocent way. She didn't know because I didn't tell her. And I didn't tell her because I was being tricky.

Let's face it.

So, in a way . . . I kind of got what was coming to me. I should have just been honest about it. If I had told her, if she'd known, there's no way she would have let him grope her and slobber all over her in broad daylight next to the campus center. Right?

It's the edge of that thought that gets interrupted when Remy comes barreling in the room, some sort of lovesick tornado. She's all over the place, bouncing off the walls.

"Sorry about the other day, I just felt like I should talk to you and I really wanted to tell you that thing about Humbert Humbert, but I should have just waited, I guess."

"Remy, look, it's okay. I have to tell you something."

No, I'm not gonna tell her I saw the make-out session with Milo. What's the point? It wasn't her fault anyway. She didn't know.

"It is? Okay, good . . . wait, what?"

"I think Milo and I are, like, boyfriend and girlfriend or something now."

"Oh. Cool."

"That's it?"

Remy looks in her bag for something she's obviously not looking for.

"Yeah, that's cool. I'm really happy for you guys. He's great."

I really wasn't going to say anything, and I'm still not going to say anything. I'm definitely not going to say anything. No way. Except that . . .

"Look, I saw you guys making out, okay?"

"What?"

"I saw you guys having a hot make-out session by the campus center."

"Oh. Well, that doesn't mean anything. I mean, we're just friends."

"Yeah, that's what he said."

"It's true. I'm obsessed with Humbert. You know that more than anyone."

"Yeah, look. I know you didn't know. But you do now, okay?"

"Of course! Now that I know, that makes everything different. Like, *everything*. Besides, I just . . . look, I'm kind of freaking out right now, actually."

And now Remy sits down, or, more accurately, floats like a piece of paper down in all her beautiful-girl-who-has-lost-too-much-weight-and-sleep-and-thus-could-be-on-the-cover-of-*Vogue* glory.

"What's wrong?"

I wish I didn't know what's coming next, but I have a feeling I know what's coming next.

"Humbert. He hasn't texted me. Or called. Or emailed. Or anything."

I want to scream, "Well, duh!" But I don't.

The fact that Remy thinks this situation is even approaching normal, this teacher-fucking thing, is really beyond. I mean, what does she think? This guy is gonna take her to the prom? "Hi, everybody, here's my date, and, by the way, he's also my teacher! And just old enough to be my father!"

And now I'm consoling Remy even though two seconds ago I thought she'd be consoling me.

"Remy, he's probably scared he's gonna be fired or something. I mean, it's just one phone call and he could go to jail. Did you ever think of that? He's probably terrified."

It's the logical explanation. It makes total sense. But not to Remy, and there's a reason for that.

I think what happened is . . . Remy was always like this little princess with everyone swarming around her and granting her wishes and obeying her every command. So, at some molecular level, she has no idea how to cope with something that doesn't go exactly the way she wants it, exactly how she wants it, exactly when she wants it.

A short way to say that is . . . she's spoiled.

Yes, ladies and gentlemen, Remy is spoiled.

But she's not a bad person. She's really not. She's just kind of way too sheltered and coddled, and there seems to be a kind of delusional aspect to her as well. At least as applies here to her affair with Humbert Humbert.

"Remy, maybe you could tell me what happened . . . ?"

"What kinda happened is I'm kinda in love with him and I kinda went to his office and looked superhot and made sure he fell in love with me."

"So, what, you, like, jumped on him?"

"Kind of."

Remy can't stop checking her phone. Putting it down. Picking it up. Checking it. Putting it down.

Outside, the sky shines lavender through the trees. By six it will be pitch-black; it's that time of year. Half-day season. Pitch-black season.

"Well, he's probably just freaking out."

"Yeah."

But she doesn't sound convinced. She digs in her pockets and finds a pill. That's the one. It's a little white pill, almost like an aspirin. Oxy. She doesn't even try to hide it this time. Just takes it right in front to me.

"Remy, you have to stop this. This is really bad. Okay. You look like some kind of stress case who's one twitch away from the rehab center. I don't even know what you're doing or how much you're doing, but I don't even want to know. And I have stuff here I need your help with. Okay? Like, Milo and I sorta went to some mysterious but possibly royal island this weekend."

"Higgs?"

"What?"

"Higgs. Higgs Island. With Milo. That's what it's called."

"I guess. I kinda never asked . . ."

"That's a big deal, actually. The fact that Milo brought you there. I mean, I've never seen Milo take anyone there. Ever, now that I think about it."

"Really?"

"Yeah. He must really like you."

We pause.

"Willa? I should probably tell you something . . . ?"

"What?"

She stares out the window for a second. Bites her lip.

"Oh, forget it."

"Wait, Remy. What?"

"No, it's nothing, I forgot."

I can't tell what's going on over there across the room in obsessive-land. Is she mad at me? Is she sad at me? Is she totally apathetic because all she is thinking about is Humbert Humbert?

Probably. So even though my heart and my brain are in a million different places, I decide I have to do something.

"Look, Remy, maybe we should get out of here. Go somewhere. Get your mind off of it."

"Really? You don't have to stay here and study all day?"

(Yes.)

"No, let's just go somewhere and do something that has nothing to do with Humbert Humbert or Milo or anyone. Okay?"

"Yeah, okay. Okay. I can do that."

I feel relief. Far more than worry about this temporary academic derailment. Remy listens to me. I know that. And I feel . . . responsible for her.

After all, there's no one else looking out for her.

And I have not exactly done a bang-up job of looking out for her, now, have I?

FORTY-NINE

The first person we see as we walk off campus is Zeb. He's still in uniform, tie askew, a little pink in his cheeks from the cold. There's something genuinely light about him. A kind of happiness. Like his swoopy blond hair just swoops all his problems away. Never to return.

"Shalom," he says, flirty.

"Why, shalom to you, too, my friend."

Remy smiles wide, blindingly, at Zeb. She is back on track. Back in make-everyone-love-her mode.

"What brings you fine lasses off campus this lucky evening?"

"Honestly, we have no idea."

"Aha! Well, come with me. I'm going into Philthy."

"Where?"

"He means Philadelphia. Or Philly," Remy explains. "But, you know, Philthy. Because it is."

This sounds like the greatest idea ever. And before I know it Zeb's getting an Uber and Remy looks at me and shrugs.

"You said you wanted adventure."

FIFTY

So, the Franklin Institute. The Liberty Bell. The Philadelphia Museum of Art. These are appropriate places to see things and get one's mind off a potential heartbreak.

But where are we? None of *those* locales! Don't be silly.

Instead we are somewhere in the middle of downtown Philly, amid cobblestone streets, at a slippery little bar called the Lamplighter. They don't card here. And everybody still smokes. It's like the Twilight Zone, and this place is stuck in what I can only imagine is the mid-'90s.

You're wondering how I let this happen. Let's play that scenario out, shall we?

Zeb: So, I know this cool dive bar—

Remy: Oh, thank God!

Willa: Bar? No, wait! Did you know that the Declaration of Independence was signed less than three miles from where we . . . guys? Guys? (Runs to catch up with friends while dodging "appreciation" from a semipro female harassment construction team.)

So, yeah. The Lamplighter.

Somewhere on the jukebox someone is playing the Stones—"Sympathy for the Devil," which I bet has been played here no less than ten thousand times.

Zeb walks right in and waves at the owner, who waves back from behind the bar.

"Um. You a regular here?" I ask.

Zeb laughs. "Oh, it's just . . . my dad shot something here so we kinda got to know the place."

It's humble. It's a shrug. He's not trying to be full of himself. He looks kind of embarrassed to state the fact.

Remy glares at me. Somehow I wasn't supposed to ask that. But what was I supposed to—

"Ladies . . ."

Zeb gestures to a red booth with a few cuts in the pleather. Obviously from all the low-down-and-dirty knife fights that are happening here on a regular basis. The entire city of Philadelphia seems to have carved their initials in our table and, also, their opinions about everybody else. My personal favorite: "Barry sucks donkey dick."

So, you see, it's a delicate place. Just made for regaining balance and serenity.

"Oh my God, Zeb. This is perfect!" Remy chirps.

I guess rich people like to pretend to be poor people. Funny, poor people don't like to pretend to be poor people. Or to be poor people.

"I know, right. I love this place. My dad made this gritty thing about south Philly criminals. You know, lots of tough guys in wifebeaters. Bada bing!"

"Like you, Zeb?"

Remy is changing the subject. To flirting.

"Oh, I'm *so* tough. Watch out." He flips his blond hair out of his eyes and strikes a karate pose.

"I could defeat those bad guys with a tofu teriyaki roll."

Now both of us are laughing. Zeb is adorable. No question. So maybe it wasn't such a bad idea coming to this place.

"So, Willa, come on. How do you like the Least Coast?"

"Boo." Remy rolls her eyes.

"I can say that, Remy, because I am from the Best Coast. Aka the West Coast. But you, my friend. You, from the unknowable middle of our nation. How do *you* like it? Or do you hate it?"

"No, I don't hate it."

"Do you have a boyfriend yet?"

"Um. Yes?"

"Too bad for the rest of the world. What's his name?"

Remy and I share a look. Should I tell him? Remy nods.

"Milo."

"Milo Hesse! Are you serious?!"

"Um. Why?"

"What about you, Zeb?" Remy raises an eyebrow.

"Come on, Remy. You know I'm head over heels for my girl."

"I know. Everyone knows. You're off-limits. Too bad."

They share a look. I definitely get the feeling there might have at one point been a Remy and Zeb flirtation.

"I'm taking Willa to Paris this summer. You should come. I think we'll try living in Le Marais. Or Oberkampf."

Zeb doesn't have a chance to answer. The owner brings over three Pabst Blue Ribbons in cans.

I stare at them, unwilling to pick one up.

Zeb's dad couldn't have filmed at a coffee place?

Thankfully, Remy doesn't take one, either. She gets up to go to the ladies' room. I shudder to think what *that* might look like.

The owner walks away, giving a nod, leaving Zeb and me alone to contemplate "Eye of the Tiger" playing on the jukebox.

"So, Willa, you do know one thing, right?"

"Um . . . what?"

"You can't trust these people."

"Which people?"

"These ones. Just . . . try not to get too attached. To anyone. Or anything. Like any outcomes."

"Why not?"

"They just don't get certain things . . . about life, you know? Like, yeah, some of it is trivial, but the rest of it matters. Like, *really* matters. And they just walk around like everything is awful and nothing counts."

"Do you really think that?"

"Honestly, I kind of do."

"But I'm supposed to trust *you*."

"No, you don't have to. But you know, I like you, Willa. You're kind of singular."

"Singular?"

"Yes, unlike any other. Totally original."

"Wow, Zeb. They definitely don't make them like you back in What Cheer."

He smiles, and that would all be perfect. Except some girl with black wiry hair comes running up to our table like the bar is exploding.

"Hey! Is that your friend in there?! You better come quick!"

FIFTY-ONE

What is happening to Remy is that she's not in the ladies' room. She is in the alley behind the Lamplighter turning into a zombie. Either that, or she is having some sort of overdose. She is turning blue, lying there on the ground, with what appears to be very little breath coming in and out of her lungs. Like she's in a deep blue sleep. In the alley. Next to the trash.

Zeb and I rush over to grab her, and the owner comes running out, too. He doesn't seem too pleased to have this zombie transformation and/or overdose happening at his establishment, no matter who Zeb's dad is.

Zeb gets down beside Remy, puts his ear next to her mouth.

"She's breathing."

"Somebody call an ambulance!" I scream.

"*No!* Look, she can't be here." That's the now-not-so-friendly owner.

But now there's a huge breath, a gasp, and Remy is breathing again. Zeb leans back on his heels with relief.

There are five zillion things running through my mind to ask, but the thing that comes out is "What do we do? What do we do?"

"I don't know. I think . . . I think she might be okay. She's breathing, at least. That's the thing."

I can't stop staring at Remy.

"Vinnie!" calls the owner.

And with that the aforementioned Vinnie appears looking exactly like an extra from Zeb's dad's movie. He's kind of tall and thin everywhere but his belly. And there's a lot of cologne involved.

He takes in the scene, nods at the boss, and with that, the undead Remy, Zeb, and I are ushered, practically flung, into a pitch-black SUV with Vinnie at the wheel.

"Where to?"

"Please! The nearest emergency room! Hurry!" I screech.

Remy leans, head lolling, on Zeb. Vinnie does not seem too excited about this errand. Zeb's eyes are glued to Remy's face, monitoring for . . . I don't even know what.

"It's okay. It's gonna be okay. You're okay, Remy." I'm holding her hand.

Her eyes are rolled back in her head, but there is a faint nod, a dispatch back from the netherworld.

I'm afraid to ask, and I think I already might know . . .

"Zeb? What is this? What was it?"

Zeb looks at me, pauses. It's like he doesn't want to be the one to cast Eve out of the Garden of Eden.

We both know what happened, though. An overdose. Yes, definitely that. I didn't pay close enough attention. I should have realized she was gone too long. And now . . .

I glance at Remy. Sleep has taken over, but she's less blue, and her chest is moving up and down.

Her eyes open briefly, just a peek, and then back to sleep.

Our ride is smooth. I can only assume Vinnie is too busy trying to dump us off as quickly as possible to freak out about his undead passenger.

"Where do you think she got it? Whatever it was."

"Some guy."

Now Vinnie from the front. "Some guy here? At the bar?"

There's a threat to it. Woe to he who deals at the Lamplighter.

Zeb shakes his head. "No, probably back home."

I'm assuming "home" means New York. And the questions are again cascading through my brain, but right now let's just concentrate on the blue-skinned zombie, okay?

Thank God, Vinnie pulls up to the ER. Awkward silence. We're just about to get out of the car and lead Remy into the hospital.

"No . . ." Remy shakes her head.

She's alive, suddenly.

"Remy, we have to make sure you're okay."

"No . . . they'll call my parents." It's slurring, but it is a sentence.

"Maybe they *should* call your parents."

"No, no. I'm fine. I'm fiiiiine."

Zeb and I look at each other.

"Remy, I really think you should see a doctor. Right, Willa?"

"Yes. Remy. Seriously."

"No. I'm fine. I'm okay now. I swear."

And the truth is, her breathing is stronger every second. She's coming back to the land of the living.

"You guys want me to drop you at the end of the block or something?"

Vinnie clearly wants us out of his SUV one way or the other. I don't blame him.

"Yeah, um. Just maybe right down there. Thanks."

"Don't worry about it."

We get out at the end of the block. Find a bench. Sit.

Zeb and I look at each other, puzzled, as Remy leans on Zeb.

"What do we do now?"

"Well, we can't exactly go back to Pembroke. Maybe we could just . . . get a couple of rooms at Rittenhouse Square or something? She should be all right by the morning, I think."

So that's it. It will be a room in a fancy hotel, then. It will not be a night in the alley. It will not be a night in the hospital.

It will not be a night in the morgue.

Not this time.

FIFTY-TWO

By the time we get back to Denbigh it's one o'clock the next day, and the reality of last night seems to have come barreling in once Zeb dropped us off. He doesn't take it on himself to issue any closing statements about the dangers of drug abuse. But as I get out, he gives me a look. I'm pretty sure the look means something along the lines of "Take care of your friend" or "Watch out." But who knows. Maybe it means "Stay away from this girl." That could be, too.

Remy is quiet now. Contemplative.

She hasn't said much all morning, and, honestly, what is there to say?

We walk up the steps to our room, which sort of seems

like climbing Mount Everest at this point. I'm pretty sure neither of us is going to acknowledge what happened now, or maybe ever.

But when I get back to the room after brushing my teeth, there is Remy, sitting on the bed.

She looks up. And I've never seen this before. Remy, shoulders shrunk down, makeup smeared, and tears in her eyes, looking up at me.

"Willa, I'm scared."

It's a little girl's voice. It's a tiny voice. It's a desperate voice.

And now I'm over there, next to her, next to her on the bed, holding her. And she lays her head on my shoulder, then my lap. "Will you help me?"

And she's crying, shuddering, and I'm there with her, trying to put it together. Trying to figure out how I can help her.

"Of course. Of course I will. We can do this, Remy. We'll do it together, okay?"

She nods, still crying.

"You won't abandon me for being a fuckup?"

"Abandon you? Why would I do that?"

"'Cause everybody does. Eventually."

Okay, I sort of don't know what she's talking about, but

I'm thinking maybe this is the heart of the matter.

"Who, Remy? Who's done that?"

"Everyone. My parents. Every guy. Like, once I like them, they're not interested. Humbert Humbert is doing it, too. You'll see. It's like I've got this disease. People get up close, and then they run away. Like I'm a leper or something."

And I am looking at this girl who has everything, who *is* everything. And I am remembering that first day, when I saw her and her name was like glittering script all around her. And the moment I was looking at the clock tower standing so tall, like an invitation, and the plan—the plan I had to climb that clock tower and make it stop.

I haven't thought about the clock tower . . . I haven't thought about it since this girl showed me people and things I would never, ever have known without her.

She reached down and pulled me up to where she was.

She saved me.

And I don't care if it sounds corny. Because given that fact—that rock-solid, unassailable fact—how could I not do the same for her?

"Remy, can I tell you something?"

"Hm." She nods.

"I am not ever going to leave you."

This stops everything in the room.

"I was in a dark place. Like, really dark. And you made me think that the world could be amazing and maybe I should try it."

"I did?"

"Yeah. It was you."

She's staring at the floor now.

She shakes her head.

"You know what's funny? When I saw you, that first day on the green, I felt like I had a chance. Like a chance at a *real* friendship. With someone real. Not these jerks, so concerned about last names and status and all that garbage. The first time I talked to you I just felt lucky. I told Milo. I was like, 'There's this girl, and she's from Iowa, and she's sort of shy and she doesn't know anybody we know or anything about us, and I want to be friends with her.'"

I smile.

"Well, look at us now. We're, like, practically lesbians."

This gets a laugh.

Remy looks out the window, the sun coming through the leaves.

"I keep saying I'm not gonna do this anymore. Like, I keep telling myself. And then I just do it again. Like I'm just watching myself. I'm just watching myself do it."

She stares at the floor.

"Willa, I think I'm really fucked."

I can't help but wonder, how did I have no idea any of this was happening? I mean, I knew Remy was gone, but I thought she was off with Humbert Humbert getting into an entirely different kind of trouble.

And what was I up to? I was seeing Milo in secret and never asking questions. Important questions. Questions that might have prevented, well, *this*.

Where was my big mouth when I needed it?

"Okay. Here. This is what we're gonna do. We're gonna stay here on campus. We're not gonna go to New York, or even Philly, and especially not Jersey. We're gonna hunker down and study. And I'm gonna find a place to go to talk to people about this. With you."

"What do you mean?"

"Like an Anonymous thing. Like Alcoholics Anonymous. But for drugs."

"Oh, that's Narcotics Anonymous. It doesn't work."

"Remy, you asked me to help you."

"What if I know someone who's there?"

"Well, it's *anonymous* for a reason. And it'll be some random place down here; no one will know. Okay?"

"Okay."

"We'll go together. Okay?"

"Yeah."

"We're gonna do this. I promise."

Remy nods. I hear myself saying these words, and I mean them, but I sound a hell of a lot like an after-school special. I know it. And I know Remy knows it, too.

"Right. You're right, Willa. I'm in."

"Good. This'll be good."

"Willa?"

"Yeah?"

"We're still going to Paris together, right?"

I smile. "Are you kidding? I wouldn't miss it for the world."

PART III

FIFTY-THREE

It's a redbrick church with red doors. A place called "The Holy Innocents," and the outside is not so bad, actually. It's the basement where they do the meetings that really makes you want to jump off the Ben Franklin Bridge.

It's a dank kind of basement with wood-paneled walls and flyers hanging off them. In the corner there's a table with coffee, half-and-half creamers, sugar, saccharine, and a few pastries. People around here drink coffee like there is going to be a worldwide coffee ban tomorrow. I've never seen people drink coffee like this. And there's a lot of smoking involved. A lot. Basically, two minutes before the meeting everybody is outside smoking and then they all hustle in last minute before the serenity prayer.

The serenity prayer is when everybody holds hands and says, "God grant me the serenity to accept the things I cannot change, the courage to change the things I can, and the wisdom to know the difference." Or, if you're Remy, the serenity prayer is when you roll your eyes and look at me like *What the fuck are we doing here?*

And I can't say I blame her. This place is a real bummer. The people are nice and all, but half of them seem like religious zealots, and half of them seem like homeless people.

This is our fifth meeting in five days.

Remy wants to stop going. I want to stop, too, but I am not going to stop, for Remy's sake.

Right now a middle-aged woman with thousand-year-old skin is talking about her last meth bender and how that was when she knew she had to stop because she almost blew up her house. I'm glad she stopped, too. She seems like a nice lady and I feel bad for her, looking at her, thinking about what her life might be like now. But she's happy. There's a kind of calm to her that surprises me. It's like she has some secret to restlessness. Some cure. Maybe there is something to this. Maybe *I* could learn something.

Someone else starts talking about God, and Remy rolls her eyes again.

I can tell it is gonna be hard to make this stick, but I don't know what else to do. Maybe it's just this meeting.

This place. Maybe there's a more glamorous meeting for fallen debutantes somewhere.

As we're leaving the meeting, a couple of nice ladies walk up to Remy to give her their numbers. They tell her she can call anytime. They look a little crazy, but there's a kindness to their eyes.

"That's nice of them. They said you can call them anytime."

"Anytime. As in, like, never."

"Remy, you have to at least give it a chance."

"I know, I know. I just wish the place weren't so fucking depressing."

"Yeah. Although . . . you know . . . ODing in an alley full of trash? More depressing."

"Touché."

There are only about ten blocks to walk back to Pembroke, and it's actually really pleasant, once you cross the train tracks. There's a sweet little park on the way and a small-town row of storefronts with expensive things no one ever buys. Overpriced candles and soaps made of thyme, tea tree, lavender. A framing store. A quilt store. Really? A quilt store? I mean, is there really that much of a demand for quilts?

"Have you thought about Thanksgiving or whatever?" Remy asks all casual-like.

Ugh, I haven't been wanting to talk about this. Milo wants me to go home with him for Thanksgiving, back to New York. And I want to. But there's a problem. I feel like if I leave Remy alone, who knows what will happen.

"Um, I'm not sure."

"Well, I think I'm gonna go with Humbert Humbert."

"What? Are you serious?"

"Yeah. It's okay. No one will know."

"Remy, does he, like, *know?*"

About NA, the OD, the OMG, is the subtext.

"No. But that's why it'll be good, you know? That's totally not his scene. I'll be . . . distracted."

"Well, where are you guys going?"

"I don't know, somewhere private, I guess."

"Well, you better make sure it's far away from here."

"I know. Don't want him to find out I'm a junkie, right?"

I grab her arm and turn her toward me. "You're not a junkie, Remy. Don't even say that."

"I think Milo is gonna ask you to come to New York with him."

My face is practically glowing with guilt as I say, "He already did." How did she know? "I'm nervous."

"Don't be nervous. Just don't mention his dad."

And that's really it, isn't it? The only rule for Milo. Don't mention his dad. Never say, "Hey, I heard your dad hung himself after his company bilked everyone in New York out of their money!" Got it.

"Listen, Remy, are you gonna be okay? Like, I'll stay with you if you want."

"Of course I'll be okay. I'll be with Humbert Humbert. I'll be more than okay. If you know what I mean."

"This can't be helping you. You know it's like a sick situation, right?"

"Yeah, but we're in love. I bet we'll get married. You can be my bridesmaid."

I frown at her. She smiles at me.

"You know, you'd actually like Humbert Humbert. He's, like, really good in bed."

"Well, that is what I look for in a teacher."

FIFTY-FOUR

I guess if you live in New York, you don't have to have your Thanksgiving dinner at home with all your relatives around watching football. No, no. Instead, you can just have a six-course meal at a fancy restaurant and invite the whole family there.

Which is what Milo's mom did. Of course.

Don't worry, though, we get the whole back room to ourselves. It's a private room with dark-wood floors, burgundy damask wallpaper, and sconces on the walls. I'm sure if you push one of the sconces, the wall flips around, revealing a secret passage to the dungeon, which is probably where they keep everyone who is cooking our food.

It's just Milo; his mom; his sister, Kitty; Kitty's new

boyfriend, who nobody seems to be talking to; Milo's grandfather and grandmother; and, of course, me. The grandfather on the other side is not in attendance. Why, you ask? Oh, because he's in jail. His wife? Um, she's in Europe. She won't be back anytime soon. So, you see, it's all a very happy family. Nothing unsaid here. The wine does go well with the chicken.

Except now the door opens and Milo's mother stands up to greet a man who must be the new stepfather.

That changes the temperature of the room considerably. Now Milo is brooding. The grandparents are pretending to inspect the wine list, and Kitty is whispering to her boyfriend, who seems slightly allergic to something. Maybe himself.

The stepfather tries to break the ice.

"So, Milo, how are things going down there at Witherspoon?"

"Not as good as they're going up here, apparently."

Kitty smiles, amused.

He's not a bad-looking man. Brown hair, thinning at the top. But a handsome face. You could see him sailing somewhere in his youth, off the coast of Nantucket. There's something kind of dry here, though. Like his veins are filled with powder. Milo's mom is a stunning woman, no two ways about it. So I'm guessing this guy is seriously loaded.

"So, you must be Willa? Named after Willa Cather, I presume."

"Yes, you presume correctly."

"And I hear you're from . . . Iowa?"

At this, the two grandparents look up, perplexed.

Kitty tries to help.

"Oh, you're so lucky! To grow up with all that land and sky and not in a city overwrought with people bumping into each other left and right!"

"I agree." Milo's mom chimes in. "I would have loved to be from someplace . . . pastoral. Like an Andrew Wyeth painting."

The grandparents look at each other but remain silent. They seem puzzled by my existence.

"So, Milo, how did you meet this belle from the Midwest?"

The stepfather is really pouring it on.

"Remy. She and Remy are BFFs."

"BFFs?" This is the grandmother.

"Best friends forever," Kitty informs. "Oh, that's lovely. Remy is practically part of the family. She and Milo went to day care together. Before she went to Spence, then Brearley, then Pembroke."

"And how is Remy these days?" Milo's mother asks.

I don't answer, "Oh, other than the obvious drug

addiction, she's just fine." Instead, I say, "Oh, she's great."

"Why didn't you invite her, MyMy?" This from Kitty.

Milo shrugs.

"She actually had plans, so . . ."

"Oh, I bet." Kitty smirks.

"Are *you* speaking of Remy Taft?" The grandmother again. This time, directly to me. Somehow as if I should not even dare to utter the name of the Remy Taft.

Milo intercedes.

"Of course she is, Grandma. They're best friends."

"Hm."

And that is all I will ever get out of that. *Hm.*

Kitty tries to lighten it. "Well, I'm so glad, Willa. Remy could use a friend like you. She needs someone grounded. You know? So she doesn't fly off into the clouds."

"Is that what they call it?" Again, the grandmother. She seems on the ball in a way I didn't expect.

"Mother, please." This is a direct order from Milo's mom.

The stepfather puts his hand on Milo's mother's arm, assuringly.

"Well, we're all happy you're here, Willa. We have a lot to be grateful for this Thanksgiving." He smiles at Milo's mother, knowingly.

And this is too much for Milo.

"Oh, really, like the fact that my dad is dead and now you

get to fuck my mother?!"

"Milo!" Kitty is as shocked as I am.

"You know what?! Enjoy your Thanksgiving." Milo stands up. "Enjoy the fact that my dad is dead. Enjoy your snobbery, too, while you're at it. God bless us, every one!"

And Milo grabs my wrist and drags me out of there. I look back at his mother, who is putting her head in her hands, and his sister, who is staring at the table. The grandparents have suddenly become very interested in the china.

Milo storms through the restaurant with me in tow. We rush through the front doors, and before you know it, we're in a cab, heading downtown.

"What was that?!" I can't help myself. I'm mortified.

"What do you mean?"

"Um . . . that Thanksgiving dinner that you just ruined?"

"What, are you kidding me? Am I supposed to sit there and—"

"Listen, what do you want to do? Make your mother cry? What for? That's not love. I mean, I know it's hard . . . but you have to let her move on. And enjoy her life. I'm sure it's been horrible for her."

"Yeah, right."

"Milo, you're being a jerk. You really are. If you love your mom, which I know you do, you'll want her to be happy."

"That fuckface has had the hots for my mother for *years*."

"Milo, that guy didn't cause what happened to your family."

Milo sits, silent, as we glide through the city streets.

"Look, Willa. You shouldn't talk about things you don't understand."

"And you should stop punching at invisible walls. Honestly, Milo, I think you need to see someone, like a therapist. To get through this."

"Oh God. It's always fucking therapy with you people."

"Who people?"

"Normal people."

"What, like commoners?"

There's a silence as we whiz past Central Park.

But I can't help myself.

"Look, all I'm saying is maybe you should stop pretending everything's okay and actually deal with it."

"And maybe you should stop pretending you're my girlfriend."

Ouch.

I look at Milo. He's facing forward in the cab, wooden.

"Do you really mean that?"

He stays facing forward, doesn't even bother to look at me.

My stomach feels as though it's suddenly filled with acid. "Let me out, please."

I can't stay in this cab one more minute.

The cabdriver pulls to the side, but Milo is the one who gets out.

"No, I'll get out. Here. Take her wherever she wants."

He hands the driver a wad of cash, practically throws it at him, and storms off into the city streets.

I sit there for a second, blindsided.

What just happened?

I was with Milo, now he's gone. I was at dinner with a table full of people and candles and wine, and now I am by myself in a cab.

"Where to?"

"Um. Uh . . . Penn Station. Thanks."

I get the feeling the cabdriver wants to say something, something kind, but thinks better of it. Maybe best to let the little girl be.

You have to wonder how many times a girl has sat in a cab, being driven through the streets of New York, crying.

I'm gonna put it at over a million.

FIFTY-FIVE

By the time I get back to Denbigh, I'm convinced Remy will be off somewhere with Humbert Humbert eloping but, no, she is there. In the room, quiet.

"Remy?"

She doesn't say anything.

"Um, hello? Remy?"

She looks up.

"What are you doing here? What's the matter?"

"He never showed up."

"Who, Humbert?"

"Yeah, he was supposed to pick me up at six and he never showed. Didn't call, didn't text. Nothing. Just fucking blew me off. On Thanksgiving."

She looks up at me, pleading somehow.

"Well, if it makes you feel any better, Milo just dropped me like a hot potato."

"Are you serious?"

"Uh, yeah. Just fucking blew up at his family and blew up at me. And then just left. I'm sort of in a state of shock right now. Which is why I'm not currently bawling my face off."

"Oh. God . . . I was hoping he'd changed."

"What?"

She's shaking her head. "He's been so angry lately. But he seemed to really like you and I thought maybe he'd grown up. Or maybe you would change him or something stupid."

"Really?"

"Yeah, I should have said something. I'm sorry. I wanted to. But I just didn't want to ruin it, you know?"

"Sort of."

"Milo is just one of those guys. Great guy. Horrible boyfriend. Why do you think I never went out with him?"

"Well, I wish you would have told me, honestly."

"I thought maybe you had a chance. I'm so sorry. God, what a fucker."

"So you think that's it? You don't think he's gonna text or anything? Or try to, like, fix it?"

I don't know why I'm asking Remy this. Except that she

obviously knows a whole lot more about this than I do. Apparently.

"Honestly, no. He sort of like . . . shuts down. You know?"

Great.

"Well, I didn't know, but I guess I know now. God, I feel like such an idiot."

"Don't. He had me fooled, and I've known him since day care. I thought he was maybe gonna be different with you."

"Why would you think that?"

"Because you're different."

"Well, apparently I'm not different enough. Ugh. I guess I should've known when he made out with you."

"He just made out with me because he felt sorry for me."

We both stay quiet for a second, contemplating our mutual pathetic society.

"God, we're a couple of sad sacks, huh?"

"Pretty much." Remy checks her phone. Puts it down.

I do not want to think of what could happen to Remy if we stay here. What kind of downward spiral seems, at this point, almost imminent.

"Okay, you know what, Remy? What if we go to a meeting?"

"I already went."

"You did?"

"Yeah."

"By yourself?"

"Yep."

"Remy, I'm proud of you. That's great."

She seems unmoved.

"Yeah, well, I don't know what I'm gonna do for these next two days. Just sitting around. Driving myself crazy."

And she's right. We have the whole weekend. And the possibility of no phone calls or texts or excuses from Humbert for two days? Will not be good. By then, from the looks of her, Remy might implode. Go catatonic.

"How do you do it, Willa?" she asks.

"Do what?"

"Like, just get up every day and get things done and think everything's gonna be okay."

"I don't think everything is gonna be okay. Are you kidding? I'm deathly afraid nothing is gonna be okay and I'm gonna end up dead in a gutter somewhere. Or like a bag lady. Or like one of those crazy people you see walking across the crosswalk, talking to themselves, gesticulating."

"Really?"

"Yeah."

"Wow. I never realized that. I just thought you were simple."

"Thanks."

"No, I mean like you don't freak out about things the way I do. Like, you don't make everything hard."

"Honestly, Remy, I don't have the luxury of making everything hard."

"What do you mean?"

"Everything is hard, like naturally, like your mom runs off with the best man and your dad is broke-ass and now you have to leave 'cause you're a hick and you want your mom's approval even though you kind of hate her guts and your dad's still in love with her and you just want to shake him and say, 'Stop it! She doesn't love you! She doesn't love anyone! She doesn't even love me!' and why would she love me because nobody fucking loves me and people just break up with me in a cab on fucking Thanksgiving!"

Something is wrong with my eyes now. They're leaking some kind of liquid substance.

"Willa? Are you okay?"

"Yes. No. Sort of. Maybe."

"I didn't mean to call you simple."

"It's okay. You know, fuck it, let's just go somewhere this weekend and hunker down and study and forget about all of this, okay? No more boy thinking."

"Yes. You're right. No boy thinking. Although technically Humbert Humbert is not a boy."

"Remy, I'm serious. I'm not gonna go anywhere with you

if you're gonna be freaking out about *him* the whole time. I can't take it."

"Okay, okay. You're right. I won't. I promise."

"Me, too. I promise. Nothing about Milo. Okay? Now where should we go?"

"We could go back to my place?"

"New York? No way."

"What about, what about the other one?"

"The other one?"

"Yeah. We could go to Old Mill."

"Old Mill?"

"Old Mill Farm. It's in Greenwich. There's, like, no one out there right now. It's deserted. In August, forget it. But right now . . . ghost town."

"And is this a farm? Like what *kind* of a farm . . . ?"

"Um. Yeah, it's totally a farm. You'll like it. You'll feel right at home because you're a farm girl who is used to churning her own butter and making out with her relatives behind the barn."

"Yes, of course. We all do that."

I know, looking at Remy, who has finally calmed down, thank God, that the place I am going to has nothing to do with the kind of farm I am accustomed to, with cows and mice and a barn cat. I know there will not be chipped paint or a tractor involved. I know there will not be a soul around named Bubba or Billy Bob or Buck or Beau. And that's okay. All that matters is that there's not a soul around.

Right? All that matters is that we get focused and don't think about boys or drugs or texts or the lack thereof and everything is going to work out perfect now.

Because I am on this.

Because we are in control.

Right?

FIFTY-SIX

You should see us on the train, Remy with her dark circles under her eyes and me with my terrarium. My plan is to open this dumb terrarium in the forest and liberate this frog. Along with Milo. Who also turned out to be a frog.

The kids across the aisle are very interested in my tree frog, that is for sure. It's sort of a funny thing. There's a little blond-haired boy, like a Little Lord Fauntleroy, who keeps crawling all over himself to get to ogle the tree frog. Then there's another boy, an African-American boy, who is also very curious, but a bit more shy. Now, it's safe to say these two moms come from very different backgrounds. Like, the Fauntleroy mom could be named Muffy. And the other mom looked like she just got done working a thousand-hour workweek, on her feet, no breaks for lunch. I mean, she looks tired. Exasperated. Over it.

The Muffy mom has a little more energy. More energy to lovingly guide her son to be curious but not impolite. To say please and thank you. To listen. To be respectful. The other mom doesn't quite have that much energy. I'm assuming because she doesn't have a nanny at home. Or maybe a chef. Or even a gardener. All things that Muffy clearly has.

So the city boy gets less patience. He doesn't get yelled at or anything. He just gets more exasperated looks and a few poignant sighs.

Both boys stare into the terrarium, which is perched on my lap. Inside, a red-eyed tree frog is looking back at them. Full of questions, these boys!

"What do you feed him?"

"Crickets."

"Eww."

"Or worms."

"Eww!"

Little Lord Fauntleroy looks at his mom. "Mommy, he eats bugs."

"Oh my goodness."

"Even worms."

"Well, well. Now, honey, next stop is our stop. So let's get ready, okay?"

The other mom, the exhausted one, calls her son over. She's had enough. The little boy grudgingly goes back but continues to stare. His mother closes her eyes.

Fauntleroy continues to marvel at the red-eyed reptile.

"Okay . . . Mom! I have a great idea!"

"Yes, dear?"

"Maybe we can get one of these?"

"One of what?"

"A frog! A tree frog!"

"Why don't we put it on the list, honey."

"Oh, Mom! Please? Pleeeeease?"

"Honey. I said we'll put it on the list."

The train comes to a stop and the little boy looks like he is just about to cry. I mean, he really does look not just like you took his Popsicle but that all the sadness in the world just became clear to him and now he is looking straight into the abyss.

I can't bear it.

I hold up the terrarium.

"Here, ma'am. Sorry, I just . . . do you want it? I wanna get rid of it. It was a gift, and I really don't want it, honestly . . ."

"Oh. Really?"

"Mommy, Mommy, please!"

The mom sighs, looking at little pleading Fauntleroy.

"We're Pembroke girls," Remy drawls.

I'm not sure if this is supposed to speak to our character and breeding, or perhaps the character and breeding of the frog.

She turns back to me. "Are you quite sure?"

"Mommy, pleeeeeeease?"

"Okay, honey, but only if you give a very polite thank-you. Like a gentleman."

"Thank you. Thank you very much for the frog."

I hand the terrarium over to the boy. He squeals with delight. "Froggy! I love you, froggy!"

The mom smiles and gives me the universal expression for "Oh, these crazy kids."

They get off the train, terrarium lifted high above the seat backs. The train pulls out of the station.

The city boy, tucked in next to his resting mother, looks at me.

Daggers in his eyes.

He wanted the frog. Of course he wanted the frog.

What did I just do? That other kid probably has a million toys in his giant toy room built only for play. And this kid, the one staring swords at me, he probably has one broken G.I. Joe or something.

I'm an idiot.

Remy says the obvious. "Maybe you should've given it to the other kid."

"Yeah, I know."

The exhausted mom doesn't notice; she's asleep. The boy continues to look plaintively.

"God, I feel so guilty."

Remy looks at me. Then she looks back at the boy.

The train pulls into the next station.

"Now you know how I feel."

FIFTY-SEVEN

If you ever wanted to live in a haunted house, go live with Remy. I'm not kidding. This place is spooky. First of all, it's definitely not a farm. Not even close. It's not even a house. Nope. Not that, either. Anybody with eyes and a semi-respectable grasp of the English language would call this a castle. Because that's what it is.

There's a train station in Greenwich that doesn't look like much. The cabdriver doesn't look like much, either. Not hideous or anything. Just ordinary. So everything is just ordinary until you go down this extremely long, curving, tree-lined street that pops you out onto what basically constitutes an oval with a shallow pool in the middle surrounded on each side by four giant plants. Topiaries, I think you call them. I, on the other hand, don't call them anything because I have never seen them before.

"That's the gazing pond." Remy smirks at me. "Don't forget to gaze into it."

The cabdriver starts to get nervous as we drive halfway down the oval to the front. Maybe he thinks we're thieves. I mean, Remy is dressed like she's wearing three outfits. Maybe he thinks we're homeless. Maybe he thinks we're about to steal the castle.

"Thanks, keep the change."

Remy pops out and I follow her. Trying not to look too impressed by the estate in front of me, where it's possible Satan was born.

The cabdriver idles and eyes the house a bit before driving off. It seems to me, and I don't think I'm making this up, that he's actually shaking his head as he drives off. I can't tell if he's shaking his head that anyone actually lives in this demonic monstrosity or if he thinks we obviously don't live here and are hoodlums attempting to fool the world!

Whatever the case may be, he glides off into the distance, around the curve, leaving Remy and me standing there in front of a place that looks like it might actually open up its mouth and eat us.

"So, this is the farm."

I try to sound vaguely humorous, but geez, this place is

really making me self-conscious. Something about the vines everywhere and the Tudor stylings and the giant mahogany door. I'm a total spazbot.

Remy seems to clock my general discomfort and, God love her, tries to deflate the whole thing.

"I know . . . I didn't want to show it to you because I knew you wouldn't come. It's ridiculous, isn't it? I have no idea why we still have this. I think it has sentimental value or something."

She heads to the door and starts rummaging through her book bag.

Is it possible that she is actually looking for a key? Is it really that simple? Oh, here's the iron key to that giant door to that zillion-dollar estate. Really? But just as I start to form the thought, she's gotten an old-fashioned iron key out and she's finagling with the keyhole.

"Isn't there an alarm system or something?"

"Of course, but we never use it."

Right. Shrug. Why would you possibly use an alarm system?

Before I know it we are in the haunted halls of horror, and let me tell you, this place is ripe for a *Scooby-Doo* reunion.

Also, I would like to note that the ceiling is basically the top of the castle, formed by these giant wooden arches in a row. You know, like you used to make with your hands in grade school saying, "This is the church, this is the steeple, open the doors, and see all the people."

Except that in this case there aren't any people.

There's an enormous Persian rug and some oil paintings embedded into the wooden walls . . . but no people. Also, I would like to point out that there's a huge marble three-dimensional fresco above the fireplace so you don't have to worry about finding a mirror or anything to put up there.

"Um, isn't there like a butler or a creepy caretaker we're supposed to run into right about now . . . ?"

Remy smiles. "You're cute. No, I told everybody to leave. But to answer your question, yes. There is a caretaker. But he's nice. Not creepy. And he's not here. At least I'm pretty sure he left already."

"Let me guess. His name is Mr. Willies."

"His full Christian name is Silly Willies."

I laugh like a total goofball.

But I'm glad we're back to being goofy. Anything but listening to that endless palaver about Humbert Humbert. *That* is a fate worse than death.

The good news is this definitely seems like the kind of quiet place where we can get some studying done.

"So, on a scale of one to ten . . . how haunted is it around here?"

"Mm, I'd say . . . about . . . nine."

FIFTY-EIGHT

The good news is Remy isn't warbling on about Humbert Humbert. Maybe she's really trying to get it together. Maybe I am even helping. Maybe I am a good person who does good things for the people around me. Maybe I am not completely pointless after all.

We're just eating in the breakfast room, not the dining room, so no need to stand on ceremony. Also, we're just eating Chinese takeout. I guess there are only two places that deliver, and the other one is pizza.

This so-called breakfast nook is what most people would consider their dining room. In fact, in Manhattan I think it would be most people's entire apartment. Remy seems almost chipper, listening to Vampire Weekend, singing along, talking about her mom without rolling her eyes even once.

"She's not all bad. She just gets kind of obsessed, mostly about textiles."

"Do they ever stay here?"

"Not really. She says it's boring. My dad likes it better, probably 'cause he grew up here."

"What about you?"

"I go back and forth. Right now I love it."

We sit there, contemplating our chopsticks. This might be one of the quietest places I've ever been. Even the crickets are slumbering, luxuriating.

There's an elephant in the room, so I'm just gonna say it.

"Hey, so . . . I'm really proud of you. That you went to that meeting on your own and that you're really sticking to it. I mean it."

Remy looks at me. I sometimes think people never talk to her about anything real. I think sometimes they just dance around everything with her.

"Yeah. I dunno. I just . . . One day at a time, right?"

"Yeah. But good job."

She nods. Smiles and gives a little cute shrug. We both sit there for a second, trying not to think about our respective heartbreaks.

"Are you still depressed?"

"I dunno."

"You know, you shouldn't be depressed. There's a lot to be thankful for."

"Like what?" she sneers.

"Like that spiders can't fly."

She laughs. "Yes, that is true. For that I am grateful."

"Also, that when you cry your tears aren't made of acid and then they burn your face and then you cry some more and then they burn your face even more and it goes on and on in an endless cycle of crying and face burning until there's nothing left but two eyeballs crying and burning themselves."

"True."

"Or that you don't have to go back in time to the Middle Ages and become the wife of a fishmonger."

Remy bats me with the seat pillow.

"Or that pillows were invented. Before pillows, everyone had to lay their sweet heads down on rusty nails. In the olden times."

"Tell me some more about the olden times."

"In the olden times, if you were grumpy . . . they would put you in jail. Also, everybody smelled bad. Because they never took a bath. Or they threw out the baby with the bathwater and then they were scared. Scared of the bath."

"*You're* scared of the bath. You are scared of haunted bathtubs."

"If you had seen what I've seen, you would be, too."

"I would be more scared of fishmongers."

"What about haunted fishmongers?"

"Terrifying."

It's getting late now. I'm already starting to imagine my harrowing room for the night.

"Thanks for coming out here with me, *mon amie*. I know it's kind of off the beaten path."

It's funny Remy thinks it would be a chore for me to come here. That just shows the universe between us.

"Are you kidding? It's incredible. The only reason I'm not drooling openly is because I don't want to come off like a hillbilly."

"You're so funny when it comes to that, Willa. You're, like, ashamed when you should be so proud."

"What? To be from Iowa?"

"Yeah. You should think that it's cool because it is."

"Why would it ever be cool?"

"Because it's different. You don't understand. All of us live in this tiny little fishbowl where everybody is the same and everybody is always gonna be the same and everyone knows everyone's business and, like, the only question marks are if you're gonna go to Harvard or Yale."

She exhales. I think that's the most Remy has ever said about anything.

She ends with a final thought. "It's . . . oppressive."

"Wow. That's so funny. I never would've—"

"So, you know . . . somebody like you, who's not from here, who's not from those circles but who's not a jerk and who's funny and who's a good person. It's almost . . . refreshing."

"Wow. Really? I'm refreshing?"

"Totally. You're like a Sprite."

"Does that mean I'm like a sprite like a wood nymph? Or a can of soda?"

"Soda can. One hundred percent."

"I guess Milo didn't think I was refreshing."

"Willa, Milo is probably totally obsessed with you and freaking out right now about how he blew it. But having Milo obsessed with you is kind of not a good thing. Because he just kind of, like, hurts everyone around him. Like he's got spikes. You remember that girl we saw at that club, remember? WTF girl?"

"Yeah. Okay, yeah. I do remember."

"Like that."

We're making our way up the stairs now, to the "sleeping

quarters." I know when we get in here there are gonna be canopies involved. I get my own room, of course, because otherwise I won't be scared to death all night.

I get what is called the blue room. Remy gets her room. You can have the Wedgwood room.

FIFTY-NINE

Remy doesn't want to study in the library because the birds annoy her. I guess there's a tree outside with scads of birds. Some people like birds and think the sound of them is a wonderful blessing signifying that everybody is happy. I am not one of those people. Birds are flying predators. If you were tied to the ground they would eat your eyeballs. That is enough for me to not like birds. And Remy, too, understands this.

What about the solarium? Oh, you don't know what a solarium is? Oh, silly! It's a sunroom with lots of grandma furniture and leaf prints and foliage where whoever has the loudest taste in the family gets to choose all the prints with a kicky abandon only suitable, I guess, for the solarium. So it's wild in here. And playful. Vibrant. It's a happy room. But Remy is not satisfied. The room is too open. Too many distractions outside.

Third time's the charm. Back to the great room. That's okay. I only study in rooms big enough to play a full-court game of basketball.

By the time we're done plopping down all our stuff and getting comfortable, it's already noon. I am not happy about this. We are losing a lot of time walking around, fussing, deciding, and generally avoiding doing what we are supposed to be doing.

"I think I'm hungry."

I can't help but roll my eyes. "Remy, no. We're studying now. We'll take a break after Contemporary Lit and Bio."

"Okay, okay."

Very unenthused.

I crack open the books, trying to demonstrate a kind of passionate responsibility. Yes, we will study! This is great!

First up: *The House of Mirth* by Edith Wharton.

The House of Mirth is a book about this girl Lily Bart, who should probably marry a rich guy because she comes from a good family with a good name, but that family is broke by now, and so the whole time they are putting all these rich guys in front of her so she will be safe and secure for the rest of her life. And the book kind of does a number on you because the whole time you think she's gonna marry this guy or that guy and you are kinda hoping she does, so that everything will be settled, but you are also kind of hoping she doesn't because all these guys are total dolts who just warble on about themselves or real estate or the best restaurants in Europe the whole time. And here's the kicker, none of the interesting guys have any money. So the choice is marry a cool guy and be poor or marry a bloviating blowhard and be set for the rest of your life but so bored you might want to put a bullet in your head. I won't tell you how it ends or the moral of the story. Although I have taken my own personal moral of the story and it is to never rely on some jerkface who talks about real estate the whole time.

Ms. Ingall tries to keep us on our toes by doing all sorts of different tests each time. Like, she'll have us write impromptu essays on the book, or the characters, or the plot, which is really hard but at least seems to have something to do with the actual novel. And one time she did something really crazy, which is she had us write a poem inspired by the book. So, you see, you have no idea what you're gonna get, so you have to be ready for any and all possibilities. And you have to read the book. You have to know the book. You have to be the book.

I can't help but like Ms. Ingall. Not just because she's taken a keen interest me. Not just that. She's enthusiastic.

She gets excited about the novel and gets a gleam in her eye talking about the story. Her eyes light up and she gesticulates, enthralled, talking about Lily Bart or Boo Radley or Holden Caulfield. She posts all sorts of words all around the classroom, on every blank part of the wall, in construction paper: "Synchronicity." "Bucolic." "Lugubrious." "Quintessential." "Louche." You can tell she authentically loves the English language. She loves the language and she wants us to love the language. To love the words.

"Maybe we should take a break before Bio. You know that's gonna be annoying."

Can't argue with Remy there. But we really shouldn't. I'm trying to demonstrate some kind of responsibility here. Or at least the ability to get something done. Just one thing.

"I dunno. Let's see if we—"

"Hold on, I'll be right back."

"Remy?"

"I have to pee."

Okay, I'll just stare out the window. There's a lot to stare at. I noticed from upstairs there's a pool somewhere out there. And a tennis court. And a horse stable. And a maze. Look, if you don't have a maze at your house, I don't know what to tell you. I think it comes in handy when you are at the end of that movie with Jack Nicholson and you need a place to lose him and escape with your life.

Looking out the window now, however, you would never know any of these features exist. Because they are tucked away, discreetly, behind the trees and the foliage and the carriage house. It's just tacky to show everyone your maze right off the bat. Clearly.

After contemplating the grounds, I take a little constitutional around the great room. Maybe I could build a fort in the fireplace.

Remy still isn't back, so I might as well wander back into the library. This place is like a shrine to old white males. Every wall has an oil painting, or three, of a sophisticated, snooty-looking, humorless old gent staring down his nose at you. Most of them are the color of chalk. I'm assuming this is the long line of Remy-ancestor blue bloods who are probably watching me now in ghost form from the attic.

And, of course, at the end . . . over the mantel. Look who. If it isn't William Howard Taft himself. President William Howard Taft. And from the looks of him, it appears he might hold the record for the president who ate the most sandwiches. For he is sturdy. And he has a mustache. A blond mustache. That curves up at the ends. Not much in the way of eyebrows, though. Maybe he used his eyebrows to make his mustache.

He is definitely the sturdiest of all these ghouls glowering down from their picture frames. Maybe that's why he got to be president. Everyone else was just too weak to make it through the campaign trail. No, William Howard Taft was definitely the only red-blooded one in the family.

Here's something.

Remy's still not back.

What is taking her? I mean, is she playing a joke on me? Some kind of Amagansett tomfoolery? Some kind of Waspy tradition meant to welcome me with a wink and a laugh over Pimms later?

It's okay. I'm not freaking out. Not at all.

I'll just look for her. I'm sure there are only a thousand rooms in the house. So I'll be back in five hours. See you then.

Honestly, I have a feeling she went back to the bedroom to get her phone. I understand this. I, too, am tempted to get my phone and fuck off the rest of the day. But no. No, we are here to be good. I can hear the water running in her bathroom. Okay, well, hm . . . I guess the best thing to do is just sit here on the bed and wait.

And wait.

And wait.

And . . . um . . . wait.

Well, now it's been ten minutes and still the water is running.

This is getting weird.

"Remy?"

Nothing.

"Remy? Hello . . . ?"

Still nothing.

Okay, now my stomach is tying itself into a million small hard knots. I am worried. Like really worried.

"Remy? I'm coming in there, okay? Don't get mad at me or think I'm weird. I totally don't want to see you, like, peeing, but I'm kind of worried and I'm coming in. Okay?"

I expect that the door's gonna be locked. Right? I mean, that's a reasonable expectation of someone in the bathroom.

But it's not.

It just comes right open.

It comes right open and there is Remy in the delicate Victorian bathroom, with the oval gilded mirror and the claw-foot tub, and everything is just so and exquisite and out of a fairy tale, except that the sink is overflowing and Remy is lying on the tile, unconscious.

SIXTY

Everybody knows you're not supposed to have a needle sticking out of your arm. But does everybody know what to do if there is an unauthorized needle sticking out of your arm?

Exactly. What?

Do you pull it out? Or is it one of those things, like moving a body after an accident, where you could possibly do more harm than good? What to do? Do I google it or call an ambulance? Yes, maybe call an ambulance. But then that definitely raises this incident to a higher level of parental involvement.

Fuck it. Remy is unconscious on the floor.

Okay, I'm gonna call an ambulance.

I notice, as I'm waiting, that there are a few things to give everyone hope. It appears that Remy is breathing. Put your ear next to her mouth and there's definitely breath there. But that is all. The lights are definitely out in all other categories.

Well, it's a good thing she stopped doing drugs.

Remy, please fucking don't die. Please fucking don't die. Please fucking don't die.

I don't even feel like I'm in this room right now. I feel like I'm up at the top of this room, looking down at someone whose best friend is lying half-dead from an overdose with a needle sticking out of her arm. Oh, but that person sitting there is me.

That appears to be me crying and generally freaking out. I think that's the normal reaction to this situation. But the me who's looking down, removed from everything? That me has just switched to the off position. Powered down. Gone into sleep mode.

Boy, those ambulances sure know how to find a place. That was fast. I guess that's what happens when you live in a castle.

There's a second where I wonder if I'll be in trouble. Like somehow I'll be busted for even being here. But no. I'm not the show. I'm not the main event.

No one ever locks the front door around here, so these

guys are yelling from downstairs and I am yelling from up here and now they are in the room. Both of these guys are pretty square-looking and they seem almost concerned about me, too, which is weird.

I think I should probably be doing something vaguely proactive or supportive, but for some reason all I can do is sit here, on the floor, staring, listening to all the commotion in a state of paralysis.

I know I should call someone. An adult. Someone responsible. Someone not me. My hand reaches into Remy's bag and pulls out her phone—a separate hand. Just doing it. Not my hand. Not my brain. Not my will.

For some reason I call Humbert Humbert.

SIXTY-ONE

Apparently, calling Humbert Humbert was not a good idea. Apparently, this got him fired, shit-canned, axed. But wait, there's more! Apparently, the whole extravaganza, between the teacher sex, the acting thing, and the OD incident, have led the Tafts to the sensible decision that maybe the Pembroke School is a bad influence on their daughter.

(If they only knew.)

But there you have it.

Pembroke is bad for Remy.

So here I sit in my giant, beautiful room, with Remy's sheets on the bed and Remy's things scattered all around.

But no more Remy.

I have desperately wanted to talk to her but then

desperately wanted not to talk to her and so on and so on to infinity.

I have kicked her stupid dirty clothes to the corner of the room in a raging fit. And I have wrapped myself up in her bedding and stared, silent, out my open door toward the maid's room.

And Milo. Well, he's AWOL, too. Just like Remy said he would be. Maybe his mom heard about the OD and took him out of Witherspoon. He hardly ever went to class anyway.

I wonder if they'll still find a way to give them both their diplomas. I mean, if they did, would any of us be surprised?

And you. Perhaps you're hoping for one of those romantic-comedy moments where one day Milo is running toward me on the quad and confessing his love and begging for forgiveness in the last minute. Nope. Sometimes life doesn't get to be a movie. Sometimes it's just weird and unsettling. Like getting dumped on Thanksgiving and then never speaking to someone ever again.

That's okay, though. I'm trying to make it okay. Maybe part of the trick is not to expect that everything is gonna turn out like a movie. Maybe if you take away that expectation and just let everything be what it is, that's how you get through this thing without tearing your hair out.

Maybe you're just supposed to let it be. Maybe you just take away the "should."

But right now there is no letting anything be, because everyone is freaking the fuck out about the play.

What to do, what to do?! All of them . . . brimming with anticipation about what's gonna happen to the play.

Apparently, Mrs. Jacobsen—who has been reinstated after Humbert's abrupt (ahem) departure—is in a real dither about the whole catastrophe. No Ophelia. No Ophelia! How can you have *Hamlet* without Ophelia?!

Maybe Mrs. Jacobsen can play Ophelia. A brilliant interpretation! *Hamlet* as Ann Taylor catalog!

But Mrs. Jacobsen will not play Ophelia. And neither will anybody else. For a moment it seems they may cancel the play altogether.

None of this would have happened if they had just stuck to *Grease*, of course.

But no, *Grease* was too pedestrian.

(I just want you to know I learned that whole Frenchy song.)

(And I'm kind of bitter about it.)

Then, finally, latest rumor. It is that Remy Taft is coming back to just do the play and only the play. A Friday-through-Sunday affair, never to be repeated again in the annals of theater. An exclusive!

And, yes, the rumors have been flying about the reason for Remy's sudden exit. Everyone is sorta wondering, sorta whispering about an inappropriate relationship between Remy and the teacher. People come up to me, their faces squished in fake sympathy, to ask: "Is it true? Did you know about it? How long has it been going on?" But I cut them off with a look and they pretend to be staring at their term papers.

It's not like Remy's image is sullied. If anything, it is enhanced. That's Remy for you. Somehow everything disgusting and depraved looks good on her. On anyone else it's gauche; on Remy it's chic. Even the overdose.

But then, no one knows about that. No one but me.

Of course I haven't heard from her. I am vanquished. I am back on the other side, looking in. I am not cool anymore. But who am I kidding? I was never cool. I was never that person. I was always just a dork from the sticks. And maybe I proved my mother right. Maybe all this was too much for me to even begin to comprehend, considering where I'm from.

But regardless, I have a ticket to *Hamlet* tonight. I'm going to sit through this goddamn play and get it over with. I'm sure it will be terrible.

I'm sure I will absolutely hate every minute of it.

I'm sure I will not long for Remy from a dark corner of the auditorium during act one, scene five. Nope. Not one bit. Why would you even ask me that?

SIXTY-TWO

This place is the perfect place for bats to fly around. And spiders. And theater ghosts. This castle turned into meeting hall turned into stage. You have to admit, it's perfect for *Hamlet*.

The opening scene, a cascading landscape, papier-mâché falling from the very back of the theater, all the way to the front, a kind of dilapidated triptych. There are rear projections. There is text on the wall. There is eerie but beautiful music under it all. Then, from the rafters: "'Tis bitter cold and I am sick at heart."

It. Is. Flabbergasting.

I guess Humbert Humbert really was more than a perverted English teacher after all. It doesn't take any of us very long to realize we are seeing something we will never see again. Something extraordinary. The temperature of the room has changed from snarky apathy before the curtain, to enthralled fascination by the end of the first scene. It's a poem somehow onstage for us and for us only.

I find myself feeling grateful I am not in the play so I can see the play. Here's the other thing. It moves all around the castle. We, the audience, move from scene to scene, entering each scene like it's a discovery, like we just happen to have stumbled upon this whispering between these walls.

When Hamlet leaves Ophelia, there is Remy, staring off into the distance, pleading, "Oh, what a noble mind is here o'erthrown." She is stunning. She is brilliant. And I am looking at her, thinking those very same words about her.

What an incredible supernova of a person is here overthrown. Spiraling downward. Driving herself crazy. There she is. Standing there in some future-past getup. Like if you made a beautiful old-fashioned dress out of gauze. It doesn't make sense, but it is exquisite. It feels like we're all awake, dreaming. Like we're all in the same hallucination. A fever dream.

Near the end of the play, in a vaulted room, Ophelia aka Remy comes in, and she is soaking wet. She's gone mad now, and she is giving flowers to everyone and saying the name of each flower.

"There's rosemary, that's for remembrance . . . And there is pansies, that's for thoughts . . ."

As the scene goes on her dress changes, like there must be dye in the dress and the wetter it gets the more dye comes out, changing the dress from white to all these beautiful blues and purples. Everyone in the audience is gasping and looking on. Amazed.

Then she looks out, directly, into the audience and says, "Good night, sweet ladies. Sweet ladies, good night." As if suddenly she sees us, actually sees us, there in the audience. As if suddenly, for a moment, Ophelia, mad Ophelia, is the smartest person in the play.

We all stand in silence, caught.

We watch, then, as she exits the room and goes outside, where we can still see her, through a giant arched window, walking all the way down the rolling hill and then all the way up the next rolling hill, into the distance, until now she's only a tiny speck far away and then, finally, we can't see her anymore. Gone. Disappeared. A magic trick.

SIXTY-THREE

I guess this is a postplay, meet-the-cast-and-drink-iced-tea-or-apple-juice-type thing. There are also crackers and cheese and a few grapes in case you forgot to eat your fruit today. Everyone is milling around in the foyer, marveling at this magnificent interpretation of Shakespeare. There are lots of scarves involved. I think a scarf was a requirement to get in, along with a ticket. The moms and dads look around, searching for their precious little geniuses to exit backstage and be adored. That's the one thing about parents. You could throw up on a piece of construction paper and they'd call it art. But then when you do something really good . . . I mean, they might as well fly up into the sky on a rainbow hot-air balloon.

Looking out at the sea of bashful kids and parents, I suddenly miss my dad. I think about all the times, all the little dumb activities I did, how he would always be standing there, after, proud as punch. "Oh, Cakey-pie, that was wonderful! I'm so proud of you!" And it didn't even matter what silly thing it was or if I fell on my face. He was just there. Like the sun and the moon and the stars. Constant.

Maybe that's what it is with Remy. Maybe her mom or dad, maybe they just kinda left out that part. Maybe they weren't *there* enough.

Or who knows, maybe they were perfect.

And maybe that didn't even matter.

Maybe we're just programmed. Preordained since birth to be this way or that way and never, ever to change.

One thing is for sure. Remy's parents are decidedly absent right now. And that is an incredible, unforgivable crime after what I just witnessed.

But out she comes anyway. She comes out from backstage, and there's a commotion, a sigh of approval, a collective gasp. A circle of heads surround her, bobbing up and down, kind words and assurances. I see she has also observed the scarf rule. A vaguely ethnic-looking scarf adorns our fledgling starlet.

And now she looks through the bobbing heads, directly at me.

I freeze, hoping to God she doesn't somehow express her disdain in this oh-most-horrible public forum.

But that's not what happens.

Remy parts the crowd like the Red Sea and comes directly to me, stands in front of me. There she is in all her postshow glory. You would never believe the last time I saw her she had tubes stuck up her nose and an IV in her arm.

She tilts her head to the side. "Proud?"

This doesn't even begin to cover it. I can feel tears prickling at the corners of my eyes. "Oh, Remy, I . . ."

She hugs me.

I accept.

"That was . . . That was incredible. Seriously."

"Really?"

"Yeah, can't you tell? Look at everybody. They don't know what to do, it was so amazing."

She blushes. (I guess people do that now.) "Thanks. It was cool, right?"

"And you were heartbreaking. I practically cried or whatever."

"I bet you stuck with 'whatever.'"

We smile at each other, both a little gun-shy.

Then Remy goes first. "Listen, Willa. I'm really sorry. I fucked up. I shouldn't have lied to you. About the meetings. About everything."

I let it all out in a whoosh. "I'm sorry, too. I was totally panicked and scared and I didn't know what to do."

"It's okay. Besides, you basically saved my life."

"Maybe."

"I think definitely."

"Well, I'm really sorry they found out about Humbert Humbert. I shouldn't have called him. I don't know what I was thinking—"

"They would have found out eventually. Don't worry about it. I sort of think maybe that was kind of the point."

"Really?"

"Yeah. At least that's what my therapist says."

Therapist? I think. Well, how about that. Not just for the commoners, after all.

We stand there for a second.

"Do you miss it here? At Pembroke?"

"No."

Ouch.

"But I miss *you*, Willa. I really do."

Okay, I can put my heart back.

"Really? Oh my God, I'm so glad you said that. I thought you hated me. I mean, I wouldn't blame you. I mean. God, I sound lame."

"I never hated you. Are you kidding? And I'm okay now.

I mean, I'm actually going to two meetings a day, if you can believe it."

"Wow, Remy."

"So, you know, even though I blew off Pembroke, I hope we can still hang out. Like, we can still go to Paris . . ."

"Wait. Paris? Really?"

"If you want to. Fuck yeah."

The bobbing heads are coming toward us now—more admirers angling for chat with the superstar.

"Well, I better not keep you from the adoring throngs."

She smiles and hugs me again. Unusual behavior for Remy. Almost normal. She is immediately enveloped when I step back. Elated masses all talking excitedly over one another.

How can I help but be proud of her? All of that under-belly—a piece of the real, vulnerable her—suddenly on display for the world to see. Everything shimmery that makes Remy unlike the rest of the humans—the stuff for which I was an audience of one—now they see it, too.

And it's not just about her parents and that she's related to this president or that scientist or that well-known novelist. It's that there's something *there*, something in *her*, something effervescent that will just give you a dress or steal a golf cart with you or whisk you off to Paris for the summer.

Something giving and vulnerable and fierce and delicate all at once.

And I love everything about it—about her, from the smudge-eyed tears to the forcible move into my room. From the beautiful Ophelia to the eye rolls at the meeting in the depressing church basement.

I love everything about her.

And now I could fly up into the stars, all the way past the Big Dipper and through Orion's belt, that she's back. We're back. And last but not least, *I'm* back. Because I get to be the person I am when I'm with her instead of the person I was when I got here.

Even though my dad is a thousand miles away, I have a feeling like I'm tucked in tonight. With a few kind words and everything in its place and the sky not falling.

And I'm about to leave the castle, walking on this excellent canopy of air, when something catches my eye.

Remember how this place was a scarf-a-thon? Well, there's something on the ground at my feet.

This is Remy's scarf. Remy's vaguely ethnic scarf. It must have fallen somewhere amid the uncharacteristic warm embrace and huddled masses.

In any case, I have no idea when exactly I'm going to see her again, since she's never coming back to Pembroke, so obviously I should just return it to her now. Simple.

Except I can't see her anywhere. She's completely swallowed up by the crowd.

No problem. I was supposed to be in this little show once upon a time, so I remember from rehearsal where the dressing rooms are backstage. I'll just tuck this scarf into Remy's stuff. Good deed for the day. Maybe I'll even leave her a little note alone with it—something funny but heartfelt, but funny.

Right?

I find the door leading to the backstage and push through it. Ah, yes. Two dressing rooms below, for the guys. Two above, for the girls. You have to go up a winding staircase to get up to the ladies' dressing room. I guess that's so the boys don't peek in.

There is not a blessed soul around. Everyone's too busy chatting over apple juice. Maybe they spiked it.

There's a janitor on the other end of the hall, but he's got his earphones in and is having a good old time without my interference.

I walk down the hall to the dressing room, and there it is, all of Remy's stuff. I would recognize that embroidered purse from Istanbul anywhere. There's probably only one on the planet. Also, it's gigantic. I mean, I'm sure *I* could fit inside it. Good, she hasn't left yet. I'll just leave the scarf.

Yep, I can just put this here. In her purse.

Except.

There is something else in her purse. Something new. It's not a new shade of lipstick or a brand-new gold compact or a new set of eyeshadow. It's not a key chain or a wallet or a vile of perfume. No, no.

It's a kit. Have you seen one of these? I haven't. Except on TV. On *Law & Order*.

If you watch *Law & Order*, you'll recognize the kit.

It's a little black bag, like a toiletry bag. Quite simple. And if you open it, which I do . . . There, look. It's got a spoon, it's got a little bottle of liquid, it's got cotton Q-tips, and, of course, it's got a couple of carefully placed syringes. All safe and snug, strapped in with elastic bands.

It's a fucking kit.

Well, it's a good thing Remy is going to two meetings a day, isn't it?

My vision clouds over.

And this is me wanting to not see this thing in my hand.

This is me wanting to never see anything again.

SIXTY-FOUR

Well, thank God I brought that scarf back, right?

If you have ever seen a heartbreak walking across a rolling green, then you will be able to picture what's going on with me. There's no running involved, just a slow lumber across a large swath of grass with no end in sight.

Just a person punched in the gut.

I keep thinking about how I should've known and how I didn't want to know. I keep thinking about how I'm an idiot and a sucker and a fool.

If you're wondering whether Remy saw me with my hand in her bag, whether there was a great, superawkward moment of recognition where curiosity finally killed the cat, the answer is no.

Nope.

She does not know.

I slunk out of there like a stray.

It was only up the cobblestone path and past the hedges where I finally allowed myself to breathe.

But here I am, my heart outside my body, wanting to turn back the clock to an hour before and live there forever. If only it were an hour before, everything would be perfect again.

An hour before, we had the world on a string.

An hour before, we were going to Paris.

An hour before, we were not a joke.

SIXTY-FIVE

My dad has been sending me a zillion text messages, but I just can't. If I talk to him, he'll hear it in my voice. My dad is like a genie. He knows everything. He'll hear it in my voice and he'll ask, "Cakey-pie, is everything okay?" and I'll try to cover but I won't be able to and then I'll break down and cry for three hours and he'll jump in a car and probably not stop driving until he is at the door of my dorm.

I just have to give it a few days. To feel better.

Maybe a week.

Or, like, a hundred years.

I saw Zeb going into the campus center. He stopped and came over to me. I could tell by the look on his face, he'd heard it all.

"She's gone now, huh?"

"Yeah, pretty much."

"And you and Milo broke up."

"If we were ever really dating to begin with." I pause. "Wait, who told you that?"

"Milo."

I sigh. "Right."

"Listen, Willa. I wanted to tell you. I'm going back to LA next semester. I just really miss it."

I shake my head. "Of course you are."

"I just really miss it, you know."

I shrug. "Yeah, I bet."

"Well, I just wanted to tell you, before I go back . . ."

He puts his hand on my shoulder and looks into my eyes. It's almost too kind and too intimate and I almost can't take it.

"You're the best person here, Willa." He nods for emphasis. "Don't forget it."

And I could cry now, but we're in the middle of the campus center, end-of-the-year rush. So I just look up and smile and nod.

"Bye, Zeb. Thanks."

When he walks off I can't help but wonder how he got to be the way he is, who raised him and what they must have done. Whoever they were, I wish I could thank them.

And so here I am, in my beautiful room, buried in a veritable mountain of books. Peeking up out of the top like the fox in the snow.

I guess I never did kill myself. I have to give myself an F in suicide.

Thank God.

That's the funny thing, isn't it? That Remy brought me back from the abyss. That she brought me back and put my head back on my shoulders and my heart back inside my body. That she stood me up again. And that's the not-so-funny thing too. That I couldn't do one thing, not any of those things, to save her. I have to give myself an F in friend-saving.

Maybe in the end she just didn't want to be saved. And maybe, somewhere deep inside, somewhere below all my dumb jokes and snark and pretending I never care about anything, maybe somewhere deep beneath my fortress of never caring, I was desperate to be saved. To be loved. To be cared for. To be accepted for all of the things wrong with me instead of constantly not living up to should.

Remy put an end to the era of should.

That's how Remy saved me.

And that's why I get to be here now. With an F in suicide.

But this. This here. Welp, this is the only thing I'm good at. Throwing myself into my books. If I can just drown myself in my tests and my papers, none of this gets to matter anymore. It gets to evaporate in a poof of superfluous gunk, and I never, ever have to care again.

Of course, it comes up.

If I stop.

Or if I have a break where I'm supposed to eat or, I don't know, use the bathroom or something.

So, I'm avoiding those things.

Eating. Not for me.

Resting. Not for me.

An occasional walk to relax the mind. No way.

That's the danger time—when Remy or Milo come flying into my brain and all of a sudden I get lost in a sea of questions and annoyances and frustration that I was stupid enough to fall for any of it.

Nope.

Instead, work. Work, work, work. Study. Write a paper. Study. Write another paper. Study. Cram for the calculus final. Read. Write another paper.

I'm even doing extra credit.

In every class.

Anything and everything a student here at Pembroke can do, I am doing. I am even visiting the teachers during office hours to ask pithy and insightful questions in order to write even better papers.

In short, I am a robot.

An academic robot.

With no heart. No soft places where I can get hurt.

There is a ten-minute shower allowed in my daily regimen, which doesn't even get to last that long because my thoughts begin to wander and I jump out, soaking wet, hustle down the hall in my towel, and throw myself into the required and not-so-required reading.

At one point I do text my dad. I tell him "it's crunch time" and "will call soon." But, honestly, it hasn't helped. It hasn't staunched the flow of communication. He really has been texting a lot. Maybe he's lonely . . .

I make up my mind to send him something. With a nice card. Maybe cupcakes. I go down the rabbit hole of the interbot finding the best cupcakes to deliver to him, and that takes me two hours, which is good, because that's two hours I don't have to think.

Except for one problem. There is a problem in my plan. Despite the fact that I have become a machine who has spent the last two weeks with blinders on and a focus on only the greatest, most impeccable achievement, grade point average and academic prose . . . there . . . somehow between my blinders, is someone standing in my doorway, someone standing right there, distracting me from my true purpose, and of course that person is the one person I am dying not to think about, and of course that person is Remy.

SIXTY-SIX

Of course, she's thinner. There's something almost somber about the way she's dressed. All black. Or maybe dark gray. All those festive, thrown-together, mismatched, kicky outfits are out the window. Now it's just make do, I guess. Now it's just whatever happens to be there when she rolls out of bed. Now it's just whatever covers her arms.

I see her, but I don't say anything. I mean, what am I supposed to say?

She is all manic energy and cheer. "Hi! Can I come in?"

"Sure."

She steps in and looks around. Books, papers everywhere. The room of a girl possessed.

"Wow, you're really going for it here, I guess."

She really doesn't look that different from how she did that night at the Lamplighter. Clammy. Purple. Sick. "I could say the same for you."

"What?"

I shake my head. "Nothing."

"Look! Look what I got us!"

And this I can't believe.

Remy is standing in front of me, all eighty pounds of her, gray skin, sunken eyes, and showing me something on her phone.

"What is that?"

"Paris! Two tickets—I just booked them. I thought we could leave right after graduation. You know, for, like, the whole summer."

I feel like I've just lit down in an alternative universe.

"Remy . . ."

"*And* I found a place in Le Marais, just like we talked about. You're gonna love it. We'll take the Eurorail. Go to Italy. Maybe even Amsterdam."

And there she is, pleading with me, with that clammy skin and those sunken eyes. This is the same Remy who appeared behind the tree that first day I got here. The same girl. But not the same girl.

I miss that girl.

"Remy . . . stop."

"What? Oh, is it Amsterdam? We don't have to go there, I can—"

"We're not going to Paris."

"What do you mean? Of course we are. I've got the tickets."

"Remy. I'm not going to Paris with you. Or anywhere."

And this look. This look that washes over her face. Like the last hope. Last train out of the station.

"Why not?"

"Remy, look at you."

"What?"

"You think it's not obvious?"

She doesn't say anything for the longest time.

And then, "Why?"

"Remy. I can't go with you. Where you're going."

I am looking at Remy and then I realize. I realize it this second. This is the last time I will ever see her. It's like I'm looking at her, but I'm looking at a person who is getting smaller and smaller, fading and fading more, until there's just an image, then the trace of an image, then nothing.

And a part of me wants to be mad at her. A part of me wants to reach out and shake her. Just shake her until she comes back to her senses.

But that would be like trying to grab a shadow.

There's a silence. The sun is starting to set, and the light in the room is a hazy lilac. Little bits of gold on the wall.

It's soft now. It's gentle.

"Are you sure? You could change your mind, you know. I mean, the ticket's in your name . . ." She trails off.

And the air in the room, heavy as stone.

Then, "Y-you said you would never leave me."

It's a sucker punch.

And it's true.

But I feel like she left me a long time ago.

"I wanted to stay with you . . ."

We both just stand there.

And I'm looking at her. There she is. That lost little girl that I would do anything to save.

But I can't. I can't save her.

"I'm sorry, Remy. I'm really fucking sorry."

And that last part comes with tears. They just come out of nowhere. And I want to grab her and bring her back, just bring her back to me. Just get her back.

This is the moment it hits her.

That this is it for us.

She nods. A kind of terrified little nod. Nothing I've ever seen before.

And now she's out the door, down the hall, down the stairs.

And there she goes, walking across the green into the

setting sun. I can see her through the arched windows, making her way toward something far away from me. There she goes, and I am jealous of the world for getting to have her, jealous of all the nights and days that get to have her. There she goes, someone great and singular and unlike anyone ever invented and the best person in the world and the worst person in the world. And, oh, what a noble mind is here o'erthrown.

I stay on her until she is tiny in the horizon, a little dot, turning the corner by the arch. And then almost gone, hidden by the gray-green stones.

There she goes, and I might as well be watching a ghost.

SIXTY-SEVEN

I get to go home for Christmas. Thank fucking God. If you had asked me a month ago if I would ever want to go back to Iowa, I would have said, "Are you kidding? No way, no how."

But not now.

Now I might as well be flying to the moon.

To be home. To be home with my dad and that sweet little farmhouse and a tree in the window and my dad will grill a steak and add a baked potato and a pecan pie and every other thing you could eat to make you fat.

The city is making way now, through the suburbs and out through Pennsylvania, starting to get white, blankets of white, the snow falling down, patient. It's gonna be about a day and a half on this thing, but I don't really mind it, rocking back and forth. There's something gentle about it, cradling, lulling you to sleep.

I sort of just threw everything in a backpack and hustled over to the train station. I didn't have time for much because the grades were given out this morning and we had to wait forever for our transcripts. They were supposed to be out by ten, but they were out by eleven, so everything was wackadoo.

Looks like all my studying paid off and I am not destined to be homeless. In fact, looks like I got a 4.0, if I may toot my own horn. That means my scholarship is intact.

Praise the Lord and pass the cornflakes.

And that's not all.

Remember how I told you about how my dad kept texting and texting like a deranged stalker? **Cakey-pie, CALL ME!! WHERE R U?! HELLOOOO, EARTH 2 Cakey-pie?! COME IN, Cakey-pie?!?!?!** Well, somehow he just wouldn't stop so I had to just pick up the phone and make sure he hadn't lost his marbles for good.

So, dear friends, I call him and this is what went down, word for word:

Ring. Ring.

"Hello?"

My dad always answers the phone very cautiously. Maybe he thinks it's a bill collector.

"Hi, Dad, it's me."

"Willa?"

"Um . . . do you have another daughter?"

"I had a daughter once. We used to speak every day."

"Sorry, Dad."

"Well, where have you been? I've been trying to get ahold of you . . ."

"Dad, it was an insane amount of studying, and I'm sorry, but it was a little bit crazy. So I'm sorry I didn't get a chance to call you. Until now. But I am calling you now, see. This is me. On the phone. Calling."

"Well, I hope it wasn't too much."

"It's okay, Dad. I did it. I got a 4.0."

"Oh, Cakey-pie, that's wonderful!"

"Thanks, Dad. Tell Mom, I guess."

"Well, I will, honey. But that's not why I was texting."

"Well, why were you texting, Dad?"

"All right, well. I'll make it quick."

"Okay . . ."

"There's an envelope for you here."

"Um, okay."

"It says it's from University of California at Berkeley."

"Oh. Oh . . . oh my God."

"*Berkeley*, honey?"

"Dad, describe the envelope."

"Huh?"

"*Describe the envelope! Please.*"

"Well, it's just a regular-size envelope."

"Oh, fuck."

"Willa Parker!"

"Sorry, Dad. I didn't mean to swear. It's just . . ."

"Well, do you want me to open it?"

"No. Not really. It's just gonna make me more depressed."

"Okay."

"Thanks anyway, Dad. I'll see you in a couple of days."

"Okay, well, you know what? I'm just gonna open it."

"Dad!"

Dads never do what you tell them. It's like they were here first or something.

Now I'm just sitting here on the phone with nothing doing. God, I hate being on the phone. Why doesn't everybody just text? Why does everybody have to talk to everybody all the time anyway?

"Willa?"

"Yes?"

"Willa?"

"Ye-es?"

"Willa."

"Dad!"

"Okay, okay. Here's what it says . . . 'Dear Willa Parker,

On behalf of the admissions committee, it is my pleasure to offer you admission to the University of California–Berkeley."

"Oh my God. Oh my God."

"Willa! What about your mother? What about Princeton?"

"You know what, Dad?" I pause, thinking it over. "Fuck Princeton."

If it's possible to hear someone smiling over the telephone, I hear that now. "You know what, sweetie? You're right. Fuck Princeton."

"Oh my God."

"You're going to Berkeley, honey! You're gonna be a radical!"

And now, I won't lie to you, there are tears in my eyes and I'm kind of hyperventilating, too, and everything from this year, everything bad and good, comes rushing over me and I can barely breathe.

"Willa, honey, what's the matter? Why are you crying? Was it your safety school?"

"No!" I can barely talk, thinking how strange it all is, how unfair and strange and hurly-burly life is that this is what *I* get, that *I* get this, and Remy gets . . . what? How none of it makes sense and none of it is ever fair and don't try to pin it down because you'll never be able to.

"Well, I'm proud of you, Willa. I'm so proud of you."

"Thanks, Dad. You should probably tell Mom. She doesn't know. I didn't tell her I was applying or anything. You know . . . 'cause either she'd forbid it or she'd try to pull strings and then I'd never really know, you know? Like if it was me who got in or the strings."

"Oh, that is so noble. You're like a noble little lion."

"Oh, Dad."

"I'm so proud of you."

Hearing that, I could walk on the clouds.

I love my dad, and now, suddenly, back on this train, I love this whole stupid year and all the horrible things in it and I love the snow falling down around me and the train chugging over and over again on the tracks.

Right before he gets off the phone, he says, "I love you so much, little Willa." He always says it. He's said it a million times. Every night before bed and then some. But for some reason this time it lands exactly in the center of my soul. And I can't wait to see him. And I can't wait to make him proud.

And I know I will.

Now it's getting dark on the train and the stars are all about to come on one by one. There's a crescent moon halfway up the sky. Here I am, looking out at all that infinite space and wondering how anything gets to be anything.

Sometimes it all just seems like a dream anyway. Like maybe I am dreaming this and you are dreaming your dream, too. Like it's a fake, somehow. A paper plane.

The snow is falling down in swirls now, getting more and more impatient. Building up. Gunning.

I think about Remy and Milo, and it's okay. They get to be who they are.

I get to let them be.

And I forgive them. I forgive them with every electron in every cell of my body. I forgive them. But you know what's funny? I know no matter what . . . they will never forgive themselves. For anything. For everything. Anything that can be made hard . . . they do. And anything that can be made easy . . . they make hard.

It's kind of preposterous now, looking out at the snow-swirled sky, all that swooshing past me now, back to that place, that time, those city lights.

All that time, all that feeling like I was in a Fitzgerald novel, wishing I could be like them, trying to be like them, being mad at myself for not being like them. Hoping somehow I could become them, never thinking, not once, not one time, that maybe, just maybe, I could become something *better*.

Maybe I could become something that wasn't about

twelve-million-dollar estates and summers in Amasandwich and people with last names like Hobbes and Peabody and Tate.

Maybe, just maybe, it wasn't so bad to be myself.

The snow is coming down in sheets now. Stirring. Nothing but the spruce and the pine and the cedars to make a say. All the way through the desolate Pennsylvania panhandle, *chugga-chugga-chugga*. It isn't until the white sheet blanket coming up through Ohio that I realize I am never going back.

ACKNOWLEDGMENTS

I am extremely grateful to the following people for helping me along the way and helping me with this book, in particular. My editor, Kristen Pettit, of course. Katie Shea Boutillier. Fred Ramey. Dan Smetanka. Rosemary Stimola. Elizabeth Lynch, and everyone over at Harper. I would like to thank my mother, as well as the rest of my family, for the incredible support and love every step along the way. I'd like to thank my best friend, Brad, for having helped me all through the years. With all of my heart I'd like to thank my husband, who is gleefully supportive and understanding of every step of the process, and of me. I tend to be a slightly strange person to actually be around, and my husband not only understands me but embraces my generally bizarre behavior. And last, but not least, my little baby boy Wyatt, who is growing now into a little boy, and who is so effervescent, curious, hilarious, and sweet that every day is a new adventure, not only out into the world but into my own heart. How infinite the heart is! For you, Wyatt, my little prince.

JOIN THE

Epic Reads

COMMUNITY

THE ULTIMATE YA DESTINATION

◀ **DISCOVER** ▶
your next favorite read

◀ **MEET** ▶
new authors to love

◀ **WIN** ▶
free books

◀ **SHARE** ▶
infographics, playlists, quizzes, and more

◀ **WATCH** ▶
the latest videos

◀ **TUNE IN** ▶
to Tea Time with Team Epic Reads

    Find us at **www.epicreads.com** and @epicreads

31901059498743